W9-CEN-232

PRAISE FOR THE FEMMES FATALES SERIES

"Delicious examples of the pulp genre, written by women and reissued by the Feminist Press. . . . When people think of pulp they generally conjure up male authors like Dashiell Hammett or Raymond Chandler. But in its heyday women were there alongside the men, sometimes subverting its conventions. . . . These stories moved fast, and they were a guilty pleasure, easy to hide under the mattress." —*New York Times*

"Femmes Fatales offers a window on another time and place. . . . It offers little details, daily dreams often overlooked by history books. . . . Pulp, after all, is about pushing limits, about revealing the edges of a culture we can't quite see. Especially at a moment when society seems to be turning backwards this may help tell us who we are." —*Los Angeles Times*

"Fascinating pulp. . . . A lot of fun to read as well as illuminating sociologically." —**"Fresh Air," National Public Radio**

"Fun sells and these books are both historic and fun. To me, the Femmes Fatales series is genius. It's the kind of thing that's going to take the Feminist Press to the end of the century." —Susan Post, owner, BookWoman, in *Publishers Weekly*

"Each of these rediscovered gems boasts its original, gleefully provocative cover art, with dayglow titles, snappy-looking 'broads' and hilarious taglines. . . . Plus, they've got spiffy new commentaries putting each title into modern perspective. . . . This isn't pulp, it's got permanence." —Caroline Leavitt, *Boston Globe*

"The feminist perspective does give these works an undeniable extra dimension." —*Village Voice*

"When we think of the pulp era today, we tend mainly to think of crime novels and male authors. The folks at the Feminist Press are here to set us straight. Their new reprint series . . . celebrates a group of female authors [who] . . . deserve a second look. . . . Damn were they cool."
Bill Ott, *Booklist*

"Sleazy does it. . . . Complete with vintage noir covers, the books feature the tough men, sex-crazed women, drugs, booze, homosexuality, and other wonderfully sleazy trappings of the genre. . . . So bad, it's good." —*Library Journal*

"While pulp fiction, which peaked from the '30s through the '60s, has been rehabilitated in the past decade, this revival has not benefited the genre's female practitioners. . . . Kudos, then, to the Feminist Press, as it launches the 'Femmes Fatales: Women Write Pulp' series in an effort to spotlight forgotten women writers."
—*Time Out New York*

"There's another kind of woman in pulp noir fiction: the kind bold enough to write it in a man's world. They not only wrote noir thrillers but in the other pulp genres as well—sometimes using male pen names to sell more books. The Feminist Press, like a good private eye, has tracked them down. . . . Check out these queens of pulp." —*Minneapolis Star Tribune*

"[A] great success. . . . The press is crossing the borders of genre, launching an unlikely series of pulp fiction . . . 'set in pivotal moments in history when there was a shift in gender roles.' "
—*Poets and Writers*

"All praise to the editors of the Feminist Press. . . . Most of us know the kings of the pulps, James M. Cain and Jim Thompson. But how many know that there were women writers who were just as much in thrall to the dark side of human nature?" —*Philadelphia Inquirer*

"The stories rate the scholarly hooray. Damn good that the Femmes at the Feminist Press are doing whatever it takes to reload the American canon." —*Bully Magazine*

"[The Femmes Fatales series offers] an intriguing look into society's fears and prejudices and the subversive means by which some authors tackled taboos and challenged conventions." —*Pages*

WOMEN'S BARRACKS

FEMMES FATALES
WOMEN WRITE PULP

WOMEN'S BARRACKS

TERESKA TORRES

AFTERWORD BY JUDITH MAYNE

INTERVIEW WITH THE AUTHOR BY JOAN SCHENKAR

FEMMES FATALES: WOMEN WRITE PULP

THE FEMINIST PRESS
AT THE CITY UNIVERSITY OF NEW YORK
NEW YORK

Published by the Feminist Press at the City University of New York
The Graduate Center, 365 Fifth Avenue
New York, NY 10016, www.feministpress.org

First Feminist Press edition, 2005

09 08 07 06 05   5 4 3 2 1

Originally published in 1950 by Fawcett Publications, Inc., New York, NY.

Library of Congress Cataloging-in-Publication Data

Torres, Tereska.
  Women's barracks / Tereska Torres ; interview with the author by Joan Schenkar
; afterword by Judith Mayne.— 1st feminist Press ed.
      p. cm.
  ISBN 1-55861-495-8 (hardcover : alk. paper) — ISBN 1-55861-494-X (pbk. :
alk. paper)
  1. World War, 1939-1945—Fiction. 2. France combattante—Fiction. 3. London
(England)—Fiction. 4. Women refugees—Fiction. 5. Women soldiers—Fiction.
I. Schenkar, Joan. II. Title.
  PS3570.O7W67 2005
  843'.914—dc22   2004025452

Text design by Dayna Navaro
Printed on acid-free paper by Transcontinental Printing
Printed in Canada

PUBLISHER'S FOREWORD: WOMEN WRITE PULP

Women write pulp? It seems like a contradiction in terms, given the tough-guy image of pulp fiction today. This image has been largely shaped by the noir revival of the past decade—by reprints of classics by Jim Thompson and bestsellers by neo-noir writer James Ellroy, the rerelease of classic film noir on video, and the revisioning of the form by Quentin Tarantino. Fans of such works would be hard pressed to name a woman pulp author, or even a character who isn't a menacing femme fatale.

But women did write pulp, in large numbers and in all the classic pulp fiction genres, from hard-boiled noirs to breathless romances to edgy science fiction and taboo lesbian pulps. And while employing the conventions of each genre, women brought a different, gendered perspective to these forms. Women writers of pulp often outpaced their male counterparts in challenging received ideas about gender, race, and class, and in exploring those forbidden territories that were hidden from view off the typed page. They were an important part of a literary phenomenon, grounded in its particular time and place, that had a powerful impact on American popular culture in the middle of the twentieth century, and continues to exert its influence today.

Pulp fiction encompasses a broader array of works, and occupies a more complex place in the literary, social, and commercial culture of its era, than the handful of contemporary revivals and tributes to pulp suggests. Pulp emerged as an alternative format for books in the 1930s, building on the popularity of pulp magazines, which flourished from the

1920s to the 1940s, and drawing on traditions established by the dime novel of the nineteenth and early twentieth centuries. The dime novel had developed the Western, the romance, the sleuth story, and the adventure story as genres, with narratives geared largely to young readers, in particular on the frontier. Pulp magazines, needing to compete with early motion pictures and to connect with an urban audience, offered similar stories with an edge. Grouping fiction or believe-it-or-not fact under themes like crime, horror, and adventure, magazines such as *Black Mask*, *Weird Tales*, and *Dime Adventure* demonstrated the existence of a market for inexpensive and provocative teen and adult reading matter. The move to book-length narratives provided an expanded scope for a voracious literature rooted in American popular culture, reflective of American obsessions, and willing to explore American underworlds.

Printed on wood-grain, or pulp, paper, and cheaply bound, the books were markedly different from hardbound editions. These first modern paperbacks served different purposes, too—entertainment, thrill, or introduction to "serious culture"—and were presumably read differently. Books intended for the pulp lists were undoubtedly produced differently, with less time given to the writing, and less money and status accruing to the authors. As pulp publishers grew in number (Fawcett, Pocket Books, Bantam, Ace, Signet, Dell), economic patterns emerged in the treatment of authors and texts: pulp authors often received one-time payment (no royalties); editors focused on keeping books short, tight, and engrossing; and author identity was often submerged beneath the publisher's pulp brand name and the lurid cover art that sold the books. Some pulp authors used pseudonyms to conceal an everyday identity behind a more saleable one, often of the opposite gender. Georgina Ann Randolph Craig (1908–1957) wrote prolifically as Craig Rice. Some used several names, each evocative of a genre they wrote in: Velma Young (1913–1997) published lesbian pulp under the name Valerie Taylor, poetry as Nacella Young, and romances as Francine Davenport. Eventually some contemporary authors emerged as brands themselves: a Faith Baldwin romance was a predictable product.

At the same time, classics and contemporary best-sellers were reincarnated as pulp, as the format absorbed and repositioned literature that might otherwise have been inaccessible to working-class readers. Pulp publishers seem to have selected classic fiction with an eye to class politics, favoring, for example, the French Revolution and Dickens. They tended to present science as an arena where good old-fashioned ingenuity and stick-to-itiveness win the day. The life of Marie Curie was a pulp hit. When classics were reprinted in pulp editions—for example, *The Count of Monte Cristo* or *The Origin of the Species*— author identity might move to the fore on covers and in descriptive copy, but in becoming pulp the works acquired a popular aura and gravitated into pulp genres such as adventure and romance. Again, when new titles like William Faulkner's *Sanctuary* or Mary McCarthy's *The Company She Keeps* were issued in pulp editions, the cover art planted the works firmly in pulp categories: ruined woman, Southern variety; the many adventures and many men of a fast city girl. The genre, more than the author's name, was the selling point.

As the stories in pulp magazines were marketed by themes, so book-length tales were distinctively packaged by genre— Dell used a red heart to mark its romance line, for instance. Over time there were Westerns, science fiction, romance, mystery, crime/noir, and various others to choose from. Genres were to a large extent gendered. Crime/noir, for instance, focused on a masculine world of detectives, crooks, femmes fatales (positioned as foils to men), corruption, and violence, all described in hard-boiled prose. Romance focused on women's problems around courtship, virginity, marriage, motherhood, and careers, earnestly or coyly described. Since genres were gendered, the implied assumption was that men wrote and read crime/noir and women wrote and read romances. In fact, this assumption proves largely false.

Because pulp genres tended to rely on formulaic treatments, it was not difficult for writers to learn the ingredients that make up noir or, for that matter, how to write a lesbian love scene. The fact that authorial name and persona were rarely linked to real-life identity further permitted writers to explore transgender, or transgenre, writing. In so doing, they might self-consciously accentuate the gendered elements of a given genre, sometimes approximating parody, or they might attempt to regender a genre—for instance, writing a Western that foregrounds a romance. These freedoms, combined with the willingness of pulp publishers to buy work from anyone with the skill to write, meant that women had the chance to write in modes that were typically considered antithetical to them, and to explore gender across all genres. Leigh Brackett (1915–1978), a premier woman author of pulp, wrote hard-boiled crime books, science fiction, and Westerns, in addition to scripting sharp repartee for Bogart and Bacall in *The Big Sleep* (director Howard Hawks hired her on the basis of her novel *No Good from a Corpse*—assuming she was a man, as did many of her fans). Other women authors wrote whodunnit mysteries with girl heroines, science fiction battles of the sexes, and romances that start with a Reno divorce. Women wrote from male perspectives, narrating from inside the head of a serial killer, a PI, or a small-town pharmacist who happens to know all the town dirt. They also wrote from places where women weren't supposed to go.

Notoriously, pulp explored U.S. subcultures, which then often generated their own pulp subgenres. Where 1930s and

1940s pulp depicted gangster life and small-town chicanery, 1950s and 1960s pulp turned its attention, often with a pseudoanthropological lens, to juvenile delinquents, lesbians (far more than gay men), and beatniks, introducing its readers to such settings as reform schools, women's prisons, and "dangerous" places like Greenwich Village. These books exploited subcultures as suggestive settings for sexuality and nonconformism, often focusing on transgressive women or "bad girls": consider *Farm Hussy* and *Shack Baby* (two of a surprisingly large group in the highly specific rural-white-trash-slut subgenre), *Reefer Girl* (and its competitor, *Marijuana Girl*), *Women's Barracks, Reform School Girl,* and *Hippie Harlot.* Other books posited menaces present in the heart of middle-class life: *Suburbia: Jungle of Sex* and *Shadow on the Hearth.* A growing African American readership generated more new lines, mysteries and romances with black protagonists. Though the numbers of these books were fairly small, their existence is significant. With a few notable exceptions, African Americans were almost never found in pulps written for white readers, except as racially stereotyped stock characters.

While a strengthened Hays Code sanitized movies in 1934, and "legitimate" publishers fought legal battles in order to get *Ulysses* and *Lady Chatterley's Lover* past the censors, pulp fiction, selling at twenty-five cents a book at newsstands, gas stations, and bus terminals, explored the taboo without provoking public outcry, or even dialogue. (Notably, though, pulp avoided the four-letter words that marked works like *Ulysses*, deploying instead hip street lingo to refer to sex, drink and drugs, and guns.) As famed lesbian pulp author Ann Bannon has noted, this "benign neglect provided a much-needed veil behind which we writers could work in peace." Pulp offered readers interracial romances during the segregation era, and blacklisted leftists encoded class struggle between pulp covers. The neglect by censors and critics had to do with the transience of pulp.

Circulating in a manner that matched the increasing mobility of American culture, pulps rarely adorned libraries, private or public. Small, slim, and ultimately disposable, they were meant for the road, or for easy access at home. They could be read furtively, in between household chores or during a lunch break. When finished, they could be left in a train compartment or casually stashed in a work shed. Publishers increasingly emphasized ease of consumption in the packaging of pulp: Ace produced "Ace Doubles," two titles reverse-bound together, so that the reader had only to flip the book over to enjoy a second colorful cover and enticing story; Bantam produced "L.A.s," specially sized to be sold from vending machines, the product's name evoking the mecca of the automobile and interstate highway culture; Fawcett launched a book club for its Gold Medal line, promising home delivery of four new sensational Gold Medal titles a month. To join, one cut out a coupon at the back of a Gold Medal book—clearly, no reluctance to damage a pulp volume would impede owners from acting on the special offer.

The mass appeal of pulp proved uncontainable by print. Characters and stories that originated in pulp soon found their way onto radio airwaves (e.g., *The Shadow*), onto the screen in the form of pre-Code sizzlers, noirs, and adventure films, and into comic books and newspaper comic strips. Through all these media, pulp penetrated the heart of the American popular imagination (and the popular image of America beyond its borders), shaping as well as reflecting the culture that consumed it.

Far more frequently than has been acknowledged, the source of these American icons, story lines, and genres were women, often working-class women who put bread on the table by creating imaginary worlds, or exploring existing but risky or taboo worlds, to fulfill the appetites of readers of both genders. But these writers, and the rich variety of work they produced, are today nearly invisible, despite the pulp revival of the last decade.

This revival has repopularized a hard-boiled, male world of pulp. Today's best-remembered pulp authors are not only male but also unapologetically misogynistic: pulp icon Jim Thompson's *A Hell of a Woman* and *A Swell-Looking Babe* are not untypical of the titles found among the noir classics recently restored to print.

In fact, it is interesting to note, even in a broader survey of the genres, how many male-authored, and presumably male-read, pulps were focused on women (remember *Shack Baby* and *Reefer Girl*)—a phenomenon not found in the highbrow literature of the period. Men even wrote a fair number of lesbian pulps. But more often than not, the women in these books are dangerous and predatory as well as irresistible, exploiting men's desire for their own purposes. Or they are wayward women who either come to a bad end, or come to their senses with the help of a man who sets them straight (in the various senses of the word). Some critics have noted that such female characters proliferated in the immediate post–World War II period, when servicemen were returning to a world in which women had occupied, briefly, a powerful position in the workplace and other areas of the public sphere—a world in which the balance between the genders had been irrevocably altered.

In contrast with these bad girls and femmes fatales were the heroines of traditional romance pulps, most of them relentlessly pretty and spunky girls-next-door. They occupied the centers of their own stories, and navigated sometimes complicated social and emotional terrain, but in the end always seemed to get—or be gotten by—their man.

Given this background, and given the strict generic dictates to which all successful pulp writers were subject, did women working in undeniably male-dominated pulp genres such as crime/noir write differently from their male counterparts? And did women writers of formulaic romances, both heterosexual and lesbian, reveal the genuine conflicts facing real women in their time and explore the limits of female agency? They could hardly fail to do so.

Relatively little scholarship has been done on pulp fiction; less still on women writers of pulp. It is not possible to speculate on the intentions of women pulp authors, and few would suggest that they were undercover feminists seeking to subvert patriarchal culture by embedding radical messages in cheap popular novels. Yet from a contemporary vantage point, some of their work certainly does seem subversive, regardless of the intention behind it.

A woman author launched the genre of lesbian pulp in 1950 when Tereska Torres's *Women's Barracks,* with its sympathetic portrayal of lesbian relationships among women soldiers in the Free French forces during World War II, sold millions of copies in the United States as a pulp paperback original. While most of the lesbian pulp novels that followed had—at the insistence of publishers hoping to deflect obscenity charges—unhappy endings, women writers provided the first happy endings for lesbians. Valerie Taylor's *The Girls in 3-B* is a prime example of this suprisingly revolutionary phenomenon, and still more intriguing for its contrast of the different options and obstacles faced by heterosexual and homo-sexual women in the 1950s (with little doubt as to which looked better to the author). The femme fatale of *In a Lonely Place,* the luscious Laurel Gray, has brains and integrity, as well as curves—and in the end, she is not the one who turns out to be deadly. In fact, Dorothy B. Hughes's bold twist on the noir genre can be seen as addressing the crisis in postwar masculinity, with its backlash taken to the furthest extremes. The protagonist of Faith Baldwin's *Skyscraper* is typically pretty and plucky;

she longs for domestic bliss and she loves her man. But she also loves the bustle and buzz of the office where she works, the rows of gleaming desks and file cabinets, the sense of being part of the larger, public world of business—and she epitomizes a new kind of heroine in a new kind of romance plot, a career girl with a wider set of choices to negotiate.

These premier books in the Feminist Press's Femmes Fatales series were selected for their bold and sometimes transgressive uses of genre forms, as well as the richness of their social and historical settings and their lively and skillful writing. We chose books that also seemed to have some impact on public consciousness in their time—in these cases, rather inexactly measured by the fact that they crossed over into different, and even more popular, media: Both *In a Lonely Place* and *Skyscraper* were made into films. And we can only speculate whether *The Girls in 3-B* played any part in inspiring *The Girls in Apartment 3-G,* the syndicated comic strip about three young working women (heterosexual, of course) living together in New York City, which debuted in 1961.

The enormous popularity of the Femmes Fatales series's first season, in 2003, confirms readers' intense interest in these rediscovered queens of pulp. In 2004, the series expanded to include a second book by the incomparable Dorothy B. Hughes: *The Blackbirder*, a World War II espionage novel with a unique hard-boiled heroine. It also added two books that achieved fame, again, primarily through the films they inspired. *Now, Voyager*, the renowned romantic melodrama that gave Bette Davis her favorite role, deals directly with issues of women's emotional, sexual, and social autonomy. The fascinating psychological thriller *Bunny Lake Is Missing*, made into a supremely creepy (and cult classic) film by Otto Preminger, introduces a hard-boiled mom, who must rapidly transform herself from a handwringer to a gunslinger when her daughter is kidnapped. We begin 2005 with two great pulp classics, *Women's Barracks,* the original lesbian pulp, and *The G-String Murders,* in which famed strip-teaser Gypsy Rose Lee provides a backstage tour of 1930s burlesque theater, replete with wise-cracking, hard-working women.

In the past three decades, feminist scholars have laid claim to women's popular fiction as a legitimate focus of attention and scholarship, and a rich source of information on women's lives and thought in various eras. Some scholars have in fact questioned the use—and the uses—of the term *popular fiction,* which seems to have been disproportionately applied to the work of women writers, especially those who wrote "women's books." The Feminist Press views the Femmes Fatales series as an important new initiative in this ongoing work of cultural reclamation. As such, it is also a natural expression of the Press's overall mission to ensure that women's voices are fully represented in the public discourse, in the literary "canon," and on bookstore and library shelves.

We leave it to scholars doing groundbreaking new work on women's pulp—including our own afterword writers—to help us fully appreciate all that these works have to offer, both as literary texts and as social documents. And we leave it to our readers to discover for themselves, as we have, all of the entertaining, disturbing, suggestive, and thoroughly fascinating work that can be found behind the juicy covers of women's pulp fiction.

Livia Tenzer, Editorial Director
Jean Casella, Publisher
New York City
January 2005

TRANSLATOR'S PREFACE

While working in the newsroom of the Office of War Information in London during World War II, I met a young woman who was our liaison with the French information services. Tereska was a volunteer in the women's division of the Free French Forces, corresponding to our WACS. We became friends, and I visited her often in the ancient mansion on Down Street that had been turned into a barracks for these Frenchwomen. I came to know Tereska's circle.

Recently I met her again in Paris, happily married and the mother of two children. Tereska had just written a book about her companions in the Free French Forces, and she showed it to me. I recognized all the girls of the little circle in Down Street, and their stories, which I knew to be true.

It seemed to me that this book, with all its tenderness, was an important book because it told a story that had not yet been truly told, the story of women in war. This was the story of the effect of living together in military barracks upon a group of young girls, many of them utterly innocent when they entered the service, where they were to encounter jaded women who had lived through every type of experience. I recognized the authenticity of every line.

The problems brought forward here are problems that must be recognized wherever women have to live together without normal emotional outlets. What is told here should help to bring understanding of these special problems, for the story of Down Street reminds us that women must be women, even in war.

—George Cummings

My husband tells me I ought to write my memoirs of the women's army in which I spent five years during World War II. It's very difficult. I don't know where to begin or how to tell it. My husband tells me laughingly that it will make a sensational book, and I really don't see myself as a writer of sensational books. But, he insists, the story will be interesting to Americans because we were a barracksful of Frenchwomen in exile, and it seems that Frenchwomen have a great deal of allure abroad.

"You know I don't like to talk about myself," I protest.

"Well, then write about the others." And he adds jokingly, "They're more interesting, anyway. Besides"—and he becomes serious—"it will be useful, it will help people understand."

It's raining. It's been raining since we arrived at the seashore. It seems that it rains a great deal in Brittany. And the rain reminds me of the summers in England when the rain fell ceaselessly.

I can still see, in every dismal detail, the big house on Down Street as it looked on those wet, cheerless days. Down Street, for all those who lived there, will always remain that big house of blackened brick in the narrow gray street, that cold and somber house bracketed between high brick walls. The dirty windows penetrated by yellowish light, the dim corridors, the large glacial assembly room, the dismal dormitories, the dining rooms with their bare tables—all had a prison-like aspect. Down Street—for me the name evokes the list of infractions and punishments posted in the entrance hallway; stairways to be swept, potatoes to be peeled, floors to be scrubbed on our knees. It evokes the little switchboard room, which someone dubbed the "Bordello," with its high walls and high grilled window. I can't count the times I stood before that window, seeking a bit of sky; but always facing us, standing there in front of the hotel across the street, was the one we called "the Ambassador of Peru," holding himself erect, tall, thin, with painted cheeks, forever watching our barracks with his strange demonic smile. He seemed to me to be an angel of evil guarding our house.

But more than all these, Down Street evokes the women with whom I lived in that house. The truth is, I'm one of those people who live a great deal in the lives of others. Perhaps that's why people seem to feel easy in telling me things about themselves. I like to listen.

Sometimes at the barracks I wondered why so many of the girls in our little group chose me as their confidante, and poured out their most intimate feelings to me, their secret thoughts, while I didn't offer mine in return. I even asked this once of little Ursula. "Perhaps it's just because it is not an exchange," she said. "When I talk to you, I feel it's not a bargain in which I leave you my troubles and you leave me yours. You take mine, and that's all."

I never felt I was taking anyone's troubles, though there were times when I terribly wished I could help my friends in some way. I felt it was wonderful to have people trust me and let me into their lives. And I will try to write of their lives, telling not only what I saw, but of the feelings and thoughts that they revealed to me, and of some of the things I divined.

Naturally I was not present myself during all of the incidents that I am about to relate. Yet I know that these things happened, and I know well the women to whom they happened. These episodes are important, because they are significant of the pressures and tensions that all of us felt, and that all women must inevitably feel when they are isolated from normal living, caught in the strange turmoil of war. And so, since I am so well acquainted with the women who experienced these things—with their characters as well as their outward lives—I shall from time to time pretend, like a novelist, that I was an invisible witness to the private moments of my comrades.

—Tereska Torres

CHAPTER 1

When the war began, I was in my last year of school at the convent of St. Celestine. I was seventeen and unobtrusive, though not really plain. I had never even gone out with a boy. I had been raised in the warm family seclusion that is characteristic of respectable French families. My mother's parents lived with us in our small house near Orléans.

My father was a sculptor, and most of the friends of our family were, I suppose, middle-class people—university professors, some minor government officials, writers, and other artists. My own school friends were a rather serious-minded set of little girls. Though we did our share of giggling, we discussed such grave problems as the emancipation of the Frenchwoman; for at that time, women in France still did not have the vote. And though we knew nothing of men, we had long discussions about the number of children we would have. I was an only child, and was therefore ambitious to become the mother of a large brood.

Then the war was upon us. Papa enlisted. During the long winter of the "phony war" we felt secure. Then the war began in earnest. Papa was at the front, and we were sure France would win.

When the Germans reached Liége, Mother said we would have to leave Paris. I said she was out of her mind. I said the Germans would never get as close to Paris as they did in the last war. A week later the Germans were at the Meuse, and my mother and my grandparents insisted that we should prepare to leave.

And so one day in May I took off the navy-blue uniform dress of my convent school, and with my mother and my grandparents I left Paris. We were in danger, my mother said, because of our origins—her parents, who had come from Poland, were Jewish.

We had heard nothing from my father for several weeks. Then there was the news of the disaster at Dunkirk. Perhaps my father was there, helping the English.

Everyone was leaving Paris—all the prominent people, and all the people in government circles, including some of our friends, and everyone who had a car. We had no car. We left on a train that was crowded like a subway. We were going to St. Jean de Luz, where we could stay with my father's cousins.

We were certain we would be back soon; so certain that my mother left the family silver and all our other possessions unlocked in the house, simply telling the concierge to keep an eye on things. And I left my Teddy bear sitting on my bed. He was just exactly my own age, and he had slept with me all his life. It was for him that I wept when I thought of the Germans taking possession of our house.

After three almost unbearable days of crowding and confusion, of trains that stopped running and trains that changed destination, we all arrived at St. Jean de Luz, where the sun shone, and there was a beautiful beach, and there was the sea. The war seemed very far away.

I was sent back to my studies, to prepare for my graduation examination, which I should have taken that year in Paris. I passed it at last, at Bayonne, and was qualified to enter college. The day of my graduation was the day when France signed her armistice of defeat.

I was only a girl, scarcely out of my childhood; I didn't understand what was happening at all, but I was shocked beyond comprehension. We had been promised victory, and we were being handed defeat. There was still no news of my father. My mother wept all day long. And the Germans were coming, everybody said, even to the south.

It was on one of those days that I met one of my mother's friends in the street, and she talked to me about General de Gaulle and his proclamation from London, asking for volunteers for his Free French army. In that moment it became clear to me that the one possible answer to the chaos in which we had been plunged was De Gaulle.

It was then that I began to beg my mother to leave. Day and night I insisted that we had to leave France. Our lives, and the lives of her parents, were in danger. And slowly she began to be persuaded.

Our fashionable little town was filling with refugees. Some of them were refugees de luxe in their big cars, but there were also bewildered remnants of troops in the streets, unshaven, distraught men—our own, and also many soldiers from a Polish regiment that had been enlisted in France. The Poles were fleeing for their lives, and no one could understand them or help them until they found us. I remember that one day we succeeded in finding civilian clothes for half a dozen Polish soldiers who wanted to try to escape into Spain.

On the twenty-fifth of June, 1940, I went with my mother to Biarritz, where there was a Portuguese consulate. We applied for visas for ourselves and my grandparents, and we were among the very last to receive them. That very night there were notices posted in St. Jean de Luz announcing that German troops would be in town the next day. In the morning all the shops were shuttered. I saw a troop carrier move through the street, and turned my face away. That same day, I hitchhiked to Hendaye, to secure transit visas through Spain. That night we packed our bags and rucksacks; even my grandparents were loaded with all they could carry.

The next day we took the train to Hendaye. We got out and approached the customs station on our side of the international bridge. We could see the Spanish flag floating across the bridge, but on our side there was no flag; our tricolor had already been taken down. But at least there was still no swastika. As the customs man stamped our passports, he said, "*Les salauds*, they won't remain here long."

We walked across the bridge, managing to lug all of our baggage. After the formalities on the other side, we took a taxi to the railway station at Irún. On the way the driver stopped at a check post, and while our papers were being examined, a carful of German soldiers drove up. Our driver gave the Hitler salute. I shuddered. But the Germans did not question us, and we drove on.

At Figueira da Foz, in Portugal, we found ourselves in a luxurious vacation center with the elite of France and Belgium: diamond merchants, movie stars, famous authors and statesmen, who sunned themselves on the golden beach, or strolled along the palm-shaded walks, or amused themselves in the cafés. We were refugees together with Danielle Darrieux, Dalio, Maurice Chevalier. We passed our days in endless gossipy discussions—should we leave for Chile, Argentina, or Brazil? Some said the United States was sending a ship for us all. Others said we would leave in a week for Canada. There were bullfights in the afternoons, movies in the evenings, and I attended my first ball.

It was there in Figueira da Foz that we received our first news of my father. Some French officers arrived and informed us that units of my father's division had escaped across the Channel.

We were overjoyed and frightened at the same time. There was a good chance that Father had escaped from France, but was he safe and well? Had he actually arrived in England at all? Nobody knew.

Mother could not leave her aged parents to go to England and search for Father, but I could. I had to do a good bit of persuading, but in the end it was agreed. My mother and her parents would sail for Canada, and I would go to England.

I left before they did. A British ship was taking volunteers for De Gaulle's forces, and place was found for me aboard.

After I reached London it took me only a few days to find an army comrade of my father's, and to learn that my father had been taken prisoner. He was to remain in prison throughout the war.

The Free French Forces had just announced that they would recruit women. Here was the very opportunity I had hoped for. I had arrived at the opportune moment, and presented myself on the first day of female recruiting. There, in the large barren hall, I felt that I would at last be transformed from a schoolgirl to a woman with a purpose.

A few score women were already on hand. I wondered just what sort of girls were to become my companions, for surely they would not be representative of the average, typical Frenchwoman. To be in London at all during the war, they had to be drawn from special groups.

There was always a certain number of students from France, but French families are extremely closely knit, and in times of stress, these students would most likely have been drawn home, so that the only ones to have remained in England would be the children of disturbed or broken families—divorced parents, disoriented homes. And then there would be some girls from the working classes—French maidservants and the French prostitutes of Soho. Another category of women were the adventuresses, emancipated women, and career women who for one reason or another had no family life.

In the end, there were to be some five hundred of us in this service during the war, and more than as many again in an ambulance and nursing corps that was formed later for service in France. Our own group was like the WACS or the ATS. We were to replace men in all sorts of jobs, so that they might be released for combat.

From that first day, we were to be united by one act—our act of volunteering. For whether we had come from Paris or the provinces, whether we had already been in London when the war broke out or had made our way there from abroad, whether we joined in 1940 or reached London in 1944, all of us were impelled by the same ideal. All of us, workers, students, servants, divorcees, secretaries, the younger and the older, volunteered with the sincere hope of giving ourselves to France—the France beloved of every Frenchwoman, the France for whom every one of us was certainly ready, on that first day in the recruiting station, to die.

From the recruiting desk I passed into a huge, cold, gloomy room where a dozen young women stood shivering, naked, waiting their turns for the medical examination. The first one with whom I became acquainted was Mickey, for, with her easy, impulsive way, she was never slow to greet a stranger. A rather tall girl, with the gawkiness of a figure just out of adolescence, she commented freely and laughingly as she looked about, finding something extremely droll in the military air that we all tried to assume. As she watched the physician, hurried and coarse, examining the teeth and eyes of the girls while keeping up a stream of questionable pleasantries, Mickey remarked that it was funny to be getting acquainted with the bodies of our future comrades before we even knew their names.

Mickey said she had just escaped from France, where she had been spending her summer holiday with her aunt and uncle. Mickey's parents were in Scotland, where her father taught French in a small college. He was French and her mother was English. They had married late in life and she was a "December child," somewhat pampered, as we were to learn, impulsive, and avid for excitement, since she had been brought up as an only child in the muted household of an aging couple. Her father was a typical absent-minded, gentle old professor, and Mickey rattled on, telling everyone within earshot about him, as we waited for our medical examination. She simply adored him, she said, slurring the accent in "adore" with a quaint tinge of English inflection. Because of her father, Mickey considered herself French rather than English. She had spent much of her young life with her father's family in France, and now she had returned on a fishing vessel to enlist in the Free French Forces.

Mickey prattled on, seemingly quite at ease in her nudity—perhaps because she knew that she was pretty. One could see that Mickey felt sure of herself in her body, as though she were wearing a Paris dress that no one could help admiring. Hers was a slim, boyish, somewhat gawky figure in perfect modern style, marred only by a few pimples on her shoulders, a temporary blemish.

"What you need is to make love. That'll get rid of those pimples for you," said a slightly older woman, winking at Mickey confidentially.

Mickey laughed, almost as though the whole thing were agreed upon; after all, she was eighteen, and the day was coming when she would "make love." The expression was obviously exciting to her, touching as it did upon something that was still mysterious and forbidden.

In a corner a little girl awaited her turn, seated on a chair. She had pulled up her slender legs and hugged them close, so that all one could see of her was her head of glossy chestnut hair, cut in a page-boy bob, falling straight and thick on both sides of her face. Her legs hid her body, while her forehead rested on her narrow, boyish knees. Trembling with cold, she hugged her legs closer to her body. The older woman's advice to Mickey and the coarseness of the woman's laughter seemed to strike the little girl, for she reacted as from a muddy-handed slap. This was Ursula.

I noticed her then, noticed how her frail body contracted at the crude words. Instinctively she passed her fingers over her face, and she turned her head away a trifle. Later, when I came to know her well, Ursula told me that this had somehow been a terrible moment for her; not that what was said was in itself so coarse, but because she had never before completely undressed in front of others, and because the ease, the very naturalness of the remark and the assumption that went with it, not only for Mickey but for all of us, gave her her first shock of reality, her first sense of what our coming life might be like. At that moment, she later told me, she felt as though a kind of dirtiness had entered her, and was sliding down her throat.

I wasn't the only one who noticed her revulsion, for a silken-looking young lady standing beside Ursula said, "I hate vulgarity, don't you? My name is Jacqueline. I'm from Grenoble. And you?"

Ursula told her name and said that she was from Paris.

"You're cold," Jacqueline said. "Take my coat. How old are you?"

Ursula seemed to hesitate. When we became friends she confessed that she was wondering, then, whether to reply with her official age, eighteen, or with her real age—just short of sixteen! She hesitated, for Ursula never learned how to lie quickly, and she ended by saying that she was seventeen. That seemed an honest compromise to little Ursula.

"You look fourteen," Jacqueline declared, with her patronizing knowingness that was to become so familiar to us. "You still look like a baby, really. Listen, I'll help you out. I'll get us assigned to the same dormitory."

Ursula thanked her. And yet, despite her frail and childlike air, she was, as we were to learn, quite a determined little person, used to living alone and managing for herself. Her parents were divorced, and she had been raised in a variety of schools and by servants, by cousins, by nurses, in the course of travel from place to place. Indeed, she showed some embarrassment at the sudden possessiveness with which Jacqueline, aristocratic even in her nudity, had taken charge of her, and she politely refused the coat Jacqueline had offered.

A door opened and a woman in uniform entered.

"All those who have completed their examinations come and get uniforms," she shouted.

Mickey led the rush to the next room, where there was a table piled with khaki garments. She was broad-shouldered, with narrow hips, long muscular legs, and diminutive pointed breasts, and she moved with a tennis-playing directness that nevertheless had a touch of the peculiarly awkward feminine charm of a girl of that age. Just after Mickey came Jacqueline, who, at the alluring call of the uniform, had momentarily deserted her new protégée. Jacqueline was, in contrast to Mickey, finely made, with delicately rounded hips and exquisite round breasts, and small altogether, as though all that was coarse in civilization had been refined away, to leave this elegant little body, a complete statement of perfection.

The corporal behind the table took our measures at a glance. "Sizes medium and large." She tossed each of us a jacket and a skirt of rough hard wool, two khaki shirts, two neckties, a pair of stockings, a rose-colored brassiere, a linen undershirt, a pair of knee-length khaki jersey panties, and shoes.

We all began to dress, emitting little cries, laughing. We tried to knot our ties, to button skirts that were too large and jackets that were too small.

The only one who seemed to know how to knot her tie properly was a strapping large girl with a boyish haircut, who looked immediately natural and in her place in uniform. When she had finished dressing she glanced around the room and called out to the corporal, "Do you want me to help you?" She had a heavy, almost masculine voice, reassuring and cheerful, and the confidence in her voice contrasted with her expression, which was a little oppressive, and predominantly sad. The oppressiveness was in her heavy chin, and there was a sadness in her very beautiful eyes, violently blue, and in her mouth with its large lips, sunken at the corners.

The corporal accepted her help, and I think that several of us noted, mentally, that the large calm girl with her air of self-possession and an ability to command would make good officer material.

"What's your name?" the corporal asked.

"Ann," the other replied in her deep voice, and the light feminine name seemed unsuited to her.

Ursula was among the girls before the counter. Ann handed her a uniform, and then helped her to dress and to knot her tie. She had a friendly, easy way of being helpful—like a big brother.

We studied each other in our uniforms. It was dainty Jacqueline who immediately drew every eye. She was instantly classified as ravishing—so ravishing that one could scarcely feel jealous. Jacqueline had the sort of impersonal beauty in which every other woman feels she is somehow represented. Jacqueline's complexion was the freshest, purest, rosiest imaginable. Her face was positively luminous, irradiated by her glamorous hazel eyes; her beautiful white teeth, bright and gleaming, were framed by a mouth with rather large sensual lips, as soft to the eye as they would be to kiss.

Jacqueline twisted her reddish-brown hair into an amusing little bun, and smiled at Ursula with a well-bred graciousness precisely suited to her appearance.

Mickey was laughing over the way we looked; she laughed over everything and over nothing, eager to find fun. Her pale blue eyes were perpetually wide-open, and her nose puckered out of sight when she laughed. Because of her mixed Anglo-French parentage, she spoke French always with that quaint little British accent which added another droll quality to her fun-loving air.

"Are you English?" Jacqueline asked her.

"No, I'm French," Mickey insisted, repeating her history. "My mother is English and my father is French, but I'm French! I just came from France. I adore France!"

With her impulsive warmth, she seemed to be establishing herself as a firm friend of Jacqueline's. And indeed, Jacqueline responded to her as to someone who was also, obviously, from a family with good breeding.

The silken, precious-looking Jacqueline came from the world of the aristocracy. Her story, too, came out soon enough. She was among us almost as a runaway, to escape a depressing family life, mangled as it can sometimes become only in high society. Jacqueline's father had died when she was a child of seven, and her mother had remarried only a year later. Jacqueline had never liked her stepfather, and as soon as she reached adolescence the child had discovered that her beauty carried with it something of disaster and doom. Her stepfather's too pressing attentions had aroused a frightened loathing in Jacqueline, and as soon as she was old enough she had seized the first opportunity to escape from her family on an exchange visit with some of their friends in England. But there too her beauty had won her too much attention, and one night she had tried to escape by dropping from the roof, and had injured herself quite seriously. As soon as she felt well enough, she had come to London to enlist.

The corporal shouted, "Form ranks in pairs, and try to march in step if you can. Forward march!"

With much confusion we managed to form ranks. The scene reminded us somehow of our classroom days.

"Silence!" cried the corporal, and our little column marched out of the room, with the women jostling each other and choking back their laughter as they squeezed through the narrow doorway.

Outdoors, in the street, it began to rain; a small, fine, clinging rain, sharp and cold. No one marched in step. I was surprised how difficult it was, since marching always looked so easy when one watched a parade of soldiers. I was in line with Ursula. "I never believed marching was something that had to be learned," she remarked, and blushed for having offered her observation.

A few passers-by turned to look at us. I wondered whether they could possibly realize how much that march meant to us. We were literally marching into a completely new life. I kept saying to myself, This is what I wanted. This is what I came for. This is the first time that I decided on something for myself, and made it come true. And it gave me a frightening sense of entering not only the Army, but life itself.

And so we marched behind the corporal, who had placed Ann at the head of the column, and it was a ridiculous column, zigzagging, with the tall and the short all jumbled together, a column of women half running, in our ill-fitting uniforms, too long, too short, too wide. But neither long-striding Ann nor the glowing Jacqueline nor the elderly woman with the coarse voice nor even the fun-loving Mickey—not any of us thought of laughing.

CHAPTER 2

A truck stood in front of our barracks, and a soldier was gesticulating for assistance; there was luggage and furniture to be unloaded.

"I want a volunteer to help unload the truck!" our corporal cried out.

The first to offer herself was tall, husky Ann. With ease she lifted a table onto her back, carrying it as though it were a feather. The rest of us were immediately assigned to clean the house.

Another corporal, dark and dry, with a face like a prune, meted out our tasks. Dainty Jacqueline and little Ursula were ordered to scrub the large entrance hall of the ancient mansion. I was to work on the main stairway that circled upward to our dormitories.

Jacqueline donned a huge beige-colored smock, rolled the sleeves up to her elbows, got down on her knees, and began to scrub. Ursula stood there staring at Jacqueline, as though she didn't know where to begin. She looked at the pail of grayish water, the wet brush, and the blackened rag. I suppose she had never been faced with such a disgusting task, and there was a dismay about her, as though she had no idea how to go about scrubbing a floor, as though she might just as well have been suddenly commanded to run a locomotive.

Jacqueline was scrubbing energetically. It seemed all the more aristocratic of her not to be upset by the most menial of tasks. But suddenly she gasped and put her hand to her back.

The prune-faced corporal, passing by, cried out, "Well, my little one, so you've already got a sore back after two minutes of work! This is a barracks, not a drawing room!" And seeing Ursula standing there confused and inactive, she was overcome with sudden rage. All these daughters of the idle rich! She poured out her anger upon Ursula. "You! You will do me the pleasure of scrubbing the hall, and after that, I've got work for you in the kitchen."

"There's no need for you to shout," Ursula murmured, red with shame and dismay. Whereupon she received a look that announced more clearly than words that this girl was already on the corporal's black list.

Jacqueline raised herself on one foot, with her hand still to her back. A lock of hair had fallen over her forehead, giving her a slightly melodramatic look. She looked a bit as though she were acting in a film, playing the part of the poor and beautiful orphan, forced to slave under the command of an ill-tempered mistress. To everyone's astonishment, Jacqueline talked back to the corporal, defending Ursula.

"Can't you give that sort of work to the stronger girls? I don't care what I do, but she's too little, she's much too frail. Why don't you find something else for her to do?"

"If she's too frail, then she's got no business joining the Army. She'll scrub the hall, and you've got no business interfering!"

The tension was eased by Ann. From the height of a ladder, on which she stood washing the high hall windows, she called out in her deep, easy voice, "Come, come, children, don't argue! It'll give the little girl some muscle to work a bit. The corporal is right."

I couldn't tell if big Ann were making fun of the corporal, or trying to help out Ursula by appeasing the corporal's anger. In any case, the result was good, for Pruneface softened a little; she even squeezed out a smile for Ann, and went off without saying any more.

Ursula got down to work near the stairs. She was furious with Jacqueline for having come to her defense. "Now the corporal hates me," she whispered.

She watched Jacqueline, who kept at her scrubbing, pausing from time to time to gasp. Mickey, who was working beside me, waxing the stairs, was also intrigued by Jacqueline's behavior. "It's an act," she said. But Ursula called to our distinguished-looking scrub lady, "Is something wrong with your back? Does it hurt all the time?"

With a resigned and rather mysterious air, Jacqueline replied, "It's nothing. Don't worry." And at the same moment the brush fell from her hand, and she toppled unconscious on the stone floor.

At our outcry, the corporal came hurrying back, with an air of supreme annoyance. She stood over us as we tried to revive Jacqueline. After all, the girl's collapse might be considered her fault.

Ursula slapped Jacqueline's hands. Ann arrived with a glass of water. Jacqueline quickly opened her eyes, apologized, and said that the fainting spell was of no consequence. She insisted that she could go on working. After a moment's hesitation, we all went back to our tasks.

Mickey, with her chattery ways and her funny little accent that made everything she said seem somehow a bit more intimate, now declared, "You know, I think she really did faint. She looks like she's acting all the time, but I think the faint was real."

One of the girls above us on the stairs began to sing *"Auprès de ma blonde"*; she had a Brittany accent. The warm, reassuring voice of Ann joined in the refrain, and then, one by one, we all picked it up. The tense and somber atmosphere that pervaded the large dim hall seemed to dissolve.

Ann paused in her singing to remark that it was still raining outdoors. This was London, where it always rained. We would get used to it, as to everything else.

A bell rang, and several women came up from the kitchen, carrying enormous steaming dishes. "Dinner!" they cried.

There were not yet enough tables and benches for all of us in the dining room. We had to crowd together on the benches. Finally everyone managed to squeeze in somewhere, and there was a kind of general sigh of relief. But just then the corporal shouted, "Attention!"

Ann was the first to jump up. The rest of us instinctively imitated her. The door opened, and several women entered.

They were dressed in impeccable uniforms, with gold stripes on their sleeves.

The Captain was in front. She was a large and handsome woman, with graying hair cut short. She had a heavy face with a self-satisfied mouth, an intelligent forehead, and impenetrable eyes. Behind her stood the warrant officer, Petit, a smallish woman who had the look of a little old man, with reddish-gray hair and a face filled with small wrinkles. She was altogether like a gallant old fellow holding himself quite erect and looking over the girls with a friendly eye.

"Everything here is still on a makeshift basis," said the Captain. "In a few days we'll have the house furnished and each of you will be assigned to a job in the forces. If any of you has any difficulty, come and see me. You know that my job is to help you, and I count on making this barracks a home for each and every one of you, since you are so far away from your families. I have some important projects in mind; I have big ambitions for you. I hope that you will put in a great deal of work these first days, and that you will get along well with your officers. France, for whose sake you have . . ."

While the Captain talked, I could see Ann studying the warrant officer, Petit. Yes, Petit had the air of an elderly man, and I suppose Ann knew that it was inevitable that Petit should notice her. She touched her tie to make sure the knot was in place; she passed her hand over her hair.

Petit was studying all the girls, smilingly, looking from one to the other of us, until her eyes met Ann's, and then her eyes remained immobile for an instant. Petit had small gray clever eyes. It seemed to me, watching her, that her little pupils were suddenly drowned in Ann's large somber blue eyes, and even I, only a bystander at this silent exchange, could sense a current passing between the two women.

They looked at each other over the heads of the rest of us, and I thought, They've never met before, but they recognize each other; they know they're the same kind. It was plain that there was no need of words or of explanations between them. It was quite simple, quite clear, and even if nothing came of it, they could count on each other in the eternal battle between themselves and other women—those of us who were subject to the needs, the fears, the weaknesses that neither Ann nor Petit felt.

We resumed our places at the tables. There was no table linen, but the food was good. After all, the cook was French, and from Normandy. She knew her work; she had operated a restaurant before the war. The cook was large and fat, with hair dyed a hard black. She didn't know how to speak without shouting, and her voice was rough.

Assigned to her in the kitchen were three little girls from Brittany who had just arrived on a fishing boat. They were young, fresh, round-cheeked; they didn't use make-up, and they looked even more unsuited to their uniforms than the rest of us.

No one ate very much. We all felt homesick. On the wall, there already hung a huge photograph of General de Gaulle. Occasionally someone would raise her head toward him, as though looking for reassurance.

CHAPTER 3

The alert sounded precisely at six o'clock, as it did every night. No one had gone out that evening. It was our first day, and we were busy arranging our things, and besides, very few of us knew anyone in London.

In the evening, a second group of a dozen women arrived, and we "old ones" experienced a certain feeling of superiority. We were already forming little groups among ourselves.

The silken Jacqueline, noisy Mickey, and little Ursula were in my dormitory, and from the first we were somehow drawn together. The reason came out, perhaps, when a young woman with a large full mouth and an absolutely round face approached our little group, and standing facing us asked, without any preliminaries, whether we were virgins.

Mickey began to laugh. Jacqueline assumed a haughty, offended air. Ursula simply blushed and said yes. On the instant, our dormitory was baptized "The Virgins' Room"— though the young woman who had asked the question could obviously not be included in that category. Her name was Ginette, and she informed us that she was a salesgirl and a divorcee. She undressed, promenading naked among the cots, and declared to Jacqueline, "You know, the best thing about my face is my legs." It was true that she had pretty legs.

Presently Ginette held up a pair of the regulation khaki panties they had handed out to us. "Just look at that! What a monstrosity! How can I expect to get a lover with that?" And on the spot, Ginette brought out a pair of scissors and a needle and thread, and began to turn the panties into briefs. At once, the rest of us followed her example. Each of us remade the regulation underwear.

A bomb fell not far away; then there was a crash of breaking glass. Mickey, sitting at the foot of her bed, was putting curlers in her hair. A woman who was a hairdresser in civilian life came over to help her, and then the hairdresser began to discuss Ursula's coiffure. She declared that Ursula ought to have her hair done up in curls, to make her look a little more mature. An argument began. Jacqueline wanted Ursula's hair put up in a bun, to make her look sophisticated, and Mickey was all for having it in short curly clusters, to make her look boyish. But Ursula rejected all of our suggestions, holding her head in her two hands as though to keep us from tearing out her hair.

At nine-thirty the corporal came to put out the lights. As soon as the door was closed, Ginette turned them on again.

Mickey, in pajamas, began teaching Ursula a dance step. Jacqueline was writing a letter, on monogrammed stationery; one of the girls was growling from under her covers that she wanted to sleep.

I could see that Ursula was beginning to feel a kind of warmth and security in the room with all these new friends— a warmth, I learned later, that she had never known in her life before. After all, the room was bright and filled with human sounds, and all these girls were like big sisters busying themselves with her. Outside, there was night, exile, bombardment, a foreign city bathed in fog and rain. Here people spoke French, laughed and worked together, and it was as though everybody had always known each other.

Mickey told her, "As soon as I heard General de Gaulle's appeal, I wanted to enlist. I'm so proud of being French, and I adore De Gaulle! I saw him once in a parade."

"What's he like?" Ursula asked.

"Oh, he's marvelous—very tall, and he looks awfully serious and sad."

Ginette spoke up. "I crossed over the Pyrenees on foot, and I got myself pinched in Spain. I told them I was a Canadian. I was with a man, an American, a good-looking fellow. He made love like a stick, but I liked him well enough. He's in America now. He's going to send me silk stockings and lipstick."

"You're lucky," sighed Mickey, puckering her little nose.

Jacqueline raised her head, pausing in her writing to mutter something about women who permitted themselves to be kept. But Jacqueline's lofty attitude didn't annoy Ginette, who was now busy tailoring the jacket of her uniform, making it over to her measure, with the help of the former hairdresser. Somehow, I felt, nothing could annoy Ginette.

The door opened again, and the face of the corporal appeared, pinched and angry. She was about to shout something when she noticed Mickey, who had her scissors in one hand and her khaki drawers in the other. The corporal glared at her. Then she announced icily, "If I see the lights burning in this room once more after lights out, the whole lot of you will stand punishment." She snapped out the light and slammed the door.

Ginette, who was caught in the middle of the room, cursed because she couldn't find her bed. The woman who had wanted to sleep grunted that at last there was justice. Jacqueline and Mickey gossiped from their beds.

Over the house, all night long, we could hear the growling of planes.

CHAPTER 4

I opened my eyes at dawn. That first morning I lay motionless for a moment, studying the large gray room. A foggy light came through the dirty windows. The rain beat on the panes and staggered down. The room must at one time have been a library, for there were empty shelves all around the walls, and the vacant shelves somehow made me think of blind eye sockets.

I could make out the figures of the other women in the narrow camp beds; here and there a head, a mass of hair, or an arm protruded from under a gray blanket. There were no sheets. There had even been a shortage of cots, and two girls were asleep on straw pallets on the floor; one of them snored. I thought, This is my life now, and I didn't mind; I felt rather proud.

I realized that Ursula was awake, and looking at me with her large quiet eyes. Mickey woke up yawning, and as she stretched she threw a joyful "Hello, baby!" to Ursula. This awakened all the others, and presently the entire room was alive with movement.

"I dreamed that the corporal made me scrub the roof," Jacqueline announced, "and I was terrified that I was going to fall. I was so frightened that I woke up."

The bell began to ring, and none of us knew whether it was ringing for reveille or for breakfast. The room was freezing cold, for the furnace had not yet been lighted. The building that had been turned into a barracks for us was an old mansion, abandoned many years ago, and almost impossible to heat properly at any time.

Most of the girls were parading back and forth to the bathroom in their dressing gowns. Ursula was dressing under her covers, complaining that she was too cold to emerge. Jacqueline went over to her, in that protective way that she had, and knotted Ursula's tie, like some society matron taking care of a waif.

The door opened and the prune-faced corporal appeared. "Everybody in the hall for inspection!"

Although it was seven in the morning, the main hall was still so dark that the electricity had to be turned on, but there was only a small yellowish bulb that gave very little light.

All of us were formed into a circle. The sergeant, two corporals, and Petit, the warrant officer, stood in the center, and called out the names of the recruits. Each of us had to reply, "Present," and come to attention.

After the roll call, the corporal whispered something to the warrant officer, who thereupon turned to glare at our little group from the "Virgins' Room."

Petit approached Ginette, commanding her to raise her skirt. Her hefty thighs appeared; high up they were rimmed in khaki. I thought of the pieces cut off from all of our regulation drawers, scattered upstairs in a corner of the dormitory. Petit said nothing to Ginette, and passed on to the next woman. Then she went beyond our group, with the same inspection. And it became evident that not only in our room, but in practically all of the dormitories, the women had had the same idea, and shortened their underwear. Petit returned to the center of the circle.

"All those who have desecrated their uniforms will be deprived of liberty during the entire week," she announced. "They will receive another pair of drawers and are required to wear them according to regulations. I am aware that they are not in the latest style, but you are soldiers, and not ladies of fashion, damn it!"

We scattered, some laughing, some muttering.

"The dirty bitch!" said Ginette, with a look at the corporal. Ann's deep voice growled a second to Ginette's outburst.

Nevertheless, a few moments later in the dining room, I noticed Ann gossiping gaily with the corporal. Ursula was sitting with me, and she too remarked on the sudden change. Like me, she was wondering whether Ann were just an opportunist, sincere only in seeking her own advancement. I took it that Ann knew how to get along with people, but as Ann came toward us I saw that sensitive little Ursula was blushing. Ann was a likable person, and I suppose, like all of us, Ursula was sorry to recognize an imperfection in someone whom she wanted to admire.

Ann sat on the other side of Ursula, setting down her plate, in which the porridge had mingled with a dollop of orange marmalade. Ann shrugged over the disagreeable mess. There simply weren't enough plates; everything had to go on one. "Well, little Ursula," she boomed, "is everything all right this morning? Do you like the soldier's life?"

Her deep voice was filled with warm comradeliness, and

Ursula instantly recovered from her doubts of a moment before. She smiled at Ann, but didn't seem to know what to answer.

In general, Ursula didn't know how to make conversation. This was probably due to the queer childhood she had had. The lone daughter of divorced parents who had wandered separately in different parts of the world, she was the little girl of no one. She had been born in France and had lived almost everywhere, raised by servants and left largely to herself. For her, France had provided an illusion not only of a homeland, but of a home. Little Ursula, as we came to know, worshiped France with all her soul, because she had nothing else to worship.

At the time of the Franco-German armistice, her mother was in America and her father in China. No one was especially interested in Ursula. In the drift of refugees from Paris, she had found her way onto a British ship that was evacuating troops from Brest. And so she had gravitated to Down Street like the rest of us.

Her heart was filled with dreams and longings, with love, with a sense of the intimacies she had missed, and all this was mingled with a strange fear of life itself. She had never felt equal to things, neither with her mother, nor with servants, nor with strangers, nor in the schools to which she had been sent, in one country or another. And here in the barracks she continued to feel lost and terrified, without knowing why. It seemed to her that all her life would be like yesterday's problem of scrubbing the floor—she would never know at what corner to begin, and no one would ever take her seriously.

"When I am grown up," she would say, and then suddenly she would realize that she was already grown up, that she was nearly sixteen and she was a soldier. And she would look terrified.

Mickey was at the end of our table; she was laughing loudly

over one of Ginette's rough jokes. Mickey's teeth were slightly pointed, like those of a puppy, and her mouth pouted forward, very red, heart-shaped in the form of a kiss. She was so eager to be part of everything.

". . . and what a *conne!*" Ginette ended her tale.

"What does that mean, *conne?*" Mickey asked, opening wide her large blue eyes.

There was a roar of laughter, and one of the women undertook an explanation.

That day, too, we were assigned to house cleaning.

Toward evening, a truck unloaded straw for mattresses— and also a batch of five new recruits, who were immediately sent off to peel vegetables in the kitchen. Ursula and I had just finished cleaning the three bathrooms. She had been chattering rather easily most of the day, and I had begun to feel that I understood this frail girl, who nevertheless was streaked through with decided, even passionate elements of character.

As we came out on the stairway we noticed one of the newcomers crossing the hall, laden with a huge pile of straw. It was a lady. A lady such as one saw in films. At first glance, the lady appeared fairly young—thirty or thirty-two. But on closer scrutiny one saw that she was somewhat older.

Ursula stood still and murmured, "Isn't she beautiful?"

The woman was tall and extremely blonde—a peroxide blonde. Her hair curled in ringlets over her forehead and fell in waves alongside her face. Her nose was fairly long, but quite narrow and very slightly arched, giving her an air of distinction. She was heavily made up. Ursula stood stock-still, a wisp of a girl wrapped in her long beige smock, watching the passage of this beautiful creature. The woman had such a marvelous scent! And in passing she threw Ursula a smile that was as perfumed as the woman herself.

At that moment our sergeant-cook appeared, roaring,

"Hey, you there, the new one—Claude! What are you doing with that straw? You're supposed to be in the kitchen!"

To our astonishment, we beheld the one called Claude raise a snarling face over her pile of straw, and from her beautifully made-up mouth there came forth one of the most violent replies that I had ever heard. As for Ursula, she stood agape. "You can go to hell!" the lady spat at the sergeant. "Just because you're a sergeant, don't think you can get away with anything! First, I'm going to fix my bed, and when I'm through, I'll come and peel your potatoes, and if you don't like it you can kiss my behind!"

The sergeant-cook must have realized that this was no little girl from Brittany, for she went away without saying a word.

Now Claude turned toward us. "Can you imagine, talking to me in such a tone of voice! What does she take me for—her servant? More likely, she'd be mine! I volunteered out of patriotism, and not to be treated like an inferior by a conne like that!"

It was strange, but the coarse words with which her speech was peppered seemed to lose their vulgarity when they were spoken by Claude. She had a very beautiful voice, cultured and modulated, the sort that could permit itself the use of slang.

"Can you tell me where to find the switchboard room?" Claude then asked. "That's where I'm to bunk. I've got to take charge of the telephone."

An assignment of this sort seemed prodigiously important to us. Full of respect for Claude, we showed her the little room near the entrance that had been set aside for the telephone operator.

Claude dropped the straw on the floor, went to the window, opened it, and leaned on her elbows, looking out into the street.

Facing our barracks was a large hotel, and in front of the hotel entrance stood the doorman, very tall, very thin, with graying hair and thin lips. His cheeks were highly rouged, his eyelids were painted a bright blue, and he bowed with feminine grace before every man who entered the hotel. Then he resumed his haughty nonchalant stance, staring directly before him at the windows of our barracks.

"You could take him for the ambassador of Peru," murmured Claude. We had no idea why "ambassador" and why "Peru," but the phrase enchanted Ursula and she started to laugh.

"How old are you, child?" Claude asked her.

This time Ursula replied, "Seventeen," without hesitation.

Claude placed her hand on Ursula's head and stroked her soft hair. I felt as though I were intruding. "You have the air of a tiny little girl, and you're ravishing—you're like a little bird," Claude said.

It was obvious that this was the first time anyone had told Ursula she was ravishing. And yet, because it was said in another person's presence—mine—it was quite normal, almost a conventional remark.

Ursula never forgot her feelings at this first meeting. When she spoke about it to me later she said that Claude's voice was so gentle, Claude's hand was so soft that she felt the very inside of her heart melting. She wanted to reply, "Oh, and you are so beautiful!" but she didn't dare, and she uttered the first banality that came to her. "I've been here since yesterday. I'm from Paris. Where are you from?"

Claude was about to answer when a corporal appeared— a third one. We seemed surrounded by corporals. This was a large girl, rather gentle and reserved; she had charge of the office. She had some forms in her hand and she gave them to Claude to fill out.

Ursula tugged at me, and we left.

CHAPTER 5

Our aristocratic Jacqueline was the first to receive a secretarial post. She would always be first everywhere, with her enchanting face and her air of being owed the best, and yet this was so natural to her that we could not resent her manner. She returned at noon, absolutely delighted with her office. Her lieutenant was a man of excellent family, she announced to us, highly cultured. And he had already invited her to have lunch with him tomorrow. Of course, he had a wife and children in France.

Soon most of us were assigned to work in various offices at GHQ. I became, for the time being, a file clerk and the operator of a mimeograph machine in the Information Bureau. But the Captain had no idea what to do with Ursula. Most of us could type, at least; Ann could drive a car; but Ursula had no accomplishments. Finally the Captain put her down as sentry for the barracks.

Ursula remained seated all day long at a little table by the entrance, keeping a registry book in which she noted down all of our comings and goings. Opposite her was the switchboard room, where Claude was stationed. Through the half-open door she could glimpse Claude's glistening blonde hair. From time to time, Claude came out of the little room for a chat. She still wore that same wonderful perfume. But with tender dismay one night Ursula asked me if I had noticed that Claude had little creases at the sides of her mouth, and white hairs mingled with the blonde. Indeed, Claude could have been her mother. And in those first days I felt that this was what drew

Ursula to Claude, the wish that she had had a mother as gay and amusing as this woman, with her inexhaustible store of gossip about all the celebrities in Paris.

But soon the stories Ursula brought back from Claude were less innocent. Ursula was fascinated and yet a little puzzled by the ease with which Claude related her bedroom experiences; she had slept with most of the currently fashionable actors and writers of the capital, and she kept up a continuous stream of intimate chatter about her lovers to the girl. Ursula would repeat Claude's gossip, somewhat in awe, and somewhat as though wanting reassurance that there was nothing wrong in her adoration of Claude. Claude would tell her, "I absolutely adored that boy, and then suddenly I had enough of him. My only love was always my husband, but he's a dog. He drinks too much, and he's a fairy, damn him! As soon as we're together, we fight. Luckily, I had Jacques. He was my great consolation. He was still a child, a high school boy. He used to come to me after school. I trained him. I made him my best lover."

Ursula couldn't get over her astonishment at this woman who adored her homosexual husband but fought with him, and who had so many lovers, and who was so much at ease about it all. The world of grownups had always seemed distant and mysterious to Ursula. With Claude, that world became even more distant, and all the values that Ursula had so painfully established for herself were overturned.

But one thing was certain: Ursula felt that the one person who really cared about her was Claude. Big Ann was pleasant and sometimes brusque; the aristocratic Jacqueline irritated her, perpetually wanting to fuss over her and take charge of her; Mickey was a clown who made her laugh; and I suppose I was just someone who listened, someone she found it easy to talk to. Ursula complained that the corporals scolded her endlessly, and the Captain could scarcely remember her name.

But Claude talked to her, confided in her as in a friend, called her her little bird, stroked her hair, smiled at her with her perfumed smile. Claude knew so many stories, she was afraid of no one, and she had a way of looking at Ursula with her black eyes, a way that made Ursula forget every desire except to remain close to Claude as much as possible.

One night there came an order for the sentry to sleep in the switchboard room with the telephone operator, so as to make sure that the service would continue in case of a serious air attack. I helped Ursula drag her iron cot into the little telephone room. Her heart must have been beating with joy. What heavenly evenings she would pass with Claude!

That same evening, Claude decided to throw a secret little party in the switchboard room. We organized it among a few of the girls, and sent Ursula out to the corner pub to fetch some bottles of beer.

Ursula put on her cap and hurried out. It was the first time she had been out since her arrival at the barracks. It was raining. Down Street was narrow and dark. Ursula found her way to the pub, which was brightly lighted and full of smoke, and crowded with soldiers in various degrees of drunkenness. They called out to her, "Oh, Frenchie! Look at the French girl!" Ursula told me later that she didn't know what to do with herself. The soldiers' eyes shone and their lips were wet with beer. They had thick red hands. Ursula's heart fluttered. She kept her eyes fixed at a point on the wall while she was being served. Finally it was finished. The soldiers tried to catch hold of her arms, but she freed herself and ran out. Ursula plunged toward the barracks as to a refuge.

I was standing in the doorway of the switchboard room when we heard Ursula's hurrying footsteps on the stairs outside. Claude brushed past me into the hall and opened the door for her. She stood there in the doorway, so shining, so blonde, with her khaki shirt partly open, revealing her white throat.

Ursula pressed herself suddenly against the woman, and Claude held her in her arms. Her hands gently caressed Ursula's hair.

I can only suppose that Claude forgot my presence, or perhaps she thought I had gone on into the switchboard room. But I remained in the doorway, and I saw Claude gently press Ursula's head against her full breasts, separated from Ursula's cheek only by the khaki shirt.

It was not hard for me, then or later, to understand Ursula's feelings. After her first, unnerving visit to a pub full of roistering soldiers, she had hurried along a dark, alien street and found again at the end of it Claude—beautiful, shining Claude—who at that moment must have seemed to her the very embodiment of warmth and safety and gentleness.

Claude raised Ursula's chin with one hand, drawing her face closer, and suddenly, in the dimly lighted hall, she kissed Ursula on the mouth. It was a quick light kiss, like a brush of a bird's wing, a kiss so discreet as not even to startle the girl.

Just then Ann and Mickey came along, with their drinking glasses hidden under the jackets of their uniforms.

In the switchboard room, a little clock sounded nine. The corporal of the guard had closed her eyes to our soiree, since Ann had given her to understand that Warrant Officer Petit was invited, and, naturally, any corporal reporting our little party would only be making trouble for herself. (I had already noticed that Ann seemed to be born with a sense of how to manage things in the Army.)

Petit was the last to arrive. The little room was filled with cigarette smoke. Claude had taken off her uniform, and was now wearing a dressing gown—blue with little white dots. She was seated on the bed with one of her legs folded under her, and the other kicking a red slipper. A lock of platinum hair fell over her forehead. A cigarette trembled in her lips, while she was engaged in reading Mickey's palm.

Petit surveyed the room, with her scrunched-up eyes of a man of the world. Petit might readily agree that Claude was beautiful, but a woman like Claude had no interest for Petit. To our warrant officer, Claude was only a dilettante. One might pass a pleasant evening with a woman like that, but nothing else. At bottom, to the Petits of the world, Claude was a pervert, a perverted woman of the sophisticated milieu, but a woman in spite of everything. As for Ursula, Petit scarcely glanced at her, obviously summing her up as a nice little thing, but nothing special. She looked at Mickey. Her expression said, "A little fool."

Ann was standing against the table with her arms crossed. She had rather thick muscular arms and broad masculine hands. Petit poured herself a glass of beer, and drank it down without stopping; she was satisfied. It was said that her last two intimate friends had remained in France on the farm where the three of them had lived before the war. She was all alone here, and felt herself aging. Soon enough she'd be fifty years old. In Ann, she must have seen herself as she had been at twenty-six—solid and robust, with a deep voice and a man's hands. Ann looked directly into her eyes, and from her relaxed and satisfied expression Petit seemed to know that everything was going well. It was probably then that Petit decided to use her influence to have Ann made a corporal as soon as possible. That would make things a lot simpler.

Much was to happen between the women who were at Claude's little party, and when I traced back their stories, I found that the threads began to be woven together on this night.

Mickey was laughing as usual and playing the little comedian. Claude knew that she was making no mistake; she had wide experience with men, with women, and with life: Mickey would go far for adventure, even though she was still a typical *demi-vierge.* She was pretty, in her gawky way, she was ready for anything, she was gay, a good comrade and well liked by everyone. Claude predicted a rich lover and a long voyage for her. Then Claude turned her gaze upon little Ursula, sitting silently at the foot of the bed, and Claude's face filled with tenderness for the child. A girl still so young, so new, altogether inexperienced and untaught. She must have thought of her own life as a little girl, for despite her bravura manner of an adventuress and a *femme fatale,* she was born of a provincial middle-class family. Ursula had already brought me Claude's story of how she had been lifted out of her small-town shell when quite young, through marriage to an elderly, dissipated Parisian who had initiated her into the city's circles of debauch. He had finally succeeded in completely disorienting a character that was at bottom healthy. Claude had left him at last, and married a younger man, an engineer by profession. But her second husband had his special passion, and had taken a job in London so as to be near one of his male friends. Claude had followed him in May, just before the fall of France, for she was in love with him despite his habits. She was a woman overfilled with love, and her love had to be dissipated. All the love that she might have had for a child had to be used somewhere. And here was this girl, this little Ursula. I think there was the same mothering desire in her love for Ursula that she had felt when that boy Jacques had come to her with his school books under his arm. And yet there was with it a devouring avidity for something as delicious as a slightly green fruit. It was strange, absurd, but when Claude talked of Jacques one could see that it had seemed to Claude as though she were carrying on in a motherly role, continuing a boy's upbringing, just as someone who had taught him to wash, to eat, to walk. She, Claude, was also a mother in her way. She had taught him to eat of another sort of food—and she was proud of his progress, with a maternal pride. And little Ursula—how wonderful it would be to watch her little mouth open for the first time, and to see her overcome with happiness, like a child to whom one has just given a beautiful toy!

Even while she kept chattering with the rest of us, Claude studied the girl through the corner of her eye. She smiled at Ursula, and drew her nearer, putting her arms around her, living again the intimate moment in the doorway.

Petit was watching, with a malicious and slightly obscene light in her eyes. She had the air of saying, "I leave her to you. That one doesn't interest me at all." But it was flattering to Claude that Petit understood at once. Claude always enjoyed the idea of being considered a dangerous woman.

CHAPTER 6

The barracks had been in existence for more than a month. Every morning we went through our drill in Down Street before hurrying off to our various jobs. One day the Captain announced that a military ball was taking place, to which all of us had been invited.

That evening we were all loaded onto trucks and carried across blacked-out London. As we bumped along, Jacqueline regaled us with tales of the formal balls she had attended before the war, dressed in white tulle. She remembered the family limousine, with the chauffeur in uniform, bowing as he opened the door for the young lady. I suppose she could not help feeling her superiority to most of the girls in the truck, who behaved with a good deal of vulgarity. And I suppose that Jacqueline really had no desire to go to a dance at a training camp, where she might be pawed by any soldier from anywhere. But neither did she want to remain alone in Down

Street. Besides, it might be amusing to see what a soldiers' dance was like, just once.

The truck made a few too many sudden stops. The driver must have found it amusing to jolt our bunch of girls so that we fell all over each other. Most of us laughed, but Jacqueline protested for her back was again giving her trouble. One of the women called her a snob, and told her to cut out her mannerisms.

When I really came to know Jacqueline, I understood that she suffered from a perverse need to impress everybody. That night, she hoped that she would faint, so as to make that woman regret her words. But it didn't happen, and she didn't quite feel like feigning a loss of consciousness, as she sometimes did by letting herself slide into a kind of feebleness that readily took hold of her. But the bouncing truck brought tortures to her back. She had been suffering these odd spells ever since that night of her flight and her accident. I knew the pain was real enough, but I sometimes wondered why she had jumped from the roof of the house in the first place. Was it really because of that pair of perverted drunkards whose children she was taking care of? Was it really to escape from them? Or had she done it because of some need she carried within herself, a need for drama and for disaster?

I was astonished, and filled with admiration for her honesty, when Jacqueline told me once that she often asked herself the same questions.

"There seems to be a tradition of melodrama in my family," she said. "One of my first memories is of being surrounded by people, all of them talking about the airplane crash that killed my father."

Soon after that, Jacqueline told me, there had been a stepfather, elegant, attentive. She recalled the household scenes, later on, between her mother and her stepfather, because he would kiss her when she came home from school. She spoke of the attempted suicide of her stepfather.

She had left home to escape this concentration of hatred and misfortune, veiled by riches and good manners. But her fate followed her wherever she went. Or was it perhaps that she carried it with her? Jacqueline wondered.

A week after her arrival in England, in the first family to which she had come on an exchange visit, the husband had died of a heart attack. After that she had lived with a couple, a man and his wife, who came in turns each night to knock on her door. She hated them. She wanted to punish them, to bring about some sort of explosion, to provoke a drama. Yes, she said, she knew now that it was drama that she wanted most of all. She could just as well have left quietly. No one would have kept her back by force. But she had preferred to stage an escape—to jump. She had had visions of herself as a beautiful corpse beside their house.

But instead, Jacqueline had howled in pain under their windows all night long and no one had come. In the morning she had dragged herself to her room. It was finished. The drama had failed.

Soon afterward, she had read a newspaper item about a feminine contingent being formed in the Free French Forces. That was her salvation. All the history of France passed before her eyes—pictures remembered from her childhood: the parades of July Fourteenth, Jeanne Hachette, Ste Geneviève, the queens of France, the *Marseillaise*, Verdun—she was going to become part of all that! To save France! To avenge the armistice, the great shame! Her father would have been proud of her—that legendary father who had fallen from the sky like Icarus.

As soon as she was well, she had volunteered. And now she was a soldier, mingled with the women of the people. There were indeed several girls of good family—Ursula, Mickey, a student of pharmacy, the daughter of a consul—but they were the exceptions. Most of Jacqueline's comrades now were women of an entirely different sort from any she had ever known before.

She spoke with contempt for all the members of her self-satisfied family—so sure of their prerogatives, so certain that it was a great distinction for anyone to be invited to their table—and yet, was she herself so different from them? Since she had come to live at the barracks, I knew that Jacqueline had her doubts. It was true that she accepted any sort of physical task without the slightest complaint, and that she did her best to accomplish it through pride—just to show us that she was perfectly capable of scrubbing the floor or peeling potatoes. But there were so many coarse women, with the tales of their cheap affairs with men already resounding through the barracks—she hated them all. They permitted themselves to be taken to filthy little hotels. They went to bed with sailors, copulating like animals. She, Jacqueline, would never permit a man to take her at his will. When the others talked of their cheap affairs, Jacqueline said nothing. But I knew she was thinking of the lieutenant in her office, so eager to please her, bringing her books and flowers and gifts, inviting her to the Mayfair or to the Claridge. All the men were in love with her; Jacqueline had become used to that, and she would have been astonished if it were not so. She loved to watch the shine come into their eyes, and to provoke their compliments. The other evening in a taxi, after being taken to dinner, she had permitted a young officer to kiss her on the mouth, and then had come running in like a child, her eyes sparkling, to tell me about it. It was fun, it was really like one read in stories, like playing with fire, to feel him burning close to her, and to be able to put him off whenever she wished. Before the war, in France, she had been engaged to a handsome lad, quite well-to-do, belonging to her own world. Jacqueline had permitted him to kiss her and to fondle her breasts, and she had found it amusing to hold him off after that, and to feel him trembling with desire, a slave of his desire for her. It was as though she had made a discovery, that in addition to being born to an aristocracy in which one always was in the position of deciding how other people should behave, she had been born into the aristocratic sex, for it was the woman who could always decide, always command, in relationships with men. It had been a pleasant discovery. Jacqueline had been seventeen at the time.

The dance was in full swing when we arrived. The men welcomed us with shouts and cries of joy; they were mostly French, though there was a scattering of uniforms from other nations—Polish, Norwegian, and Belgian. I liked dancing, and found myself in a little circle of swing enthusiasts. Everybody was learning the Lindy, and I danced with one after another in a strange exhilaration, so that I scarcely knew or remembered with which boy the dancing went well. They were still all boys to me.

Mickey was seized by a master sergeant of the Air Corps, who squeezed her tightly as they danced. He was short and slightly bald, but Mickey said he was nice enough. Mickey was never especially particular. She liked to have fun and was willing to taste out of any dish, finding them all pleasant. As she danced, soldiers called to her. They assessed her with an expert air. Her mouth especially excited them—an arched red mouth with the upper lip slightly advanced, as though the girl were constantly ready to be kissed.

While they danced, the sergeant kissed her throat. For form's sake, Mickey pretended to be shocked. But even the sergeant could see well enough that she was not at all offended.

I looked around for Ursula, but she didn't seem to be anywhere in the room. I learned later that, after having danced with a fat soldier who was nearly drunk, she felt that she had had enough, and sought to escape. The cigarette smoke was so thick that it stung her eyes almost to the point of tears. She was afraid of these men, didn't know what to say to them, and was terrified merely at the idea of being touched by any one of them. She saw a door and fled outside. There was a little courtyard, and the fresh evening air made her shiver. Ursula sat down on the steps. The cool air caressed her cheeks, and she shook out her hair, relieved in her escape. Then she noticed that a soldier, quite young, was sitting on a crate in the courtyard, and watching her. There it is, she thought. I have to leave this place, too.

But in order not to appear ridiculous, she told me with her quaint nicety, she remained for another moment, planning to get up and leave as though she had just come out for a breath of air.

She kept her eyes averted from the soldier so as not to give him an excuse to speak to her. The music came from the hall— muted, but reaching them nevertheless. In there, a voice was bellowing "Madelon."

Suddenly the soldier said to her, "It's better out here than inside, don't you think?" And as soon as she heard his calm voice, tinged with a slight foreign accent, Ursula felt reassured. Now she looked at the soldier. She could scarcely see him in the darkness, but he had a very young air and seemed rather small in stature. She replied, "Yes," and didn't know what else to say.

They remained silent for a long while. Ursula was suddenly quite astonished to hear her own voice break the silence.

She said, "Have you been in England long?"

The soldier answered, "I've been here three days. Last week I was in Spain, and it's only about fifteen days since I was in France."

Now Ursula looked at him with a kind of awe. He came

from France! Only fifteen days ago, he had walked on the earth of France and spoken to the people of France and looked at the trees, the sky of France. It seemed to her that she had been in London for years rather than months.

She raised her head and watched the searchlights sweeping the sky. It was beautiful to see. The alert had sounded, just as it did every evening, but there had been no sound of aircraft. The German planes must have headed somewhere else instead of coming over London.

"Aren't you cold?" the soldier asked. He spoke so nicely, with so much gentleness in his voice, that Ursula said she was touched. She shook her head. He was probably not French. He had an accent, but Ursula couldn't tell from what country. And yet he spoke perfect French.

He was silent again for a little while, and then he said, "I admire you for joining the Army. It's not much fun for the men, but for women it must really be hard."

And now Ursula began to speak. Whenever she knew she was to be in the company of young men, she worried her head for days in advance to prepare some conversation. And she confessed that her voice always sounded affected to her own ears. Young men had always seemed members of another race to her, mysterious beings with whom she had no point of contact.

But this evening in the dim courtyard, Ursula found herself talking freely to the unknown soldier. She told him about her life in Down Street. She described Jacqueline, "absolutely ravishing, but a little bit artificial"; Mickey, "a good comrade, and so funny"; Ann, "everybody thinks she'll be the first to get her corporal's stripes"; Ginette, who "talks nothing but slang, used to be a salesgirl, and can sew her own uniforms to measure." She spoke of Claude, "very intelligent, very generous," who was her protectress. Then suddenly she saw us all, all of her comrades as we were in the mornings, tense, badly adapted to this life, ready to find distraction in anything, hungry for love, each hiding her homesickness at the bottom of her heart. Ursula saw the main hall of Down Street, and her little sentry table. And all day long the phonograph that we had just acquired kept playing the same records, "Violetta" and *"Mon coeur a besoin d'aimer."* She spoke about our captain, hurried and distant, a smirk always on her lips, calling us her "dear girls," always giving the impression that she was really going to do something, that she was going to help us somehow, that she was going to create an atmosphere of friendship in Down Street. She talked about this at every opportunity, but after each of her speeches one found oneself just as lonesome and empty as before.

The soldier listened without interrupting her, and when she had finished all he said was, "I understand," and Ursula felt herself to be truly understood, although she didn't really know what there was to understand. It seemed to her that this boy comprehended things even before she had grasped them herself. This comforted her, like finding a schoolroom problem solved without having to trouble over it.

We were all ready to go home, and had been hunting for Ursula. Jacqueline opened the door to the courtyard and called, "Ursula, are you there? Ursula, where are you?"

Several voices shouted, "Blackout!" But we just had time to make out two forms, like little children clutched together in the dark. They started up, coming toward us.

"Hurry!" Jacqueline called. "What a relief! At last we can leave," she said to me.

Ursula came slipping through the door.

The truck was waiting outside, and we piled in. This time I suppose the driver was too tired for his game of jolting us against one another. It was far past midnight, and some of the girls slept, leaning their heads on each other's shoulders.

Suddenly I heard Ursula murmur, "Oh. I forgot to tell the soldier good-by."

Just across from us sat Claude; she was holding Mickey's head on her shoulder. I could feel Ursula stir unhappily. It must have seemed to her that Mickey had stolen her place.

CHAPTER 7

We jumped from the truck, one after the other, and were swallowed in the barracks hall. The house seemed to come awake, invaded like a beehive. Doors slammed, women ran up the stairway, women called to each other from room to room.

Mickey, in pajamas, began to dance in the middle of our dormitory. Jacqueline was dressed in one of her elegant flowered linen nightgowns. She sat massaging her face with cold cream. Ann, who was already carrying out the duties of a corporal, even before being promoted, came to remind us that the reveille for tomorrow was for six o'clock, as usual, and to put out the lights. One door after another was heard closing, and the night quieted. There were still a few whispers from bed to bed.

"I was dancing with a sailor, and he's crazy about me."

"He's a perfect dancer. He wants to take me out someplace where we can have fun. You know."

"He's going to phone me tomorrow."

"But honey—it's amazing—he knows my brother! They went to the same school in Lyons."

As for myself, I hadn't met anyone special. I had given my name to a few of the men, perhaps for one of those evenings when a girl is so lonesome she'll go out with anyone. I'd seen some of the girls do things they probably wouldn't do otherwise, out of this loneliness, and I hoped it wouldn't happen to me.

The whispering gradually ceased. Ursula slipped through the room in the dark. She had been in the bathroom, as she was still modest about undressing; she had put on her regulation rose-colored pajamas. This was one of the nights when she slept in the switchboard room, and she slipped out of the dormitory, going downstairs.

When Ursula reached the little switchboard room, Claude was already stretched out on her narrow camp bed. A storm lamp stood on the floor. In the feeble light, Claude's bright hair shone. Everything else was in shadow. Outside, the guns began to roar.

Ursula went to sit on the edge of Claude's bed. The alternate nights that Ursula was assigned to sleep in this room were impatiently awaited. For on these occasions Claude talked to her at length about her husband, about her lovers, about her life before the war. Claude told about places where opium was smoked, and about her travels, and about her pets. It was always passionately absorbing, and Ursula would listen without saying a word, extremely impressed by the number of important people Claude knew, by her countless adventures, and flattered to be spoken to with such intimacy. No one else had ever been like a real friend to her. Especially a really grown-up mature woman.

Ursula adored Claude, and was attracted to her in a special way she could not explain to herself. Sometimes it seemed to her that Claude took particular pains to charm her, as though she, Ursula, were a man. But that would be absurd, and Ursula rejected so ridiculous an idea.

That night as she sat on the edge of the cot Claude said to her, "What a whorehouse that dance was! Where did you hide yourself? I drank I don't know how many glasses of port. Everyone offered me port to drink. I'm sleepy. Kiss me,

Ursulita." She drew Ursula against her as she had that evening by the door, and suddenly she kissed her on the mouth. But this time the kiss was not so short. Ursula felt Claude's lips burning hers. She didn't know what was happening to her. She was lost, invaded, inflamed. She tried to get hold of herself as though she were drowning, dissolving in Claude's arms. Claude drew her into the bed.

Ursula felt herself very small, tiny against Claude, and at last she felt warm. She placed her cheek on Claude's breast. Her heart beat violently, but she didn't feel afraid. She didn't understand what was happening to her. Claude was not a man; then what was she doing to her? What strange movements! What could they mean? Claude unbuttoned the jacket of her pajamas, and enclosed one of Ursula's little breasts in her hand, and then gently, very gently, her hand began to caress all of Ursula's body, her throat, her shoulders, and her belly. Ursula remembered a novel that she had read that said of a woman who was making love, "Her body vibrated like a violin." Ursula had been highly pleased by this phrase, and now her body recalled the expression and it too began to vibrate. She was stretched out with her eyes closed, motionless, not daring to make the slightest gesture, indeed not knowing what she should do. And Claude kissed her gently, and caressed her.

How amusing she was, this motionless girl with her eyelids trembling, with her inexperienced mouth, with her child's body! How touching and amusing and exciting! Claude ventured still further in discovering the body of the child. Then, so as not to frighten the little one, her hand waited while she whispered to her, "Ursula, my darling child, my little girl, how pretty you are!" The hand moved again.

Ursula didn't feel any special pleasure, only an immense astonishment. She had loved Claude's mouth, but now she felt somewhat scandalized. But little by little, as Claude continued her slow caressing, Ursula lost her astonishment. She kept saying to herself, I adore her, I adore her. And nothing else counted. All at once, her insignificant and monotonous life had become full, rich, and marvelous. Claude held her in her arms, Claude had invented these strange caresses, Claude could do no wrong. Ursula wanted only one thing, to keep this refuge forever, this warmth, this security.

Outdoors, the antiaircraft guns continued their booming, and the planes growled in the sky. Outside, it was a December night, cold and foggy, while here there were two arms that held her tight, there was a voice that cradled her, and soft hair touched her face.

CHAPTER 8

Sometime during the night, Claude shook Ursula, telling her to return to her own bed. Ursula was so tired that she moved as though in sleep to the other cot.

At seven o'clock the corporal came on her tour of inspection. Claude was singing in the bathroom. She had a beautiful voice, rather low. She sang:

"Tel qu'il est,
Il me plaît.
Il me fait
De l'effet
Et je l'aime!"

The corporal glanced at Ursula, who was polishing the buttons of her jacket, and Ursula blushed. It seemed to her as though "that" must be visible on her face, as though the whole world would notice the change that had taken place in her, for she had made love, and now she was a woman. She was

Claude's woman. And Claude seemed to her extraordinary and marvelous.

Now there came back to her mind certain phrases that she had heard in the barracks. Disagreeable remarks about Ann and Petit, about Claude too. Expressions she had read in books. She had never paid much attention to them, she had never quite understood them, but now everything was clear. She understood. No, Claude had invented nothing last night. Just as there were homosexual men, so there were homosexual women. Ursula had known it about men for a long time, because one year when they were rich her mother had employed a chauffeur, and he had been like that, and everybody had made jokes about the man. But she had not known about women. Now she understood. And yet a mystery remained. If Claude were "that" way, how was it that she had so many male lovers? And how could she still love her husband, as she said she did?

It was so difficult to learn about life all alone. Yet she didn't come to me then with her story. Much of what I now relate to you was revealed to me later.

What hurt Ursula most of all, that morning, as she later expressed it to me in her pain and perplexity, was Claude's indifference. For when Ursula turned to her Claude seemed cold and distant, as though what had happened during the night were insignificant, common. Ursula didn't dare to touch upon the thousand questions that trembled in her. Claude, humming, went off to breakfast.

I noticed how miserable Ursula looked that morning, and wondered what had happened. But we all had to rush off to our jobs, and it was not until evening that I had an opportunity to talk with her, and by then she had told a good deal to Mickey.

For Ursula had been off duty in the afternoon, and she had gone out. She didn't know a soul in London, and walked haphazardly through the foggy streets, wanting only to find a corner somewhere, to hide away and cry. Huge red busses passed, and the policemen at the crossings seemed to her immense and majestic, and they seemed to know something about her.

She walked along Piccadilly, looking at the marvelous shop windows, and for a moment she thought of buying Claude a beautiful gift. But her Army pay was very small. She had only five shillings in her pocket, and besides, she knew so little English that she didn't dare go into a shop.

A house that had been hit during the night was still smoldering. A few firemen were at work in the ruins. The passers-by didn't even glance at the house. Because it was done for, because it was lost, and because one should never remember the night before, in the day.

At Piccadilly Circus, Ursula bumped into Mickey. It was five o'clock, and Mickey had left her office an hour early to go to the dentist. At last, a familiar face! As Mickey hailed her with her usual enthusiasm, Ursula felt as though she had met someone of her own family. Out of the anonymous, out of this strange city from which she had expected nothing, at last a face emerged that had a point of connection for her. And Mickey was so excited at seeing her, so friendly, always in good humor, with her turned-up nose, her clear eyes, and her heart-shaped mouth. She took hold of Ursula's arm and pulled her along.

Then all at once Ursula unburdened herself. The need to speak was almost a physical compulsion. She began to talk about Claude, and little by little she described what had happened in the night. She said, "I was so happy, Mickey, it was so marvelous and so strange! And yet I feel as if it can't be right. What does it mean? She's a homosexual, isn't she?"

Mickey laughed with superior knowledge, then grew sober at the perplexity and worry in Ursula's face. "You mustn't do it again, Ursula. You'll get sick. And besides, you mustn't go around talking about it. Don't tell another soul!"

Ursula didn't feel that she knew any more than before. Yet Mickey seemed to take it for granted now that everything was explained. And Mickey, too, had a story to tell. Just before the dance, in the canteen at GHQ, she had met an officer who was absolutely wonderful. "Handsome as a god!" She was in love with him. Whenever she had to go into his office, Mickey felt chills and fevers running up and down her spine, she began to perspire, she couldn't stand still, and she was sure that he noticed all this. He had invited her to go to the movies tomorrow. He liked her. But Mickey had noticed that he liked all women. He was very dark, with green eyes, a rather strong nose, and thin lips. His name was Robert. He was nervous and disorderly. He often appeared in Mickey's office. He'd arrive in a rush, kiss the typist on the neck, call Mickey "darling," and pass his hand down the back of another secretary. The women laughed, and scolded him without conviction.

It crossed Ursula's mind that she would die of fright in the presence of such a man, but Mickey adored him. They had reached the dentist's door, where they separated. Ursula didn't know what to do with herself or where to go. It was six o'clock, and night had fallen. In the blackout, one could scarcely see the pavement. Everything was black and depressing. The alert sounded; no one paid any attention.

Ursula readjusted her gas mask and helmet. They were heavy and clumsy, but regulations required that they be worn in the street. She waited for a bus and mounted to the top. In the day, it was amusing to sit up there and look down into the street. But at this hour one could no longer see anything beyond the windows.

Everybody noticed her French uniform. Ursula was proud of her uniform. A woman nearby leaned toward her and said with a strong English accent, *"Vive la France!"*

"Merci," said Ursula. "Thank you very much."

A man said to her, "I was in France in 1914, at Douai, Verdun, Valenciennes."

Ursula smiled. It was amazing how many Englishmen had already stopped her in the street to tell her things like that. They had all been at Douai, Verdun, Valenciennes. Indeed, Englishmen often pressed my hands in the street, repeating the same words. The English are nice.

Ursula got down from the bus. For a moment it was diffi-cult for her to orient herself in the dark, but she managed to find her way toward Down Street.

That night there were fewer of us at dinner than usual. It was a Saturday, and many of the girls had begun to make friends and to go out. In the rooms at night, there were always some who talked about their lovers, recounting their experiences in full detail, while laughing and often ridiculing the men. I sup-pose for some of us, this served to increase our curiosity, and at the same time to decrease the importance of such things, to lower the barriers to love affairs, so that it didn't matter much if one went out and did the same. After all, all this was tem-porary. The war would soon be over. In the spring of 1941 there would surely be a second front. And then our exile would be ended, together with all these local love affairs and the loneliness of Down Street. But for others of us, this easy talk had another effect, making promiscuity repulsive.

<X>The talk went on when we went down to supper, and while we stood in line for our food. Sergeant Machou, the cook, dished out the portions according to her preferences. The best servings were handed to the women who flattered her, or who could talk back with her own vulgarity. She also had respect for those who were friendly with the officers, and so she was always generous with Ann.

Ursula stood in line for her soup, and then she looked around, and I knew that she was looking for Claude. But

Claude had liberty, and had gone out to dinner. Mickey was gossiping at another table. She kept whispering to Ginette and glancing at Ursula. I had already heard a bit of Mickey's tale upstairs. Although Mickey had warned Ursula to keep silent, she apparently felt no need to follow her own advice. As Ursula hesitated, looking so isolated, missing Claude, I motioned her over to the place beside me.

That evening in the dormitory, the women all looked at her coldly, and scarcely anyone spoke to her. I helped her carry her bedding up from the switchboard room.

Ginette made a remark about *gousses*, and there was a general burst of laughter. But Ursula didn't know what it meant. She went to bed early, and in spite of the light and the noise, she closed her eyes, trying to sleep. Poor girl; she had told me everything, as we trundled her bedding from the switchboard room, and I knew that she could not sleep, and that she was lying there with a cold feeling oppressing her heart.

CHAPTER 9

I had been given more interesting work to do. Every day our contacts with France grew better, and some of the resistance reports came to me, to be adapted for use in propaganda. I became deeply absorbed, excited by my work, and it was perhaps because of the excitement of my task that I felt less need for a personal emotional life than so many of the girls. Or perhaps I was only slower to develop, emotionally.

Jacqueline, doing the same sort of work, nevertheless was soon personally enmeshed. She was in an office next door to mine, for her chief, Lieutenant de Prade, was working on establishing more contacts with the resistance movement.

From the day when she had been assigned to his office, Jacqueline had told herself that she was fated, and that it was her fate always to be unlucky. For here she had discovered the man of her life. He was intelligent, elegant, cultivated, handsome, and they had the same tastes in everything. But he was married, and he adored his young wife and children, whom he had had to leave in France. Moreover, De Prade was a devout Catholic, and he treated Jacqueline like a young sister. Nevertheless, she was certain that he was desperately attracted to her.

As for De Prade, he struggled against Jacqueline's attraction with all his strength. He knew that she was in love with him, but he tried to persuade himself that this was only a youthful infatuation, and that she would find another man to love. She was so pretty, and she was so much sought after by all the officers at GHQ, that things would certainly arrange themselves.

De Prade had rented a little house in Kensington where he lived with three other officers and a servant. Every weekend Jacqueline visited them. She had become a sort of mascot, a symbol of home for the group. Jacqueline knew how to manage a house, and the men had grown quite accustomed to having her take charge of their servant. She played the lady of the house, arranged all the menus, and acted as hostess when they had guests.

With her distinguished grace, with the beautiful manners of a young Frenchwoman of good family, Jacqueline reminded De Prade's comrades of their sisters, their wives, or their daughters. All of them were more or less in love with her, and they deluged her with flowers and candy.

But Jacqueline loved De Prade. Beneath her air of pampered urbanity, she had a will of iron. She wanted De Prade; in spite of and against everything, she wanted him. During the course of weeks, she had been working on him, playing the innocent young girl, calling him Uncle Alain (he was twelve years older than she). And every day she felt that she was gaining ground, that he was slipping closer to intimacy in their seemingly innocent relationship. She had her own room in the house in Kensington, and slept there on Saturdays and Sundays. De Prade would come to say good night, tucking her into bed and kissing her cheek. Then he would leave.

He was still a young man, and each weekend this game grew more unendurable. But he too was stubborn. He was determined to remain faithful to his wife. For some time the struggle continued. Inevitably, it had to come to an issue.

While for Jacqueline and for most of us there was a growing life outside the barracks, in our jobs or in love affairs, Ursula was still there at her little table in the hall, on duty, and all her life seemed to be enclosed in the switchboard room with Claude, only a few steps away.

One afternoon Ursula was seated with her check list as we went back to our jobs from lunch. It was not long after the famous night with Claude. We hurried past her. Most of us got into one of the trucks that were waiting outside, but the richer ones went to the corner to take the bus, and the most ambitious marched off on foot for the exercise.

Ursula wrote down the names of the last to leave, as they hurried past, running because they were late.

The Captain walked rapidly by. Ursula rose to attention. The Captain gave her a condescending little nod, and went into her office.

Ursula could hear Machou yelling in the kitchen; she was probably cursing out one of the girls on K.P. The poor things! Of all the punishments, this was the one Ursula most dreaded. She preferred the heaviest labor to spending five minutes in the presence of Machou.

She couldn't understand how the regular kitchen helpers

could bear their slavery. There were several little girls from Brittany permanently assigned to Machou, and somehow they seemed to have adjusted themselves well enough to their kitchen tasks, and also to life outside the barracks, in London. On their smooth round cheeks their newly employed rouge appeared almost obscene, and their heavily reddened lips seemed to be bleeding. Ursula wondered about them, and she talked to me about them, for they were girls of about her own age, and they seemed to find this life agreeable enough, while she learned so painfully.

The little girls from Brittany had arrived in different ways, mostly from Brest. Some had come on the fishing boats of their brothers or cousins; others had arrived after wild adventures, stowed away in naval craft. One of them had found herself running along the quay during a bombardment of Lorient in 1940. She was deathly frightened. A sailor ran alongside her. He told her to jump into his boat for shelter. The girl had followed his advice, screaming as each bomb fell. The sailor had put her down in the hold, and in the meantime the captain had raised anchor for England. On arriving, he had been startled to discover his stowaway.

The little girl had been even more astonished, but there she was in England, together with a number of French sailors, who advised her to stay. She had wept, imagining that her mother would believe her to be dead, but she had decided to remain, hearing the call of General de Gaulle. A woman's army was about to be formed—and at home there was the Boche.

That was how most of these daughters of the fishermen and peasants of Brittany had arrived, to be assigned by the Captain to kitchen work or to the daily cleaning of the barracks. The little girls from Brittany went out with the sailors from their own province, who took them dancing in sordid little halls and slept with them in disreputable hotels. Otherwise, they'd have been left alone, always stuck at the barracks. With the sailors they could talk of home, of St. Malo, of Brest, of Cherbourg. What else could they have done, in a London filled with heretics who had never even set foot in Brittany?

As assistants, these girls had the women who were on punishment. The penalties were posted in the hall. One could read:

Jeanne, 50 lbs. of potatoes to peel, for being drunk.
Louise, dishwashing, for painting her nails red.
Andrée, confined to quarters for a week, for disrespect to an officer.

Two or three times, Ursula had been punished. Once she had appeared late for morning roll call. Another time the corporal had found her hair too long. Ursula peeled potatoes to atone for her long hair—it had reached to the collar of her jacket, which was forbidden. This regulation was relaxed later on, and Ursula again let her hair grow; but at first this rule, like all the others, was rigidly enforced.

Seated on the kitchen stool, enveloped in a long yellow smock of rough canvas, she had endured the jesting and the ribaldry of Machou and her acolytes for two hours. No one spoke directly to her, but their voices, which seemed to be purposely raucous, and their descriptions of their affairs with men disgusted Ursula. She felt sick and dirty. There was no feeling of superiority in her, as in Jacqueline. On the contrary, Ursula was embarrassed by her own feeling of revulsion. She would have liked to be able to hide it, as though it were some disability, and to laugh with the others, and to be treated as one of them. She wanted so much to be liked, but there was nothing to be done. Whenever she opened her mouth, her voice seemed to come out false, strange, and forced, so that Ursula herself couldn't recognize it, and she was sure that the others were not deceived. They called her a sissy, and gave their tales an extra seasoning so as to make her blush.

All this was not purposely vicious; except for Machou, they weren't badhearted. But they were bored in the kitchen, and the presence of a timid little girl who blushed was a diversion. Their cruelty was only childish. Actually most of them were of the same age, or scarcely older than Ursula. And they knew well enough what would be thought of them at home if their mothers or fathers were aware of the life they were leading in London.

At her table in the hall, Ursula heard the coarse voice of Machou, and the voice of one of the Brittany girls answering in the same tone. She sighed and opened a book that she had taken from the barracks library. The door of the switchboard room was closed. Claude was angry with her, and wasn't speaking to her, for it was generally known how the news had spread of their night together, even though Mickey swore that she hadn't said a word. And for Ursula there was another complication. The women were no longer speaking to her. Claude, nevertheless, had lost none of her popularity. She was admired and rather feared by the girls. It was Ursula whom they all held in disfavor, and every night Ursula wept in her bed.

For the first time in her life, she was aware of her body. It had a special independent life of its own. It longed for the warmth of Claude and for Claude's hands. It twisted in every direction in the narrow little bed, hungry and cold, in search of the other body that had awakened it.

The evening before, a new order had been issued: The sentinel was no longer to sleep in the switchboard room. Ursula thought she would fall sick with frustration. If at least Claude would talk to her or smile . . . But Claude didn't even look at her.

Miserably, she tried to fix her attention on her book. She didn't know what she was reading. Then suddenly the half-open door of the barracks was pushed open, and a soldier entered. He wore a Polish uniform. He was a very young man, small in stature, a little chubby, not handsome, with a round childish face, a thick mouth, and very large black eyes. He looked all around, with his brows raised, and this gave his face the expression of a questioning, astonished child.

Realizing that Ursula was looking at him, he asked in a foreign accent, "Isn't this the barracks of the Free French—the women's barracks?"

It was only then that Ursula recognized him, and she felt a rush of joy in her heart, as at recovering a friend.

"Yes, it's me!" she cried, and at the same moment she grew very red, for there was really no way for her to know that it was she whom he sought. But the young soldier smiled and approached her.

"Now, that's really lucky! I was wondering how I would manage to find you, because I only knew your first name."

"But how did you know my first name?" Ursula asked.

"Why, when you were leaving, your friend called you Ursula."

Ursula gave him a chair and he sat down beside her. Once he had got that sentence out of him, he fell silent again, and Ursula found him a little dull. Claude, for instance, always had something to say. She kept you continuously hanging on her words.

The young soldier asked her what she was doing and whether she was free for dinner that evening. Ursula said she was. It would be better than to stay in the barracks when Claude wasn't even speaking to her.

Then he arose, and asked her pardon for having come without warning, and left.

Nevertheless, Ursula felt more cheerful because of his visit.

Her turn of duty was over at five o'clock and it was still

daylight, gray and rainy as usual. Ursula went up to the empty dormitory. It was cold; the window was open. The cots were made up as in men's barracks, with the sheets and blankets carefully folded at the head of the bed in a square packet with no overhanging edges. The mattress was folded double, so there was nowhere to sit except on the bedsprings.

Ursula stood in the middle of the room. Although the women were still forbidden to put things on the empty shelves around the walls, the officers had relaxed their attention to this regulation during the past few days, and little by little, photographs, holy images, little vases, and books had appeared next to the beds. But there was nothing at all by Ursula's bed. She had no mementos. She decided that she would buy herself a bunch of violets to put in the toothbrush glass above her cot, as Jacqueline had done. She would go out right away for the violets.

In the street, Ursula bought the violets for sixpence, and suddenly she had the idea of giving them to Claude. As soon as the thought came to her, she couldn't wait. She began to run in the street, holding tight to the little bouquet, which consisted mostly of leaves around four or five violets. She arrived at the barracks out of breath and knocked at the door of the switchboard room. Claude's melodious voice said, "Come in."

Claude was seated in front of the switchboard, manipulating the plugs. She kept her back erect, as always. The blonde hair was brushed back. She turned her head toward Ursula, slightly contracting her plucked brows in an annoyed manner. Ursula, her head lowered and her heart full of uncertainty, held out her little bouquet to Claude, without saying a word.

Claude's frown dissolved in a smile. "Oh, how nice!" she cried. "What lovely violets! Come let me kiss you!"

And drawing Ursula to her, she kissed her eyes. In that second Ursula came back to life. Her brown eyes were once more alight, her heart was like honey. She felt happy and light.

Everything was beautiful, everything was perfect, her life, the barracks, London—since Claude still liked her, since Claude didn't hold anything against her. She sat down on the camp bed, and between two telephone calls Claude recounted her woes—she had seen her husband again, she was desperately in love with him, she would never love anyone else. Claude drew a photograph out of her pocket and showed it to Ursula.

Claude's husband had an air of self-confidence and cruelty. Claude began once more to relate how she had met him, and how they had married after years of quarreling and love-making. Her voice became feverish as she spoke, and all at once she seemed almost an old woman; a woman showing age, filled with agitation, with dark reflections in her eyes, with bitterness against everything—against herself, against her husband, against the barracks. And suddenly she began to quarrel with Ursula, complaining that the evening before, in Claude's absence, Ursula had failed to note down a telephone call from Ann. Then it was finished. Ursula could never again be happy for more than a few seconds with this strange and ever beautiful woman. The dinner bell sounded. A voice called Ursula.

She went out sadly, trying to hold back her tears. In the hall, the young soldier waited for her.

CHAPTER 10

There was no secrecy in our dormitory. It had become almost a law to announce whom you were going out with, and on returning to describe the results.

One evening Mickey perfumed herself with chypre, borrowed from Ginette. She used a depilatory under her arms, and selected her best khaki silk tie. She said that she had a date with Robert. Ann laughed, because Mickey had gone through all these preparations a few evenings before, for a movie date with Robert, only to have him call it off at the last moment.

Mickey hadn't even been angry. She had told us that she was sure he had a date with another woman, but it was all the same to her. She had nothing against him for standing her up. She was neither susceptible nor vengeful—and Robert had invited her to dinner for tonight.

"Where are you meeting him?" Ginette demanded.

"At his hotel," Mickey said.

"Well! Something's going to happen!" Ginette predicted.

Something's going to happen, Mickey thought while dressing. Something is certainly going to happen. I can't go on in this state.

She had felt sick with excitement for several days. She no longer ate or slept. She wanted "something" to happen. It was Robert. When he came into the office, Mickey's whole body reacted. Her typing became scrambled, and she didn't hear what was being said to her.

She had had enough of waiting and holding back. She had been playing at the approaches to love for three years now. She remembered a certain actor she had known, and the recollection, agreeable enough until then, suddenly became disgusting to her. She had, indeed, rather bragged of her "affair with an actor" to all of us in the dormitory. He had taught her everything, without ever going to the very end. He had taken her, one summer day, to a field filled with daisies, and he had caressed her, and then he had said, "You're too young. Go home, quickly!" She had been satisfied to go home then, for at that time she had not wanted to explore any further.

Now she had had enough of these sterile caresses. Before putting on her uniform shirt, Mickey glanced at her back in the mirror. All those pimples were so ugly. Soon, now, she would-n't have them any more, and Ginette would treat her as an equal, and she would know, she would really know what it was like.

She had met the actor at the home of some friends. He had been performing in a small theatre in the provinces. Backstage, where she had gone to see him, he had bent her against a pile of ropes and kissed her while caressing her thighs. She had found it amusing. This sort of thing had continued for a year. He had of course been much older than she.

Afterward, she had flirted with a number of boys, but still she knew no more than she had ever known. The men saw only little pieces of her and she gave herself in little pieces, laughing, wrinkling her nose, opening wide her large innocent blue eyes, so that all of them felt a little bit remorseful, and treated her like a little girl, without insisting too much.

After a few months in Down Street, Mickey was beginning to feel tired of being treated like a child—especially by Ginette. Ginette was very fond of her. They often went out together, and sometimes Ginette took a few others of us along, when her men friends wanted dates for their friends. Ginette was ugly, but she was a great success with men. She had sex appeal. From their first look at her, men seemed to know that she liked to make love.

But Mickey had a certain lack of success when she went out with Ginette. Ginette used the same trick with all of us— "They're virgins," she would say with a kind of pitying scorn. For a while the idea of being out with a virgin would amuse a man on a casual date, but after some time he became irritated, and even seemed to find the circumstance humiliating.

Ginette was a pure type of Paris *midinette*. She was coarse, logical, practical, intelligent, and goodhearted when she wanted to be. Her husband had beaten and deceived her. He was a handsome lad, a champion cyclist. Ginette had divorced him at nineteen. She had worked as a salesgirl and supported her parents, who were old and sick. She had become hardened by life, she was afraid of no one, and she knew how to get along. At the barracks she was in the good graces of all her superiors, and even Machou feared her a little. Everybody said that she would be promoted to private first class at Christmas. Petit had confidence in her and often assigned her to special tasks.

Somewhat to our surprise, Ginette advised Mickey against taking the great step.

"Marry as a virgin, Mickey, it's better," Ginette declared, though with the air of someone who expects that her advice will not be taken, and indeed, would be just as pleased. "If you begin by sleeping with some fellow, you won't be able to stop, and you'll go to bed with everybody."

Mickey studied herself in the little mirror on the wall of the Virgins' Room. She thought, I'm making myself ready for my wedding night. And it seemed to her comical to see herself in a khaki uniform with cotton stockings, and wearing a necktie, instead of being dressed in a long white gown. It seemed so comical to her that she began to laugh out loud; although at the bottom of her heart she suddenly felt sad. There were so many romantic dreams that little girls had when they were fifteen, when they went walking and stopped in front of the shop windows to study the mannequins dressed in white satin and tulle. Now she had definitely to separate herself from those dreams. It was a bit terrifying and sorrowful to pass in this way from girlhood to womanhood. In this way, all alone, and without ceremony. And, Mickey thought, without love, either. No, she was quite sure that she didn't love Robert. She only wanted him. She wanted him, and she wanted to know, and besides, it would be so agreeable to have a lover, like a real woman. And yet she said to herself, I hope I'll love him afterward.

Slowly she climbed the stairs. She knocked at the door.

Robert opened it. He was in civilian clothes, and it was odd to see him dressed so; he appeared a little less cruel. His green eyes covered Mickey with caresses. Without saying a word, he seized her in his arms and began to kiss her. Mickey freed herself and began hurriedly to undress. She wanted to seem experienced. Robert watched her, probably astonished. Things were going almost too fast. But she was already nude, and he was good enough to praise her, as a connoisseur. Long-muscled narrow limbs, a supple, well-built body with hand-some shoulders, scarcely any hips, and small pointed breasts. He undressed just as quickly, flinging his clothes over a chair.

His body was cold when he lay down next to her. He was very bronzed and very hairy. He kissed her again, but hurriedly. Mickey looked about her. The hotel room was violently lighted by a bare electric bulb. There were jonquils fading in a vase. She felt alone, utterly isolated from this man who was going through a ritual that did not affect her.

He was astonished to encounter a physical barrier. He had not believed her to be a virgin. When he hurt her, Mickey uttered a short cry. It was all so quick, so strange, she felt disappointed. Nothing but that! All that fuss about such a little thing.

Robert still had said scarcely anything, nor had she. And now it seemed that there was even less reason to talk.

Robert arose; he was very handsome, with his air of arrogance. He smiled at her and said, "Come to the bathroom, honey." His suddenly intimate manner of speech gave her a sensation of horror. There was no reason for his now assuming the right to say *tu* instead of *vous*. Why did he use the intimate form of address as soon as she had made love with him?

They dined almost in silence in the hotel restaurant, like strangers exchanging banalities. Nevertheless, Mickey felt better. She was freed now from that storm within herself—

from that thirst and from desire. She felt herself calm and appeased. It was done. She was a woman.

CHAPTER 11

Mickey returned to Down Street. Faithfully, almost as though she had gone through the experience in order to tell us about it, she recounted the scene. She felt disappointed, but like all of her feelings, this didn't penetrate deeply. "It's life," she concluded, and she was satisfied.

That night, when the phonograph had finally become silent, and when the last bed-to-bed whisperings were over, Mickey could not get to sleep. The roaring planes above the barracks and the regular explosions of the bombs didn't disturb her; she was used to all that. But she was thinking of Robert, of the hotel room, of the faded jonquils in the vase.

I was on fire-watch duty that night on the roof, and suddenly I found Mickey sitting beside me on the parapet in the dark; a pensive Mickey, who talked almost as though to herself.

"It's life," she repeated musingly, and then she told me what she had been thinking, and somehow she was led back to a childhood memory, a very distant memory. It was of the time when she had first realized that lies were a part of life, that it was necessary to lie.

One summer she had been in the mountains with some of her father's family in France. Mickey had then been six or seven years old. One day in August her uncle and aunt had taken her along on an excursion. Mickey loved the mountains, and she loved these walks.

Toward midday they had picnicked in a little clearing at

the edge of a stream, in bright sunlight. They were all alone in the sunlit silence of the mountain.

They had finished the lunch of boiled eggs, potatoes, and fruit that her aunt had prepared. Mickey's uncle, a thin little man, jaundiced and bad-tempered, was standing looking at the slope across the valley. His sharp silhouette was outlined against the cloudless sky. He pointed with his cane to something in front of him and said, "Look at the goats over there."

Mickey's aunt rose, joined her husband, shaded her eyes, and said, "Where?" And following her husband's directions, she finally discovered the goats, tiny black and white spots, going down the opposite slope of the mountain.

Then Mickey too rose and slipped to her uncle's side, trying to see what he saw. She sought everywhere, inspecting every rock, every tree, every bush, following his every indication, but she couldn't find any goats. At first her uncle had tried to help her out. "But look, look there, right in front of you. You see the tree, the small round tree, you see it?"

"Yes."

"Good. Now look to the right, and down a little. You see the white stone? Good. To the right now, a little lower, you'll see them, eight goats with a black one in front. You see them now?"

Mickey saw nothing.

Then her aunt had joined in, adding her explanations. "But pay attention to what you are told, my dear. Don't you see the rock that your uncle showed you? And the three trees in a diagonal line? Then drop your eyes six feet to the right, and you'll see a white stone. And still to the right, a sort of reddish spot—you see the red spot? There, there, a whole flock of goats!"

Mickey tried desperately to see them, her eyes searching in all directions, going up, going down. She didn't see any goats anywhere at all. There was nothing to be done.

Her uncle lost his temper. "She's doing it on purpose!" he shouted. "She's making fun of us. Why, it's impossible! She's not blind."

And then, in order to put an end to the shouting, and simply to please them and to have some peace, Mickey told a lie. She announced that she saw the goats at last. "Oh, yes, there! Of course! To the right. I see them now."

Her uncle and aunt smiled upon her again, and her aunt gave her chocolates. For the first time in her life, and at the age of seven, Mickey had discovered that in the world of grownups, it was necessary to lie. She was astonished and a little sad. She had just discovered that the world was different from what she had thought until then, and that life was different. People had always told her, "You mustn't lie." And that itself was false, because it was necessary to lie. Therefore probably everything that she had been told was false.

From that time on, she had listened with skepticism to the moral counsel of her parents. Besides, they were both so old, as old as other children's grandparents. And her aunt and uncle were also aged. Mickey did not like old people. She was always wanting to laugh, to have fun, and that made noise. And so she was always in rebellion. But among the things that she still believed in at the age of eighteen, there had been love with a capital L, such as one read about in novels.

That night she decided that love, too, was like the rest. Still another lie. And she laughed in the dark.

"Oh, after all, it's not important. One can be satisfied with what it is and have fun. It's not serious."

She didn't want to pity herself like an old woman. She declared, "Since it's necessary to lie and to say that it's wonderful, I'll learn to do it. I'll learn to make love."

She didn't yet know how she was going to go about this, but she knew that she was going to begin on the very next occasion. She wanted to get to be like Ginette, like Claude.

And already, her scene with Robert, as she remembered it, seemed less sad. Robert was handsome. The jonquils hadn't been so faded after all.

I was thankful to Mickey that night, not only because I felt she had at last shown me her true self, but because, in a way, she had been through something for me, for every one of us, and perhaps she had spared me pain.

CHAPTER 12

It was the first Christmas of the war. A huge fir tree had been set up in our assembly room, and the chaplain was celebrating Mass in the barracks chapel. More than two hundred of us were there. Our captain stood in the front row, with her officers beside her. Then came the two warrant officers, Petit and Morvan, the sergeants, and the corporals. Ann, Ginette, and several others had just received their stripes. Claude had made quite a scene, for she had not even been promoted to private first class. She was furious, and refused to sing in the choir. Still, she had come to Mass like all the others.

Every woman had her eyes fixed on the little manger with its figurines of the Holy Family, and on the priest with his slow beautiful movements. We listened to the tinkling of the bell, and each of us wanted to weep, wanting to be pure and clean and small—to be a little girl, to be in France.

Before coming to the service, Claude had had one of her moments of warmth and candor, when she could be so touching. I had been in her little telephone room with Ursula, and admired the sprigs of green that Claude had put on the walls of the narrow chamber and over her switchboard. And suddenly Claude had told us that for years she had been promising herself every Christmas to return to the faith, to have no more lovers, neither men nor women. She would again become the pure little girl that she once had been. We had come together to Mass.

"Les anges dans les campagnes," sang the choir, and Claude, sitting beside me, bowed her head and clutched her missal till her knuckles shone white through the thin skin of her lovely hands, and a tremor passed through her. Then with a little sigh she relaxed and raised her eyes. Seeing me watching her, she gave a little smile and shrugged.

Jacqueline was staring straight ahead of her, a look of intense concentration on her face. But I knew it wasn't the Mass that Jacqueline was concentrating on. Jacqueline could think of little these days but her fated love. In these last days her back had been paining her more than ever, and early this evening she had complained that the pain was intolerable. She took it as a punishment in advance, as an exchange for what she so desperately wanted. As the choir sang, she suddenly bent her head in prayer, and I thought I could divine her prayer. "Dear God, give him to me. I love him, I won't do anything to hurt him. There's a war, and it will be a long time before he'll see his wife again. She won't know anything at all about what happens here. I don't want him to leave her for me. I only want to have him once. At least once. I want it to be with him. That will be enough for me. Forgive me, I know it's bad, but what can I do? Forgive me, help me."

Ursula had no religion. No one had thought of providing her with anything of the kind. She had been given neither education nor faith. She must have felt a stranger to what was taking place here, and yet been drawn into the wondrous prayerful atmosphere that had been created by all these women, her comrades.

All at once everyone had changed. All the faces had suddenly become peaceful. As I watched Ursula scanning the altered faces of her friends, I knew she was wondering what the feeling of this religion could be. Was it something so good? Would she never know it? She studied Petit, her arms folded like a man's, her eyes closed. It was strange that Petit too was religious. She had to ask someone—as she asked me later—whether someone like Petit weren't disowned by her religion. And she herself, Ursula reflected—was she like Petit? Was she too disowned?

Claude had rented a little room in the city, and several times Ursula had gone there to be with her. She adored Claude more than ever, and permitted herself to be bullied, without the slightest resistance. Claude was never in the state of humor that one expected to find, and Ursula always felt herself to be walking a tightrope with her. One day, Ursula knew, she would fall and hurt herself badly.

As the singing voices rose, Ursula felt doomed. She was lost, there was no hope for her, she would end up like Ann. She wanted to cry, for she would never love anyone other than Claude. Not even someone like Michel—for she knew his name now, Michel Levy. He was so generous, so intelligent, so calm, and so gentle. He had never even tried to kiss her. Ursula felt secure in his presence, and yet she was sure that she was not in love with him. She didn't like his small hands and his chubby body. He bored her sometimes, and he was timid. She preferred the caprices, the angry moods, and the phantasies of Claude. She was ready to endure anything for the pleasure of half an hour of Claude's gaiety and charm.

And I—I thought of my dear father, somewhere in a German prison camp, of my mother and grandparents in Canada. Would we ever be together again for Christmas in our little house near Orléans? It was better to lose myself in the thoughts of the other girls. . . .

The priest raised the Host. All the heads were bowed. A few women were weeping in their hands. I saw tears drop between the fingers of one of the little Brittany girls.

It was already being rumored that the invasion would not take place in the coming spring. Our exile was being prolonged. Over there in France, little brothers were growing up, parents were hungry and cold, the Boche contaminated Paris, and here we were so far away—so lost. Would all this never come to an end? *"Noël, Noël, Il est né, le Divin Enfant."* The season of joy was even more difficult to endure than the gray days.

Michel Levy was waiting for Ursula as she came out of the chapel. He had a gift for her—a book of poems. Several times in the last few days, when Michel asked her to go out with him, Ursula had put him off in order to be with Claude. But tonight Claude was celebrating Christmas in her room in town with some English friends and a few of us from the barracks, and Ursula had promised to have supper with Michel. Claude always teased her about her "lover," and Ursula would have liked to stop seeing him, but she didn't know how to manage it without hurting his feelings.

All the women who had asked for leave were scattering down the street with their friends, soldiers, officers, and there were little groups of girls going out together. Ann and Petit went out arm in arm.

Ginette was spending Christmas respectably with a married couple she knew. Jacqueline left for Kensington. Mickey, in a sudden access of remorse, had not wanted to spend Christmas night with Robert. She had asked Claude if she could come to her party.

Hot chocolate had been prepared in the barracks for those who were staying in. Down Street went to bed late, and when the women slipped into their cold cots they sighed, *"C'est la guerre."*

Others were dancing all through the night, and drinking.

And all of us, wherever we were, were thinking, Next Christmas, surely, we'll be in France and we'll make up for all this. How glorious it will be to return in uniform, we, the volunteers of Free France! Everyone will honor us. Our parents will be so proud, the bells will ring *Noël, Noël* for us, *Noël* for liberated France, and we'll march under the Arch of Triumph! Oh, France, France, our next Christmas will be in the France that we will have freed!

Yes, our life here was only temporary; another few months to pass, at most a year, and it would certainly be over.

CHAPTER 13

There was a little Italian restaurant that we had discovered on Greek Street. It was modest and cheap, and it was there that Michel took Ursula, for he had very little money. And yet, despite his poverty as an ordinary recruit, he never seemed to be able to think of enough things to do to give Ursula pleasure.

Before the war he had been a student. He wanted to take his degree in philosophy, he told Ursula. In 1937, his parents had got out of Poland, and he had continued his studies in Belgium.

That was nearly all that Ursula knew of him, and she was not enough interested in Michel to wonder about his history. She liked him well enough and she was touched by his gentleness and his discretion. Sometimes when Ursula talked to him about Claude, Michel gazed at her with his childlike eyes, so unreally pure, and the black eyes, with their thick brows always raised in a startled expression, seemed to look at her with so complete a comprehension that Ursula thought that he must know everything, must have divined everything, for he never asked her any questions.

This evening he seemed gay. It was Christmas. Neither he nor Ursula was Catholic. Ursula was nothing at all, and Michel said he was in search of truth. And yet Christmas made them both happy.

After dinner they went out into the black street, where groups of people passed singing. They walked without any special destination, and Michel took hold of Ursula's arm. At first she wanted to withdraw it. She couldn't understand why the slightest physical contact with Michel frightened her. But not wanting to offend him, she did nothing, and they continued to walk like that.

"Merry Christmas!" people in the streets called out to them, and once more Ursula felt her heart heavy and sad. She wasn't thinking of Christmas in France, for she had had neither childhood nor holidays nor a family in her past. There was almost nothing. It was as though she had been born only the day before; her heart and her spirit were still unmarked and they floated in a sort of prenatal obscurity.

But Michel was happy to feel her near him. She was so young. She was the only woman who didn't frighten him; because she seemed so defenseless, because she didn't know how to chatter or to laugh like most women, who always either had an air of being on the defensive or were aggressive. Until now he had told himself, I don't have the right to touch her, or to take her with me, for I have nothing to offer her, neither God, nor a home, nor security, nor even myself—a self that wanted only to die until I met her, a self that still wants to die. He beheld her again in the courtyard, opening the door and halting on the lighted doorstep, a black hazy shadow against a background of light. He saw her sitting on the steps and saw the little movement of fear that she had had upon noticing him—like that of a little wild animal that trembles on seeing a man. He saw again her odd, small face, framed by her glossy hair falling thick and straight like that of a little Indian. And an immense tenderness more powerful even than love invaded him again.

He thought, Do I still want to die? And Michel had to answer himself that it was still so, despite his knowing her. He loved her, but he couldn't draw from her the nourishment that he needed. She could not silence the questioning in him and the agony in him. He knew that he had found nothing and that he still wanted to die, as on that day some months ago in Switzerland, in Fribourg, when he had decided to kill himself. Solemnly, his great eyes open with their strange candor, he told her all that was in his mind.

Michel, interned with several other Poles in a camp in Fribourg, had been granted the exceptional privilege of being permitted to take courses at the university. Scarcely seventeen, he felt as though he carried the moral weight of the whole world on his shoulders. He lived in profound despair, telling himself that there was no hope, that human stupidity and the cowardice of the human mass was so great that one could never change anything, that there would always be wars and barriers of hatred. He wished that somehow he could speak to mankind, explain that only humanity itself could put an end to these horrors. But how, and in the name of what could he speak? He was timid and ugly and he had no power of leadership. Then of what use was it to take part in the human farce and to love when love did not exist, and to bring children into the world in order that they might be killed in the next war in the name of some country that pretended to be more important than another? What for?

The boy Michel had decided to kill himself. He had bought some veronal, and was on his way to his rooming house when he met a fellow student from the university. This student was a monk, and strangely enough, a Jewish monk, a convert—a huge, handsome lad who enjoyed great popularity among the other students. He walked along with Michel, his white robe brushing the boy at every step. The sun warmed the snow on the mountaintops, and the air was so clear and so pure that one might almost have washed in it. Suddenly Michel began to talk. He told the monk that he had found his own truth and that it gave him a will to die. He told of his decision.

There are people who always talk about committing suicide but who never do it. But on Michel's face there was something so serious, his black eyes raised toward the monk were filled with such agony, that the monk realized that Michel had made up his mind.

Instead of moralizing, he proposed a sort of bargain to Michel. "You want to die," he said. "Agreed. But you don't have the right to die in cowardice, or stupidly. There is a war going on. Every day there are men who die, though they want to live. Leave Switzerland. Go to Spain and then to England. Enlist, and let yourself be killed while fighting. Perhaps you will die in place of the father of a family. Perhaps your death will save others. Perhaps your death will hasten the peace. Go get yourself killed, Michel. But only there, through England."

Three days later, Michel was in unoccupied France. He managed to get across France without much difficulty, arrived without mishap in Spain, and passed through without being noticed by the police. This voyage, which took months for others, took him scarcely fifteen days. From Gibraltar he embarked for Liverpool. For Michel, everything proved easy and simple.

Now he walked in the blackout with Ursula, who was silent. Ursula's thin arm was enlaced in his, and once more a flood of tenderness for her invaded him. He wanted to help her, to be with her, to take her face in his hands. She was so little, so gentle. She would never make him unhappy. He would take her away from that miserable house, and from that woman who held this child in fascination and would surely bring her suffering.

Michel halted, and with the sudden courage of the timid, he brusquely drew Ursula to him and kissed her on the mouth.

Ursula had expected nothing of the kind. An immense disgust welled up in her mouth upon the touch of Michel's lips. She felt his full lips crushing her own, and his masculine breath, and his cheeks scratching a little. Claude, Claude! she cried inwardly. She freed herself, and with her eyes filled with tears she began to run in the blackout, running blindly. She had only one thought: Claude. Claude's gentleness, her perfume, Claude's soft body close to her own. Ursula cried as she ran, surrounded by the thick night.

To reach Claude's house was her only aim. She turned into one street after the other, got lost, crossed a square into another street. "Merry Christmas!" people cried in the night. And then suddenly she was in front of Claude's house.

The house was filled with noise. It was Christmas Eve. The Christmas dawn would soon be born. The little room was crowded, and men and women were laced together, some drunk, some half drunk, some boisterous, and over everything there was a gloss of alcoholic jollity. We shouted when the bell rang, as though some great and wonderful friend would now appear.

Claude went to the door, her glass of whisky in her hand.

Ursula mounted the stairs, running. At the top of the stairs stood Claude. She was wearing gray trousers and a rose silk shirt. One could see her round breasts pressing against the silk. Ursula threw herself into her arms, sobbing.

"What is it, Ursulita, my little girl, what's wrong?" Claude repeated. She drew Ursula into the room.

When she was a little quieted, with her face against Claude's breast, feeling calm against her, against this maternal refuge, Ursula told Claude that Michel had kissed her.

Claude laughed, pressed the child in her arms, and told her she was a little fool. But deep in her eyes, it seemed to me, I saw a glint of triumph.

CHAPTER 14

One day in January, in the midst of drill, Jacqueline fainted. Ginette, who was near me, said, "There she goes again, our fancy lady!" Others were saying, "Jacqueline must have something wrong with her heart. She ought to be discharged."

As soon as Jacqueline had regained consciousness, Corporal Ann told Mickey and me to take her back to the barracks to rest. The doctor happened to be in the building just then, talking to the Captain. The Captain asked us why we had left drill, and we explained that Jacqueline had fainted. This was a wonderful occasion for the Captain to display her concern for "her dear girls," and she had the doctor examine Jacqueline right away.

We took her up to the infirmary. The doctor was in a hurry. He thought Jacqueline must have had a simple attack of vertigo. But in examining her he touched her back, and she let out a cry. Then he realized that there was something wrong with her, and sent her to be X-rayed.

Two days later Jacqueline was taken to a hospital, where she was put in a plaster cast for several months. She had a spinal fracture.

Jacqueline's cot in the barracks was at once occupied by a new recruit, a student, whose only passion was chemistry. Every evening, amidst the noise of the dormitory, our newcomer, Monique, calmly devoured her chemistry manuals, just as some of us read novels. During the first days the noncoms regarded her with suspicion; then they classified her as crazy but harmless, and left her in peace. After three days, we talked no more about Jacqueline. No one mentioned her. The hospital to which she had been taken was too far away for us to visit. The girls said, "She's just unlucky," or "How did she manage to do that to herself?" Only a few of us knew the history of that melodramatic night, before she entered the Army, when she had fled from her too ardent hosts. It was true that she now was gossiped about, like the others, for her weekend ménage and her numerous suitors, but this other matter seemed to touch upon the more remote and mysterious areas of life, and it was left undiscussed. Indeed, Jacqueline was soon forgotten. Each of us had her own worries, her own preoccupations, her own problems, and then came those of one's closest friend. There was no time to think about anyone who was gone.

Ursula had received a letter from her little soldier, Michel, filled with apologies, in which he begged to see her again. She had not replied. Just now, Ursula was happy, for Claude was in a good mood these days. Whenever Ursula was free and Claude was off duty, Ursula went to Claude's place.

The little room was on the fifth floor, reached by a narrow stairway. Civilian dresses, blue silk sets of underwear and stockings were scattered over the chairs. Claude made toast in front of a gas radiator. On those days Claude wiped off her make-up, and then her face took on a touchingly youthful look. As soon as she was relaxed, there was a kind of childishness that returned to her face, which became fresh and clear. Despite all of her habits, her lovers, her opium, her women, her whisky, one had only to scrape off this veneer of debauch in order to uncover in her a simple little bourgeoise, filled with a foggy remainder of "principles." She had been born to be a good wife and a good mother in some provincial town, and at bottom her lack of equilibrium was due to her having been turned away from this life by a series of circumstances.

She was religious, superstitious, and fairly well cultivated. She considered that a girl ought to be a virgin when she married. Another of her principles was that a decent woman would never permit a man to come to her place to make love. She preferred to come home alone from her lovers in the middle of the night, rather than to allow a man to sleep in her room. All the perversions seemed acceptable to her in love, but this one thing she could not allow. And why that one rather than another? Perhaps only to preserve for herself a sort of token of rectitude.

In the afternoons, when Ursula came to her room, Claude busied herself with little womanly tasks, mending her dresses, repairing stocking runs, washing her clothes, knitting pullovers for herself. If she had had a kitchen, she would have cooked excellent dinners. Claude was nearing forty and she had been leading a dissolute life for twenty years. Nevertheless, one felt that all that was basic in her came from her peaceful childhood and from her provincial adolescence. She was not a good drinker—even one drink went to her head right away—and yet she drank a great deal. Then she would do anything, scarcely knowing what she was doing.

In the evenings, in the dormitory, Mickey kept us posted on her affair with Robert. She was seeing him fairly frequently. She told us that he had several other mistresses, but she wasn't jealous. Despite her excitement at the beginning of the affair, her senses were slow in awakening. She found it agreeable to make love with him, but the experience aroused no particular feeling in her. It was a sort of game, with a touch of gymnastics in it. And she practiced this sport mostly to be able to say that she had a lover.

When spring came, everybody began to say that the second front would not take place that year either, and a wave of depression swept through Down Street. We would have to spend still another winter in London. Our exile was thickening on us like a crust. Every morning we marched through our drill, commanded by Petit; we marched around automatically, dreaming of our families, or of the landscape at home.

Hyde Park was covered with blossoms. In her strong, deep voice, Petit called out her commands: "To the left, march!" We obeyed, expert automatons now, though sleepy after the all-night bombardments.

And the bombardments grew in intensity. One night, as I stood fire watch on the roof with Ginette, Ann, and two other girls, we decided to relieve the monotony by telephoning down to Claude, who was on duty at the switchboard, and asking her to sing something for us. Pressed together around the receiver, we heard the distant melodious voice of Claude as she sang:

"C'est toujours l'onde
Qui m'a charmé,
Vagues profondes
Aux flots legers.
Aussi toujours,
La nuit, le jour,
Je veux chanter
L'onde, mon seul amour."

And all of us on the roof joined in the refrain:

"Bonsoir, Madame la Lune, bonsoir,
C'est votre ami Gerbault qui vient vous voir.
Bonsoir, Madame la Lune, bonsoir."

One day, years later, I opened a newspaper and read that the poet Alain Gerbault had just died. In the same moment, I saw all of us again on the dark roof, and I heard myself singing, together with the distant voice that rose to us from below:

> *"Bonsoir, Madame la Lune, bonsoir,*
> *C'est votre ami Gerbault qui vient vous voir."*

On that small roof, weren't we also afloat in a little boat, like the poet? And this night-gray stormy sky that surrounded us—wasn't it the immense sea with which Gerbault was in love?

The noise of the planes became deafening, and the DCA sounded on all sides. When we spotted a flare falling in our vicinity, Ginette immediately telephoned down to Claude, giving the direction in which it had fallen, and Claude transmitted the information to the local ARP. We were by now so accustomed to these alerts that the bombardment at first did not seem to us heavier than usual. But presently one of the Brittany girls remarked that this time all the bombs seemed to be incendiaries, and that they were all falling some distance away into a single area. It seemed to be the part of London known as the "City." Fires began to show there.

On the roof, we had sacks of sand ready. Ann peered out into the night, whistling the refrain from Alain Gerbault's song. From below, Claude informed us that the ARP had just come around to tell her that the entire City was on fire, that bombs were falling there like rain. The duty officer, Claude said, had ordered all the girls to get up and assemble in the kitchen. Our kitchen was in the basement and served as a shelter during the heavy raids.

Ann said she thanked heaven she was on watch that night. She had an absolute horror of any sort of shelter. Such places filled her with a mysterious terror and a sense of suffocation. She preferred a thousand times to be out in the open where she could see what was happening; if there was any danger, she wanted to see it.

The sky became dark red as though it were a lighted fireplace, with a flame that increased in intensity every moment. The spectacle had so extraordinary and horrible a quality of beauty that it filled all of us with awe. We all left our sandbags and forgot every principle of defense as we leaned against the railing of the roof, watching the scene.

London was on fire.

The sea of Gerbault was now all around us, a sea of fire. Not for a moment was any one of us free of the agonized consciousness of all those whose homes were collapsing and of those who were dying at this instant. And yet we could not take our eyes from this immense pyre whose flames seemed to be great enough to consume the world. Ann remarked that we were like Nero watching Rome burn, and because it was so conventional, her statement seemed somehow appropriate, with a historic grandeur that matched the grandeur of the scene.

The holocaust continued all night long. And somewhere deep in that night of flame, Ann began to talk to me. Though Ann was one of those people who seem entirely explained by their very appearance, I realized that I had known little of her until that night. It was as though the purgatory all around us were the purgatory of her life.

I recalled that other night when Mickey had come up onto the open roof, after her experience with Robert. But what Ann had to tell belonged to this night when all was unreal. In her husky voice, held down to a quiet monotone, Ann talked of her life as though she had to communicate it to destiny itself, in the face of this holocaust. Like most of the girls in the barracks, I had taken Ann and all Lesbians somehow as freaks, even to be considered amusing. Listening to her in that tragic purgatory, I wanted to weep.

Ann had spent her childhood in France, raised by her mother in poverty. She was an illegitimate child. She had shown unusual sexual tendencies when she was still scarcely grown. She had left her mother, and little by little cut herself away from all her early connections as she entered the spheres of her particular passion. She had come to England with a woman. When she had broken with her, Ann had found herself alone and penniless in London. It was just at the time of the defeat of France, and Ann had volunteered for De Gaulle's forces. As soon as she had seen Petit, she had felt herself to be at home.

Ann could not live without a liaison. It wasn't so much a need of love as a need of an affair with all its accompaniment of intrigue, mystery, and the consequent pleasure. By herself, she was not outside the normal; she was only so when she had a partner. And yet this departure from normalcy was necessary to her, as she had found out when scarcely more than a child. She could not live otherwise. Without a partner she felt as though something were amputated from her.

CHAPTER 15

A woman like Claude offered no interest either to Petit or to Ann. They rather disdained her, with the disdain of the true artist for the dilettante. They never considered her a Lesbian. They said of her, "She's a pervert, a curiosity seeker." And as to Claude's Lesbianism, this was true.

We had known so little of these matters when we came to the barracks, and now we were able to distinguish between the various grades. Through Ann, I realized that Claude made love with women not because of an absolute physical necessity, but through snobbism, and in order to excite her masculine lovers. She also felt that she was revenging herself on them, through feeling that she was just as strong as they in winning women. Several times in her life she had found men unfaithful to her. As soon as she discovered herself in such a situation, Claude sought out her rival and appropriated the girl. It was then she who became the lover, the taker. This was her strength, in the face of men.

Moreover, she was fond of her role as a dangerous woman. Love-making with women, opium-smoking, group love-making—all this was part of her role. She had learned to be a Lesbian, just as she had learned to smoke opium. For her it was the same sort of excitement. Claude had never suffered from this condition as Ann and Petit had suffered. She was married, she had numerous lovers, and she could have lived a normal life as wife and mother if she chose. As for the rest, it was nothing but a game that satisfied her vanity and provided her with amusement. She played being the man. The women of her circle, before the war, all played at that game. And the men of their acquaintance took them seriously, being unable to perceive that it was only a game. The men believed that they were making love with real Lesbians, and felt flattered and proud. What a man I am! they would think. I can even arouse a Lesbian! In the great comedy of love, in which everybody lied, this was only one more lie.

But to Ann, the love of women was no game. Ann had memories of her solitary childhood, when she had continually been reprimanded for not conducting herself like a good little girl who plays with her dolls. She remembered when all of her girlhood friends started going out with boys, and her own shame at being always alone with nothing but a secret love for her teachers, or for her mother's women friends.

One summer she had visited Sweden, and there she had met a woman for whom she had felt an instant adoration. Soon enough the woman had called Ann into her room and explained certain things that Ann had not yet known about herself. She had listened in fear, and yet with a terrible joy. For at last she knew that she was not alone, and that there was a way in which she too could love. The woman had become her mistress and her lover. It was an exhausting love, compounded of jealousies, of quarrels, of petty intrigue, but nevertheless it brought her the possibility of loving someone.

Ann was then seventeen. She had her hair cut, and looked absolutely like a boy. She had never experienced any desire for a man. For her, men were good comrades; she felt herself their equal. She was never in need of their help or of their presence.

Since that time, Ann had come to know well the contempt, the closing doors, and the hardening faces of respectable people. But most intensely she had known that exhausting love which dies of its own sterility between brief flashes of passion. It was a love that circled on itself, like a cat chasing its own tail. But that was how she was made. And Petit also. And the childhood of Petit had been the same. And the youth of all these women had been the same, and no one could ever change things for them.

At Down Street there was never any question of a true Lesbian pursuing a normal woman. Normal women were rarely interested in the real Lesbians. Claude could play at such games, for the subject of her attachment was of little interest to her. It was not the woman that she desired, but her own self-excitement; or, as in the case of Ursula, it was the child that she desired.

Ann and Petit enjoyed passing an occasional evening with Claude, for at least with her everything was clear. They could be their own selves, without having to hide anything. Claude served as a bridge between the Lesbians and the other women. Only by this bridge could the Lesbians approach other women, and in this way come to feel themselves less isolated in the world.

There were several other Lesbians in Down Street. In their group, every slightest incident became exaggerated into immense proportions, and there were the most violent discussions of the smallest bits of gossip, the mildest adventure. The taste for intrigue was the one feminine trait that seemed to remain with them, and it was developed to the maximum.

There were also Lesbians from outside, Englishwomen, ambulance drivers, women from the ARP and ATS, who came to visit the bar that had been set up in the main assembly room of our barracks.

The rest of the girls, the "real" girls, dancing to the eternal "Violetta" in the arms of sailors or soldiers from the Free French Forces, laughed among themselves as they watched the Lesbians.

It was at the bar that Ann met Lee. We all saw this happen. A tall Englishwoman, thin, long-limbed, with a very pale unreal white face and yellow catlike eyes, she had the air of a young Oxford student. Lee belonged to an aristocratic Scottish family. She was working as an ambulance driver. She had come to Down Street that evening wearing navy-blue trousers; her short hair glistened; her long hands trembled a little as she raised one glass of whisky after another. Ann, too, was standing at the bar, and it was plain to us all that she was intensely attracted to the Englishwoman.

CHAPTER 16

My long talk with Ann on the night of the fire of London had given me a deeper insight into the behavior of my comrades—of Claude and Mickey as well as of Ann herself.

There were many ways in which Mickey resembled
Claude. She, too, liked to play the dangerous woman. But
while Claude knew exactly when she was doing good or evil,
and while she called her actions by their right names, Mickey
didn't have the least moral sense. It had little to do with her
youthfulness; she simply knew no wrong. Occasionally she
liked to offer some of the girls what seemed to her to be serious advice and moral counsel. She would rattle off any number of catch phrases, platitudes, and it could be seen that they
had no significance whatever to her, and that she never related
these precepts to her own behavior. In her own life, Mickey
was always carefree and gay. She was not a very demanding
girl and life was easy for her. She liked novelty, adventure, and
a little danger. If she burned herself, she cried for a few minutes and then began again. Moreover, she was quite practical
and realistic and didn't get mixed up in things for the sake of
ideas.

She was immensely taken with Claude, for in her eyes
Claude represented the ideal woman. She wished she could be
like Claude.

Before long Mickey was chattering to us about her
unfaithfulness to Robert, and for a time she made love haphazardly with one man or another. Each time she wanted to
feel more and more ravished, and so she would come back and
tell us that her new lover was "handsome as a god!" She was
learning the technique of love, like a dutiful student. Presently
she began to report to us that men were telling her she was an
excellent mistress, and in the end Mickey even believed that
she was happy.

Claude and Mickey made an excellent pair, and went out
a good deal together. Claude began to see less of Ursula. She
sensed that Ursula was not really made for Lesbianism, and
even felt a little guilty about having started the girl toward perversion. Lately, when Ursula had come to her, this feeling of

guilt toward the girl had made Claude ill-tempered and petulant. Often she had sent the child away. Ursula would suffer, without understanding these changes of mood in the woman she adored. But with Mickey, things were easier for Claude; with Mickey she had no feelings of guilt. Mickey was made of the same stuff as she was, and so Claude got into the habit of taking Mickey along on her dates. The blonde and blue-eyed youthfulness of Mickey contrasted attractively with Claude's air of the mature *femme fatale*. Mickey was amusing, very gay, and universally pleasing.

One day, when Claude was drunk, she made a little game of kissing Mickey on the mouth in front of her current lover, and from Claude's mouth Mickey passed to the mouth of the lover.

That evening Mickey described her afternoon to me. Ursula was sitting on her cot, in her pajamas, and Mickey somehow included her, though not speaking directly to her.

Mickey had gone with Claude to visit a colonel whom Claude had met at the house of some friends, and who had invited her to come to his place for a drink. Mickey, as a second-class private, had felt flattered and impressed at going along to the house of a real ranking officer.

After a few whiskies, Claude began to undress. Her eyes grew quite small, as always when she was drunk. The colonel was what is known as a fine specimen of a man, according to Mickey's description: about forty, graying elegantly, fairly large and tall. He was a good officer and probably a good family man. But his family was in France, and there was no end to his exile. Besides, here was a woman undressing in front of him without even having to be asked. He studied her, nude. Claude was very beautiful. She was rather large, with fully rounded muscular shoulders and magnificent breasts, round and firm. Her skin was soft as though polished by years of caresses. She had a hard belly and a long back. Only her legs were a little short, but altogether, for a woman of forty, she was extraordinary. Seeing Claude nude, Mickey said she considered that she ought to keep her company, and began to undress in her turn. The colonel kept on only a funny little undershirt that reached to his thighs. One could sense that actually he was a little shocked by Mickey's youthfulness, for, as he told them, he had a daughter of Mickey's age. But Claude gave him no time for recollections.

A brief spring sunlight came through the windows. Mickey remembered a photograph of a woman, smiling in a frame. A man's glove lay open-handed on the floor.

In spite of everything, it was Claude whom the colonel preferred. Mickey probably reminded him too much of his daughter.

But, "He's handsome as a god!" Mickey declared. "He makes love marvelously. It was very amusing."

Ursula had listened without saying a word, sitting there with her bare feet swinging a little above the floor. She lowered her head, watching her feet so that we might not see anything in her eyes. But one could see into her heart. Ursula was pained, unable to accept this abandonment.

Ginette recounted the tale of her latest love, a Canadian. Two women whispered together, laughing. From the hall below came the sound of the record that was most often played after "Violetta," *"Mon coeur a besoin d'aimer."* Ursula too went to bed. She buried her head in her pillow. Her heart beat fast. She told herself, She just used me for amusement. And all at once she recalled the black eyes, the melancholy eyes of Michel, and the thought came to her that Michel would never have made use of her. But he had left, gone out of her life. She herself had driven him away. A longing rose in her for the calm voice of a man, and for the security that a woman feels because of a man's being in love with her—a man like Michel. Until now she had been a little girl all alone. But after her experience with Claude, Ursula had come to know the need of another being. She no longer knew how to be alone; she was afraid to be alone. And yet she was not resentful of Mickey. It was not in her nature to be resentful, and she liked Mickey very much.

The idea of evil arose in Ursula's mind. No one had ever taught her what was right. Whatever morality she possessed was instinctive. When she felt happy, she had told me once, it seemed to her that her actions were good, and when she felt unhappy, she thought of evil. And it seemed to her that the fear and the sense of solitude and the suffering within her were the result of evil. She did not know how to cry. Her tears never emerged, but seemed to remain at the bottom of her throat. Once again Ursula felt herself crushed by this world of grown-up people who took little girls and covered them with lies that were disguised as shining words, and then discarded them. She felt no resentment against either Claude or Mickey. She resented only the gestures, the false gestures that were made in the name of love, and that were used by grown-up people in life as in a play. Every gesture she had made had been pure, but now her own actions were tarnished, because all that people did was tarnished.

CHAPTER 17

The following evening we had gas-mask practice. We were all assembled in the dining room, and there was a great deal of whispering and laughing and nudging back and forth while a handsome officer, young and blond, solemnly explained how to make use of a gas mask, as though we had never been told before.

Each of us had to put on her mask and keep it on for half an hour. There were two hundred women in the large hall, and we might have been taken for a school of monsters from beneath the sea. The rubber tubes slanted comically in all directions. We talked to each other with our hands. Inside the masks, we felt hot, and a fine haze covered the glass panes.

Claude was sitting next to Mickey. It was one of her days of remorse in regard to Ursula. She had again decided not to have any more to do with the girl, and she had not even looked at her all through the evening.

Behind the little window of her mask, Ursula saw Claude and Mickey pressed one against the other on a single chair. Their rubber tubes kept bumping, their masks had an air of laughter. Claude's arm was around Mickey to keep her from falling off the chair.

Ursula was sitting behind them, and it seemed to her that she was entirely enclosed and locked in a huge grotesque mask that isolated her from the rest of the world. She didn't know what to do, but she had to do something. She couldn't remain abandoned like this. She was too miserable. And then all at once, as she afterward confessed to me, Ursula had the idea of pretending to lose consciousness. If she fainted, the way Jacqueline used to faint, then Claude would be forced to notice her, to run to her, to pay attention to her. At the thought of such an action, she blushed in her mask. What if everybody understood that it was a fraud? What if everybody made fun of her? Worst of all, what if Claude didn't even come to her?

It doesn't matter, she told herself. I have to try. And overcoming all of her inner resistance, Ursula suddenly caused herself to slip from the bench to the floor. There was a turmoil around her. All the masks pressed against her, pulling and pushing at her. Petit roared in her commanding voice, "Quiet!

Return to your places!" Ann had removed her own mask and was pushing away all the women who were crushing Ursula. Finally Petit leaned over and undid her mask.

Ursula immediately opened her eyes. Ann held Ursula's head in her lap and said, "It's nothing, baby. You were too hot, that's all. There, it's all over."

And Claude, Claude was there, her anxious face bent over her. It was marvelous. It had succeeded after all. Claude was there.

We helped Ursula upstairs to the dormitory. She lay down on her bed. Claude followed us and sat down by Ursula, calling her Ursulita and stroking her forehead. Ursula looked at her without saying anything. She felt tranquil, almost happy, but with a tiny point of contempt for Claude within her happiness. For it had been necessary to deceive her, and Claude had let herself be taken in the trap.

But at least Claude was paying attention to her. Ursula sighed and closed her eyes. For the first time in her life, she felt as though she had accomplished a grown-up action.

Nevertheless, this brought only a short respite. Several times Claude took Ursula out with her in the evening, but Ursula felt lost in the night clubs. Unlike Mickey, she didn't explode into laughter over the jokes of Claude's friends. She was not talkative. She didn't know how to drink. Men found her nice but dull. They rarely found her pretty. Her pale little face with its huge brown eyes had a sort of style, it is true. But in those years in London, what men wanted of women was to make them forget the war, forget their problems and their nostalgia, and Ursula, without wishing to, reminded them of all those things. They much preferred Mickey.

And for Ursula, these excursions were a torture. One evening, in a bar near Grosvenor Street, when a drunken soldier seized her in his arms and tried to kiss her, she let out a cry of terror that brought laughter to the entire club.

Summer had come, another rainy London summer. The only hope for breaking the tension and the monotony was to go on leave. But where? Some of the girls went as guests of English families. Ursula dreaded going to stay with strangers. And Claude was becoming more and more nervous. Claude had spells of violent rage for no reason at all. In the switchboard room the atmosphere was always tense and stormy. She swore at the other women. One day, in the middle of the dining room, Claude started an argument with Ginette and called her a slut. Ginette slapped Claude's face.

Every day Ursula told me that she was going to ask for her eight-day leave, and every day she held back, hoping there would be a change in Claude.

One evening it seemed to Ursula that the change had arrived, and that everything would be again as it had been. And as always, it was not because of a sexual need in Ursula for Claude; it was simply a thirst for tenderness, in which the sexual aspect was only incidental.

It was a Saturday evening, and Claude was off duty. A group of us had decided to go out on a hen party, just by ourselves, to have dinner somewhere and then go to a movie. Claude had invited Mickey and Ursula to come and spend the night at her place afterward. Ursula asked for weekend leave. Claude was in excellent humor, and as always when a party was in sight, she seemed to regain her youth.

The beginning of the evening passed well. We went to dinner at a place called Rose's, a little restaurant in Soho kept by a sort of witch—a fat Belgian woman who never served anyone she didn't like. At her place, the only dish was horse-meat steak with fried potatoes. Fifteen people at most could get into the restaurant. Most of the clientele consisted of sailors of Free France; sometimes there were a few Belgian officers, and occasionally there was a party of high society people in search of exotic atmosphere. The radio played, and people yelled and sang. On the wall there was a photograph of King Leopold, covered with grease spots. Rose served everybody herself, growling continuously. Beer had to be fetched from the pub across the street; it cost two shillings six. And the meal was finished off with a dish of apple sauce. It was always very gay there, and the food was quite good.

Claude performed imitations and sang *"Ah, que c'est done bête un homme!"* and Rose's large ill-tempered face wrinkled up in a smile. When Claude was in this mood, there was no one on earth who could resist her charm. Ursula ate with great appetite, and laughed with all her soul. And Claude was full of attention for her, refilling her plate with fried potatoes, asking her opinion about everything, treating her like an intimate friend.

Then someone suggested that it would be dull to go to the movies after this, so we decided to make a tour of the pubs and bars.

And then Claude began to drink.

At eleven o'clock all of us went off to the barracks, except for Mickey and Ursula, who were to sleep at Claude's. The next day, Ursula told me what happened.

The alert had sounded. Alerts had been rather rare the last few months. The searchlight swept the sky over their heads, but not a sound was to be heard. The three women walked home along the length of Hyde Park.

Claude was no longer paying attention to Ursula. She had taken Mickey's arm in the dark, and she talked only to Mickey. From time to time she stopped and kissed Mickey, and Ursula stopped too, not knowing what to do or say. It didn't occur to her to make a scene. It seemed to her that Claude was free to kiss whomever she liked.

They arrived at Claude's. Mickey went to take a bath. Claude followed her, laughing, and Ursula undressed and slipped into Claude's large bed. Like a suffering animal, she could think only of closing her eyes and burying her head in a hole. She rolled herself into a ball in the empty bed, and little by little the laughter of Claude and Mickey became more distant, and she fell asleep.

Ursula didn't know what awakened her. She found herself still alone in the bed. The room was dark except for a luminous circle on the floor, a reddish illumination shining from underneath the lighted gas heater. Ursula raised her head and looked about. Claude and Mickey were stretched on the carpet in front of the fire. They were nude, and the firelight gilded their bodies. They were extremely beautiful, both of them. Both very blonde, one with her slender young body and tiny little pointed breasts, the other with her womanly body and her round breasts, heavy and firm. There was a strange plastic beauty in these two sleeping women. Their arms and legs mingled until they looked almost as though they formed a single monster with two heads.

At that moment, Claude opened her eyes and looked at Mickey. Ursula clearly saw Claude's face. It was directly in the firelight. Her eyes seemed to be two dark holes, immense as chasms, and deep, deep within, there was a red burning light.

All at once a horrible terror hit Ursula. She said to herself, It's a demon! From the deepest part of her being, a primitive comprehension flooded her. This was a demon.

A kind of shiver mounted all through Ursula, shaking her. She slid back under the sheet, covering her head, terrified, her heart beating wildly. She stuffed her ears and bit the sheet, and for the first time since her very early childhood, tears began to flow.

Ursula finally fell asleep like that, hidden almost at the

bottom of the bed, her face inundated with tears, all curled within herself, and feeling her body filled with pain, as though she had been battered by a demonic fist.

On Monday she asked for her eight-day leave, and left to visit one of the many English families that kindly opened their homes to the troops of other countries.

CHAPTER 18

It was impossible that Ursula's leave should go by uneventfully. What happened to her seems to me quite beautiful, very strange, and rather mad. It could not have happened except during the war, and to Ursula. She told me all about it in detail, and I shall try to recall everything and to describe those days without the slightest change. I wish I could recover Ursula's very words.

She was visiting in a small harbor town that was forever filled with wind, a great wind that undid Ursula's hair, and that sometimes sent her flying into the arms of passers-by.

The family was charming. Ursula consumed great quantities of lamb, boiled cabbage, boiled potatoes, excellent meat pies, and rose-colored trembling gelatin. For two days she wandered around the port and the beach, amusing herself watching the boats, and thinking of Down Street as seldom as possible.

The port was a wonder to behold, and for childlike Ursula it was paradise. Bearded sailors, crates being unloaded, monkeys that the sailors were bringing home leaping about the gangways, people speaking in all sorts of languages, shops where one could buy the loudest Chinese silks and little rows of ivory elephants, trunk to tail, one behind the other on an ivory bridge. Ursula would have loved to buy herself a red and black kimono or an elephant or a monkey. But as she didn't have enough money, she contented herself with looking at these treasures.

In the evenings, the entire family took French lessons from her. The father repeated, *"La porte est ouverte. La demoiselle est jolie."* The mother, with great difficulty, managed to read a Free French newspaper, and the children had Ursula do their French exercises for them.

At night she slept with the three girls, and the mother came to hear them say their prayers and to kiss them all good night.

All the aunts, uncles, and cousins came to see the French girl, and to ask her if she liked England and if it were true that the French ate frogs.

Ursula acquired all the latest news about Princess Elizabeth, which the family read in the *Tatler*, and together with the three young daughters she knitted small squares of multicolored wool, to be assembled into blankets for soldiers.

The three girls had three boy friends, all freckled and timid, who appeared on Saturday afternoon to take them to the movies with their mother's permission. Once one of the boys had even kissed the eldest daughter, who was fifteen, very swiftly on the edge of her lips as a sign of engagement, and had bought her a brooch in one of the harbor shops.

On the third day, Ursula, in uniform, was walking along the jetty when a voice asked her in French:

"Aren't you French, mademoiselle?"

She turned, and as there was a sudden heavy gust of wind against her, she almost fell into the arms of a French naval officer. He began to laugh. He seemed to be about thirty-five. He had regular white teeth, thick lips, and brown eyes. Ursula found him big and handsome and nice.

They walked along the port talking. He was attached to a

French vessel, a warship that had been there three months for repairs. He had not seen a Frenchwoman for months and months. He had just returned from the Orient and had been in China, in Haiti, and in America.

They talked a great deal, each delighted to find a compatriot. He took her along the pier to show her his ship, and he told her the names of all the ships, and he took her to tea in a curious little establishment that had all sorts of weird souvenirs hanging from the ceiling.

During the entire year that she had passed in worshiping Claude, Ursula had never gone out with a man, except Michel. She avoided men, considering herself definitely outside the normal, like Petit and Ann. But now with Philippe, everything was so simple, so amusing. He didn't frighten her, as all the other men did. There was a comradeship about him, almost as though he were a big brother, and he was so huge next to tiny Ursula that she felt sure that he would treat her as a child, and this was reassuring to her.

Seated there in the strange café, Philippe told her about his voyages, and to Ursula they all sounded marvelous and strange. He declared that the life of a sailor was the most beautiful of all and that his only bride would always be the sea. This expression pleased Ursula greatly.

She listened to his tales of China, where he had smoked opium and made love to Chinese women, and of America, where he had actually eaten meals in pharmacies, and of Haiti, where one covers oneself with flowers.

Suddenly he asked her to excuse him for a moment, went out, and presently returned to tell her that he had requested the commander of his ship to invite the little French soldier girl to lunch the next day—to lunch aboard ship, at the officers' mess. There would be a special feast in her honor.

Ursula blushed with joy. She accepted, but confessed that she was a little worried because of the English family. What would they say? Would they be shocked at her going out with a stranger? Would they understand that in this exile every Frenchman was a brother? Philippe suggested telling them that he was her cousin, or indeed her brother. Ursula thought "brother" would make a more correct impression, and so they made an appointment for lunch the next day.

The good folk were delighted when she told of her amazing encounter. They found the coincidence quite within the normal range of fortunes of war—especially for the French, an exciting sort of people. What luck to have met her brother in this out-of-the-way port! Sometimes there were good things, even in war.

CHAPTER 19

It was a happy girl who arrived the following day at the gangway to Philippe's ship. Ursula had carefully polished the buttons of her uniform, put on her best khaki silk tie and the silk stockings forbidden in the regulations, and brushed her chestnut-colored hair, which hung thick and straight at both sides of her face, like the hair of little girls on their way to school.

It was twelve-thirty and the sun burned the length of the quay. The warship seemed so spotlessly clean, and its flag was so blue, so white, so red! At the gangway the sentry came to attention for her, and for a second Ursula felt like an admiral. Philippe was already advancing toward her, followed by a group of midshipmen, all young, all smiling, all overjoyed at seeing a French girl.

Ursula, with her hair mussed by the wind, was surrounded

by all the blue uniforms and taken to the commander's cabin. The commander offered her sherry and showed her his Chinese engravings. Then they went in to dinner. There was an immense table, and around it sat twelve officers. Ursula was the only woman. She laughed ceaselessly and Philippe poured out white wine for her, and then red wine, and this made her laugh and chatter even more. A dark sailor, a native from the colonies, served chicken with rice while smiling at the nice young lady.

She had never drunk so much or eaten so much. The pastries were perfect, and the black coffee made her heart beat faster. After that there was brandy in lovely stemless glasses, altogether round like little bowls. Ursula was seated on the couch, the radio played, the uniforms chattered, and Philippe sat down next to her and began to ask her questions. Ursula talked about Down Street. It had been the limit of her horizon for many months; but she said nothing of Claude.

Philippe asked her if she had a boy friend. She said no, blushing, and she saw that Philippe didn't believe her. Suddenly it was as though a light had dawned on her. She comprehended, though vaguely, that all these nice officers, seeing her in uniform, told themselves that she was certainly used to drinking, used to freedom, to men, and to life. To them, she was a little girl in appearance only, for everybody knew perfectly well that women in the Army were no babies. The whole idea barely crossed her mind; her head whirled, the radio played, and the midshipmen began to sing, and Ursula took up the refrain with them, *"En allant glaner des joncs."*

Most of the afternoon went by like this, in laughter and song. The commander had gone back to his cabin. The slant-eyed sailor had brought in tea and cookies, and some of the officers left to go ashore. Philippe explained to her that most of them came to sleep in their cabins only on their day of guard duty. During the three months of waiting for their motor to be repaired, they had rented apartments in the city, and they spent their free hours and their nights in town.

Then Philippe suggested that he take her around the ship. They left the dining room. Ursula climbed up ladders, went down ladders, crossed over narrow passageways, and stepped into the broiling galley, where sailors were at work half naked. Afterward she leaned against the railing on the bridge while Philippe showed her all the directions on the compass. That way was America, and that way was Iceland, and down there was Brazil.

They sat down on a coil of rope, and Philippe showed her how to make sailor's knots and Ursula tried to make them the way he did. She wished that she were a man so that she could be a sailor.

As they rose, Ursula looked at her hands. After climbing all the ladders, leaning against smokestacks, and hanging onto ropes and rails, her hands were completely black. "I must wash my hands," she said to Philippe.

Philippe led her down more ladders and through long corridors, and finally stopped before a closed door. He opened it and gestured her inside. "This is my cabin," he said.

CHAPTER 20

It was a very pretty little chamber, and at first Ursula had no thought but to admire it. Philippe showed her his work table, his books, his pictures on the walls, some Japanese engravings, little reproductions of Egyptian statues, a reproduction of a Van Gogh painting, photographs of the Orient with palm trees and camels, and a handsome map of the world over his bunk.

Then he gave her soap and a towel and she began to wash her hands. Philippe sat on a chair watching her. A ray of sunlight entered through the porthole and blue motes of dust danced in the sunbeams. When she had finished, Ursula hung up the towel and turned around.

Philippe rose and came toward her and very casually said, "But you still have some dirt on your face."

She raised her chin innocently. "Where?"

Philippe came still closer. "There," he said, and before Ursula could realize what he was doing, he was holding her in his arms and kissing her on the mouth.

It was very strange for her, and at first repulsive, as with Michel. She detested the taste of tobacco in the mouth that took possession of hers, and the thickness of the lips, and the slightly brutal force of this kiss, which she neither expected nor desired. But at the same time, she wanted to know. She wanted to know how it was, this kiss of a man, and in the depths of her heart she wanted to know if she couldn't respond to it.

She didn't resist. Philippe lifted her in his arms and stretched her on the bunk. Then, sitting next to her, he continued to kiss her. Little by little Ursula sensed that her mouth was becoming habituated to the strong lips, to the taste of tobacco, and to the stubborn tongue, which was as knowing as Claude's, but thicker and more insistent in its ideas. She went so far as to put forward the point of her small tongue, but the first contact shocked it so that it withdrew immediately. Philippe laughed, raised his face from hers, studied her unlaughing brown eyes.

Then he began to kiss her again with swift little kisses; and then again for a long time with long kisses. And Ursula began to like his kissing very much.

Then he slipped his hand toward her body, and immediately Ursula's entire body contracted. It was like an electric shock. She seized Philippe's hand and pushed it away, and raised herself ready to leap from the bunk. But Philippe only laughed, not in the least embarrassed, and promised not to touch her again. Then Ursula relaxed and he began once more to kiss her.

A bell rang. Philippe got up. Ursula raised herself from the bunk. He gave her his comb and she straightened her hair. Then they went out together, returning to the open deck. It was nearly six o'clock, and Ursula said she had to go.

They went down the gangplank and along the quay. Philippe held her arm as though from now on she was in his possession. This pleased and displeased Ursula at the same time.

He asked to see her the next day for dinner. He was very formal and said there would be another officer with an Englishwoman. This reassured Ursula, and she accepted.

They made no further allusion to his kisses. Philippe began to talk of the sea again, and as they walked along the harbor road they kept stopping like typical French citizens to study the people and the shop windows, to criticize the women's clothing and their hats. Englishwomen, they remarked, had a particular gift for wearing any color from mauve to rose to green to orange without the least embarrassment. This made Ursula laugh, but Philippe was indignant. He didn't like the English; he didn't like Englishwomen, or English cooking, or the English climate.

"The women don't know how to make love," he declared. "Their cooking is horrible, and it rains all the time." As though to contradict him, the sun continued to shine, but a violent wind threw them against each other, and for an instant he held Ursula in his arms.

When Philippe left her at the house where she was staying, Ursula wanted to reflect for a while, to put her ideas in order, but the three sisters surrounded her, the dog began to jump all over her, the mother appeared to ask all about her brother, and she had to tell about the ship, describe the luncheon, and then do the French lessons of the girls.

It was only in the evening after prayers, when the sisters had grown tired of talking about their boy friends and had fallen asleep, that Ursula was able to return to her thoughts of Philippe. And so, she reflected, she had kissed a man and found it agreeable. Philippe was nice and gay, and not complicated or hysterical like Claude. What a good smile he had, and what nice warm eyes! He hadn't tried to force her, when he saw she didn't like his touching her. Yes, Ursula decided that she could see him again with pleasure and without any risk, and that it would do her good, it would help her forget Claude.

CHAPTER 21

She spent the whole day on the beach, gathering mussels among the rocks, for she had taken it into her head to cook them and give the British family a taste of this delicacy. The dog, Vicky, accompanied her, and halted before each mussel-covered rock with the patient air of a good English dog.

The sun was quite warm. Ursula took off her shorts and sunbathed in her swimming suit, and then she ran into the water, splashing, swimming, floating, as happy as the great dog whose head stuck out of the water beside hers.

When Ursula came out of the water she found a deserted crevice among the rocks, and there she rolled in the sand with Vicky. He leaped about and rubbed himself joyfully against the rocks, and it seemed to Ursula that life was beautiful.

The mussels were received with a good deal of suspicion. Each member of the family ate one out of politeness toward the little French girl, saying, "It's odd, isn't it?" Ursula emptied the plate all by herself, because she was very hungry, and for the honor of France.

In the afternoon she returned to the beach. The sea was mounting, with a constant roar of breaking waves. A plane passed far overhead and later there was the distant sound of antiaircraft fire. Ursula had almost forgotten that there was a war. A goat was browsing on a hillock, and from time to time the goat raised its head with a graceful movement. Ursula thought of Philippe, and a strange shiver passed down her back. Her heart began to beat faster, she felt cold, and her throat contracted.

What's the matter with me? she wondered.

From that moment until evening, the strange shivering continued ceaselessly up and down her back, and her heart kept beating, beating. She wished that it were already seven o'clock, and at the same time she wanted to run away, no matter where. Or perhaps to the soft arms of Claude, resting her head on Claude's breast.

She dressed nervously, telling herself she was an idiot. She couldn't manage to make a respectable knot in her tie, and her hair was full of sand. Her hostess gave her a key in case she should return late. She left at last, quite a bit early, and arrived ahead of time at the church in the central square where they had agreed to meet. The wind was so strong that she was barely able to keep erect. She went into the church to wait.

Ursula had rarely had occasion to enter a church. She sat down in a corner and looked about. It must have been a Catholic or an Anglican church, for there were statues and flowers. There was the odor of incense and of candles. It was very calm. It must be so strange, she thought, to belong to a church and to feel at home in this huge house. And this little girl without religion, without a creed, without a past, left to herself in a world of which she was ignorant, felt herself in some way linked to a deity who received the prayers of mankind. Not a special god called by a certain name, and endowed by mankind with a list of attributes, but simply that unknown and mysterious force to which people everywhere build temples and toward whom prayers are raised. "God of Mankind," she said, in a very low voice, "you see, I am here. My name is Ursula. I don't know anything about anything. Please make it so that I can understand—so that someone explains to me why everything is, and what I must do. And thank you, God of Mankind, for the sea, the sun, and the sand."

She felt quite content and much reassured when she went out into the daylight. Just outside the church, Philippe waited, turning over his uniform cap, which was covered with gold braid.

The other officer was a friend of Philippe's. He was the ship's doctor, and quite naturally Philippe called him Doc. The young woman with him was a very pretty English girl, highly self-assured, very feminine, smartly dressed, and well made up. She examined Ursula with an air of superiority. Philippe, like Doc, seemed to go out of his way to please this young woman, and Ursula found herself with nothing to say. She felt awkward, embarrassed by her heavy khaki clothes and her hair falling into her eyes, and conscious of her hands with the nails cut short. She wished that she also were a grown woman, knowing how to laugh with self-assurance and how to look men in the eye without blinking, and wearing a low-cut black dress, revealing her provoking breasts. She wished she could dance perfectly, wearing high heels and transparent stockings. But instead of being like that, there she was saying nothing, feeling queasy ever since yesterday's meal on the boat, and not able to eat anything.

Philippe exclaimed at her leaving her plate untouched. He was very fond of eating, and it seemed to him a sacrilege to refuse smoked salmon and to leave a roast untasted. To please him, Ursula managed to drink the wine that was served to her.

The young Englishwoman had the art of turning the conversation easily around all sorts of obvious subjects, which one couldn't remember a moment afterward. The dinner was rather long. Afterward, Philippe suggested that they finish the evening at his place in town. And since there were four of them, Ursula accepted, reassured by the presence of the other woman.

They took a taxi to Philippe's apartment. It was a modern three-room flat filled with Chinese and Indian knickknacks that Philippe had brought back from his voyages. They all made themselves comfortable in the living room. Philippe brought out whisky glasses. The conversation languished. Doc and the young woman exchanged glances and whispered to each other. Suddenly the young woman rose and left the room. Doc followed her, and Ursula found herself alone with Philippe.

CHAPTER 22

She was seated on the couch. Philippe leaned over her and, as on the day before, began to kiss her. Ursula was astonished to discover that his mouth was already familiar to her. How warm and good it was, penetrating her own!

With his free hand, Philippe put out the bright lamp and snapped on another, which suffused the room with a dim rosy light, in which everything was intimate and soft. Ursula felt tranquil, happy. After all, his nearness was natural, not frightening at all, quite normal and reassuring.

Perhaps half an hour passed. Philippe's hand began to explore Ursula. It touched her very lightly, but at the same time much more determinedly than yesterday; a hand that had a will of its own. And as on the day before, a mad panic seized the girl. In the same instant she became rigid and filled with tremors. She didn't want this. She didn't want it at all.

Philippe sighed, took his hand away, and resumed his kissing. But very quickly he returned to the charge. For quite a while, in silence, the struggle continued. Ursula would become rigid, and then would relax slightly, murmuring only, "No, no." Finally Philippe sat back on the couch next to her. He looked at her queerly, with an air that was neither angry nor astonished. With a quick motion of his hand he brushed back the mass of brown hair that fell in disorder over his forehead. He said, "Why don't you want me to make love to you?"

In very low broken words, Ursula said that she was afraid, that as yet no man had ever touched her, that she didn't want it. She begged him not to be angry. She liked his kisses well enough, but nothing else. "I beg you, nothing else."

She didn't tell him that in the depths of her being there was also an infantile panic at being found ignorant, at failing like a schoolboy who hasn't prepared his lesson; a fear that he would make fun of her as of the Englishwomen who didn't know how to make love. She didn't tell him that she was still in terror of the unknown thing before her, of that which came after the kisses, and which could not be in any way like what she had learned from Claude—certainly altogether different.

Philippe looked at her with astonishment. In his eyes, Ursula could see that he didn't believe she was a virgin—a virgin after a year in the Army! He certainly believed that she was just a little teaser playing the ingenue. After all, she knew how to kiss well enough; it just wasn't possible. He didn't believe it. And this thought pained her very much. She really liked him. She wished she could prove to him that she was telling the truth, and she wished that she could make him happy, but she was afraid, and her fear was stronger than any other feeling.

At first, Philippe said nothing. He took her in his arms again and resumed his kissing, as though his kisses could convince her better than words. But when it became clear that nothing was going to change her, he studied her attentively with a reflective air, as though asking himself whether she was after all telling the truth, and whether she was indeed a virgin, a naïve little girl.

Then he said gently, "Why are you afraid, Ursula? I won't hurt you. Why are you afraid to make the jump? Afterward you will be a woman. You have to become a woman someday, and it will make you very happy, you know."

He said the things that all men say on this occasion, but he said them sincerely, gently, and Ursula was hearing these words for the first time.

She wanted to cry and to ask his forgiveness. He was so gentle and nice, and she was probably behaving very badly, letting him kiss her and then refusing to go further, like those frightful teasers that Claude was always talking about in disgust.

She wanted to; she wanted to; but she simply could not.

Philippe rose, poured himself a glass of whisky, and returned to sit next to her. He no longer attempted to kiss her, but he began to speak of his childhood, of his home and his parents, of their small estate in the Pyrenees, of his brother and sisters, and of a way that his mother had when he was bad of saying that it wasn't he who had misbehaved, but "Popaul." He turned toward Ursula smiling, and said that it probably wasn't Philippe, but still Popaul who wanted to go to bed with her. Philippe didn't want to annoy her, or hurt her in any way. He was so good, so simple this way, and Ursula didn't know how to explain the gratitude and the tenderness that she felt toward him.

They talked quietly the rest of the evening. He spoke again of his voyages. It was always to this that he returned most easily. And Ursula described the barracks, and our warrant officers, and Mickey, Jacqueline, and me, but without ever speaking of Claude. She sensed that Philippe would never have understood, that he would have been terribly shocked.

It was past midnight. There was a discreet knock on the door. Doc entered with his young woman, who was as elegant and as well made up as before. The young woman gave Ursula a little glance of complicity filled with secret understanding. Doc assumed the well-bred air of a gentleman who deliberately ignores the obvious.

They played the phonograph and danced a little, and then Doc said that he and the young woman were going to leave. Philippe helped Ursula into her coat, and the four of them left together.

The streets were black. There was no more wind, and the sky was filled with stars. Doc and the English girl hailed a taxi and drove off. Philippe and Ursula walked on without speaking.

At her door Philippe asked her to meet him the following day for dinner. He apologized again and said that everything was Popaul's fault, and then he took her in his arms and kissed her very long and gently.

CHAPTER 23

For the first time in her life, Ursula failed to close her eyes all night long.

She listened to the regular breathing of the three sisters and heard them sigh in their sleep. She saw the stars fade little by little and the dawn inundate the sky.

Well, then, she wasn't normal. For how could Ursula know, all by herself, that she was behaving exactly as any pure young girl behaves the first time a man tries to make love to her? She told herself that she would never get out of her difficulty, that she would never have a home or children, that she would remain doomed to solitude all her life, like Ann, like Petit. She couldn't rid herself of Philippe's words: "Why are you afraid to make the jump?"

But she *wanted* to make the jump, she wanted to love a man, to know what a man's love was like, to be linked with that endless chain of human beings who joined with each other in the same way, and told each other the same words, always entirely new since the first man and the first woman.

Why was it, while she found Philippe so good, so handsome, and so nice, that his hand frightened her so, that she contracted so at his touch? Could it be because of an idea she had from Mickey's and Claude's descriptions, that there would be pain in losing her virginity? Perhaps it was only that—a simple fear of pain.

And then, if she should prove to Philippe that what she had said was true? For she sensed that at bottom Philippe continued to disbelieve her. He would then really know that she was a virgin. He would be ashamed of having doubted her word.

To vanquish her deep fear, to prove to herself that she was normal—that was it. It was the only way to save herself. Otherwise it would be too late. This was her last chance. If she didn't take it now, she would never be able to accept intimacy with a man.

Ursula struggled all by herself, groping for an answer, searching in her immature and uninstructed mind, encumbered as it was with all the false ideas that she had gleaned haphazardly during all her life, searching with her primitive consciousness, and calling upon the most profound instinct of creation.

That night, without knowing it, Ursula told herself the things that Catholics tell their priests during confession, and that Americans tell their psychoanalysts. But she had no one to counsel her and to clarify her idea of herself.

The day pierced through the net curtains. The three girls stretched like cats.

Ursula had made up her mind.

She didn't eat anything all day long. She couldn't. Her throat was so contracted that it was impossible for her to swallow.

She went to the beach, crouched against a rock, and tried to think of nothing at all. The dog laid his head on her bronzed knees, waiting for her to play with him.

A little green hill rose just behind her. Ursula climbed it with the dog. Once on top, she beheld the immense sea, open in all the directions that Philippe had shown her, Newfoundland, New York, Rio de Janeiro.

On the hill there were queer little stakes projecting from the ground all about. Ursula tried to pull one out, but it wouldn't give way. She finally abandoned it and went down the other side of the hill, with loose stones rolling under her feet. Some fishermen in a little boat made signals to her, shouting. Ursula couldn't understand their cries, but she waved her hand in greeting to them.

It was only when she reached the bottom that she saw a large sign barring the way up the hill: "Do Not Climb. Mortal Danger. Mined Hill."

It was at least something to tell the family. They all gasped. They didn't cry out, for they were after all British, but the mother and father grew pale, and the three little girls sighed, "Oh, dear." But Ursula, after her original fright, had from the incident a strange sense of being protected, a mystical sense of sureness, as though this were a sign that her prayer had been heard.

That evening before dinner, Ursula said good-by to the

family. She had already informed them earlier in the day that her leave was ending and that she had to return to London. Her brother would take her to the station. They didn't have to worry about her.

She packed her little valise, shook hands all around, promised to write, and thanked them. They told her they would come to see her in France after the war; they would bring Vicky.

Ursula left, clutching her valise. She checked it at the station and then went back into town. Philippe was already waiting in front of the church. He was the same: polite, well mannered, nice, although perhaps a little constrained.

They went to dinner in a different restaurant, just the two of them, and Philippe danced with her during dinner, and taught her some new steps.

Ursula forced herself to eat in order not to offend him, but each mouthful was a torture. The food simply stuck in her throat. Happily, there was a desert of strawberries and cream, and that went better. Philippe seemed not to know what to do with her. He prolonged their stay at the table after dinner, ordering liqueurs, and finally he asked her if she would like to go to the movies.

Taking her courage in both hands, Ursula said clearly, "No, I'd rather go to your place."

Philippe seemed astonished. He looked at her hesitatingly, and then he took her hand without saying anything.

They rose and went out.

CHAPTER 24

They entered the living room as they had the night before, but this time, as soon as the door was closed, Ursula asked

Philippe to wait a moment, and went into the bathroom. She had no notion of preparatory caresses, of love play, of delays. Since she had decided to make love tonight, then it might as well be done, and quickly.

Alone, she undressed hastily, took off her medallion, folded her clothes, and placed the medallion on top. Although she had been raised without religion, it seemed to her that she could not wear the medallion—which one of her governesses had given her long ago—under these circumstances. Then, altogether nude, she returned to the living room.

Philippe had certainly not expected this. He was still standing there, in uniform, smoking. He saw the door open, and the girl enter and remain standing silently before him with her head lowered and her straight hair veiling her cheeks. He saw her childish little body, her tiny breasts, her thin arms, her round knees, and the demarcations of her bathing suit, leaving her breasts and her hips all white in the midst of her bronzed body.

He approached, taking her face in his hands, and he raised her head and said, "Don't be ashamed, Ursula. Look at me. You are beautiful."

The radio was playing. It must have been the BBC's French program, for a solemn voice was discussing Alphonse Daudet's *Moulin.*

Philippe undressed and put on a woolen robe with green squares. He had not yet recovered from his astonishment, and seemed to be asking himself if he were dreaming. He picked Ursula up in his arms and carried her into his bedroom, placing her on the bed. Then in the dimness Ursula felt the naked body of a man touching her body. And now the terrible fear returned. The child began to tremble like a leaf; she trembled in all her limbs. Her teeth chattered, and she trembled and shivered without being able to control herself. Philippe kissed her and pressed her in his arms, but he felt the fear and resistance in her.

A sob of utter sorrow broke from the girl. Philippe began to rock her as one rocks tiny, frightened children. "My dear little girl, don't cry. Don't be afraid of anything. I won't touch you any more. You see that I can't touch you when you tremble like that. It stops everything in me. Look, little one, my baby, don't be afraid of anything. You are too small, you're still just a little girl. I don't want to hurt you. Now you're going to sleep with me, just nicely, without anything. Do you want to?"

Little by little Ursula calmed herself. She pressed herself against him. Philippe hugged her in his arms and talked to her soothingly, like a big brother, and she fell asleep.

In the middle of the night she awoke. Philippe was not asleep. He got up, turned on the bed lamp, and put on his dressing gown. He went to the kitchen and brought back a glass of milk for Ursula, and for himself a large glass of whisky.

Philippe watched her drink, sitting altogether naked in his bed, holding the glass in her two hands with her hair falling over her eyes. He got back into bed; they talked a little and fell asleep.

The morning found them pressed innocently against one another. Philippe awoke, gay and playful. He licked Ursula's brown shoulder and told her that she was all salty. They took their bath together, and Philippe prepared their breakfast of boiled eggs, buttered toast, and coffee. Then he dressed and went off, leaving her in the apartment with some books and magazines.

In the evening they went out again with Doc and his mistress, who obviously accepted them as lovers. Afterward, Philippe took Ursula to the theatre. They went to the station for her valise and brought it back to Philippe's apartment, for Ursula still had two days of leave.

During those two days she lived at Philippe's, treated like

a little sister; he never attempted again to make love to her.

Philippe would take her on his knees and say to her, "You remind me of the sea, the sun, and the sand. You do me good. You make me a better person. You've got rid of the Popaul in me. Someday you will love a man, and he'll marry you, and when you have a flock of children you'll think about old Philippe. As for me, you see I could never marry you because my only bride will always be the sea. And so it's better the way we are."

He had the most tender affection for her, and above anything, did not want to hurt her in any way. Now that he knew she was still a little girl, he told her that it seemed to him that it would have been a sacrilege to change her, and then to leave her, as he knew he would have to do soon enough.

During those two days, Ursula was like a normal woman who busies herself with a man and lives with him. She found this to her liking and amused herself with shopping and preparing his meals.

Despite the setback of this last experience, she no longer had any fears about herself. It was a strange thing, but in spite of everything, she now felt herself to be normal. And she was at peace. She couldn't understand why, but it was so. Perhaps it was because Philippe treated her as he did, and because he didn't seem to find anything strange in her, or to believe that she was anything but normal.

On the last day, Philippe took her to the station. He installed her in her compartment and bought her some sandwiches for the journey. Ursula leaned out of the window for his last kiss. Both knew that they would never see each other again and that they had lived through a strange episode together.

The train began to move. She saw Philippe on the platform in his blue uniform, standing straight, watching the train disappear.

CHAPTER 25

In spite of everything, Down Street, when Ursula entered again after a week of absence, had something of an aspect of home for her. She glanced into the assembly room, cold and somber as ever, and then went up to the dormitory with its uncovered beds and the photograph of General de Gaulle on the wall. Ursula listened, and as he had expected, the phonograph was playing "Violetta." Machou's raucous voice was heard from the kitchen, and the sound of a typewriter came from the Captain's office.

It was the barracks; it was the unhappy barracks, in this country of exile, with everyone longing for the end of this period of military life that had brought nothing but a series of disillusions.

And still in that immense and strange city of London, it was the only refuge any of us had. It was at least a lively place, filled every night with French voices and familiar faces, with smoke and babble. We had all in a measure become part of this house, which seemed to have taken flesh, not only through our physical presence, but through the private life of each one of us, through each one's history, through each one's pain and joy.

And yet, what had we succeeded in accomplishing? Nothing, nothing at all. We had become classified numerals. Not one of us really believed she had done any real soldiering. Even the lucky few who, like myself, had jobs in which they were interested could not help but feel that they were doing little to free their country. It was said in some quarters that De Gaulle was against a women's section in the Army. Sometimes we reasoned that our presence in the service freed the male recruits for more useful activities. Very well, then, as Ursula used to say with her touching, pessimistic wisdom, that meant that three or four hundred soldiers were thus free to go and get themselves killed. The whole thought was maddening.

We had imagined that the uniform would somehow put us right into the middle of the war, but it was not at all like that. The war was taking place far from us; we were not participating in it. Bombs were bursting over our heads, but no more over ours than the civilians', and we worked in offices with civilian women who were much better paid and who were free to do what they wished when the office day was over.

And what was the use of all this? What was the use of going on blindly for months, living in the midst of all these women, not one of whom felt any real reason or purpose in what she was doing?

Still Down Street was our barracks, almost a corner of France.

It was five o'clock in the afternoon when Ursula came home; most of us were not yet free from our jobs. Ursula noticed that there was a suitcase on what had once been Jacqueline's bed, and that the chemistry student's books were no longer behind that bed, but in another corner of the room. So there had been a change during her absence. Ursula began to arrange her things. The door opened and someone cried out, "Ursula baby!"

She turned. It was Jacqueline.

She looked as fresh and pretty as ever. She threw herself on Ursula's neck, and they sat down on the bed, both talking at once, delighted to see each other again.

Jacqueline was cured. She had found the hospital extremely tiresome, but she had been a great success there, too. Her doctor and several of the patients had, naturally, fallen in love with her. Fortunately, De Prade, now a captain, with a car at his command, had been able to come and see her often. He had been simply marvelous to her, bringing her fruit, flowers, and other gifts.

Jacqueline chattered on, bringing Ursula up to date in the affairs with which we were all so familiar. De Prade was still her great love, but she still enjoyed getting every man she met to pay court to her. And there still wasn't a man who failed to succumb as soon as he laid eyes on Jacqueline's rosy face with her pretty mouth, her regular teeth, and her shining hazel eyes. For she, too, couldn't live without at least an illusion of love, and she used all of her power to create this illusion, employing her expert eyes, her sensual mouth, and her supple young body.

But now Jacqueline turned all her attention on Ursula, resuming her old protective air. "You don't look well, my dear child, you've become thinner. I'm sure you don't eat at all. It's a good thing I've come back. I'm going to take care of you."

Ursula, of course, detested having anyone officiously take care of her; this had always irritated her in Jacqueline, but she said nothing, for life in the barracks had already made her more indulgent toward the faults of others. After all, it was part of Jacqueline's character.

Now the girls began to come home, one after the other.

I scarcely had a moment to talk with Ursula before Mickey arrived, shouting, "Ursula! How glad I am to see you!" She danced around Ursula, with her excited, disjointed gestures, and then sat down on the edge of the bed, swinging a long khaki-clad leg. Ursula was delighted to see her, to hear Mickey talk with her slight English accent, and to hear her laugh. Mickey had a gift for making a room seem warm.

Ginette asked Ursula if she had had a good time, and if she had gone out with any boys. Ginette had already set herself to polishing the buttons of her uniform. When they were bright enough to suit her, she began to clean her shoes for tomorrow; she was meticulously neat. And Ursula was duly surprised at Ginette's new hair-do; but actually the new arrangement only made Ginette's face, her eyes, her nose, and her mouth seem rounder and flatter than ever.

The dinner bell sounded. We took our places in the queue, plates in one hand, mugs and utensils in the other. Machou was shouting as usual, "Move along, move along! That's enough, there's someone else here besides you! If you don't like it, go to the Ritz!"

So Ursula was resuming her life, her real life, her life in war.

After dinner, she sat in the assembly room with us. Mickey and Jacqueline were there. Jacqueline decided that we ought to have a drink in honor of Ursula's return, and of her own, and she went to order Dubonnets at the bar. Her walk was as distinguished, as worldly as ever.

Just then Claude entered. According to the new schedule, she was on twenty-four-hour duty on alternate days, from eight in the evening to eight the following evening; she had just finished her stint. Ursula had not seen her at dinner. Now Ursula studied Claude as she stood at the door, talking to Ann. Claude carried herself straight, as always, with her blonde hair pushed back, and she gestured gracefully with her hands as she talked. She noticed Ursula and made her a distant sign, smiling. Ursula rose and went toward her, and suddenly, as she was approaching Claude, she told me later, it was as though someone had at that instant cut a cord between them. Suddenly Ursula had a physical sensation as of a weight dropping away from her, setting her free. It was over in a second; she was advancing toward Claude, and in the next instant she knew that it was finished, that she was not in love with her any more.

And as Claude went on talking, Ursula saw her for the first time objectively.

Claude's magic power no longer worked on her. Ursula saw nothing more than a woman of forty, a handsome woman, very well made up, but with little lines at the sides of her mouth and a scattering of white hair. Her voice was feverish. What Claude was saying no longer interested her. When Claude began to recount her last dispute with one of the girls, Ursula found the story tiresome and felt that Claude made trouble over nothing.

Claude left for the switchboard room, and Ursula remained standing where she was. She had the impression of having suddenly grown. It was a strange impression, leaving her with a sort of pride in no longer being a little girl.

She looked around. Now she was free.

CHAPTER 26

Claude soon noticed that Ursula was no longer in love with her. She was delighted. An adventure with a woman was amusing to her so long as it wasn't serious, so long as it was only a game, considered as an unusual excitement by both partners; but the mute and passionate love of this child who was too young, too pure, and too sincere had embarrassed and irritated Claude. This love affair had confronted her with utterly unwanted problems, needlessly complicating her existence. There were indeed moments when Ursula's clear little face, so filled with love and admiration for her, flattered Claude and even touched her. There had indeed been days when Ursula had reawakened in her that desperate tenderness which needed to be directed toward children, and as she had caressed the girl's glistening hair, her own heart had been filled with hunger and regret. But most of the time Claude had

felt only one desire, and that was to discharge all of her irrita-
tion upon the nearest victim, and the victim had nearly always
been Ursula.

And so the change that had taken place delighted her. At
last she found a good little comrade in Ursula. Claude liked to
watch the girl's serious face. And she found again the silent
little girl to whom she had been attracted that first day, but
now purged of all sexual desire. That side was quite finished
for Claude too. After all, the pleasure of watching the child's
first reactions to love, and the enjoyment she had experienced
in educating the girl in this direction, had passed. She was not
a man; she couldn't marry Ursula. She was not Petit; the idea
would never have occurred to Claude to live in union with a
woman. Therefore, she told me in one of her surprisingly can-
did moments, everything had "fortunately gone back the way
it should be."

But I sensed that in the depths of her being, Claude
retained a vague remorse over having initiated Ursula to a vice
for which there was no true natural leaning in the girl. And I
wondered what it was that Claude sought so devouringly in
one girl after another, since it was clear that she did not seek
to develop a Lesbian liaison. First she had seduced Ursula,
then Mickey, and recently there had been a fresh young
recruit, Renée. What was this unappeasable hunger for the
young, the innocent?

And then I remembered a story Claude had confided to
Ursula, in their most intimate days. They had been talking
inconsequentially about things that made one feel guilty, and
Claude had told, first, of a cat she had once picked up on the
street and brought home, a skinny half-grown cat with no
charm whatever. Her lover of the moment had leaped with disgust at the sight of the animal, and had advised Claude to
throw it out the window. Finally she had put it out in the street.
Her guilt over abandoning that cat had haunted her for years,

Claude told Ursula, just like her guilt over an abortion.

And then, in the tumbling way in which Claude had of linking the most trivial and the most consequential of events, as though they were of equal importance, Claude had related how she had once found herself pregnant, and had suppressed the birth of the child. She had been living with the same lover who had objected to the cat—a dissipated journalist whom she had met shortly before her divorce from her first husband. When she found herself pregnant she vacillated for two months, unsure in her own mind about having the child. Not that she had any fear of scandal. But the inconvenience . . . Still, she had been tempted, feeling something marvelously warm growing within her. Day by day she had studied her breasts, which seemed to grow fuller and harder, and her belly, which was soon to fill itself with child. She had almost decided to have the baby; and then suddenly, after the incident with the cat, she had sought out a doctor and had an abortion. She had done that like almost everything she did, on impulse, without reflection. When she found herself stretched on the operating table, with two nurses strapping down her legs and the doctor bending over her with the chloroform, she had realized that she was about to kill her child, and it was too late. Remorse had entered her with the odor of the chloroform, and she awakened, empty and alone, with this remorse within her. Since then, Claude had tried to have another child—she had tried with lovers, with her second husband—but she had never again conceived.

As I recalled this story, it seemed to me that Claude's first instincts toward Ursula, and probably to all of her girls, had been nothing but maternal. And while with girls like Mickey the adventure quickly turned to erotic sport, there had been in Ursula a truly childlike response, and this had touched Claude more than she knew. It seemed to me that she felt guilty toward Ursula and at the same time resented the girl for having let her have her way, for having allowed herself to be drawn into the game. It was almost a motherly resentment over the bad behavior of her child. Claude would have loved to find an Ursula who was faithful to her childhood, and who would remain only a child for her—her little girl.

All these unhappy feelings in Claude were augmented by her boredom in the little switchboard room where she had spent the last two years. Almost daily she was becoming more irritable. Her rages were proverbial in Down Street. One encountered less of the charming, smiling, and beautiful Claude, as her place was taken by a nervous, aging woman, always quarreling with someone or other. All the discontented souls of the barracks came to her switchboard room to complain and conspire. Claude was continually discovering new enemies.

At the same time, her liaison with the colonel continued. She went out often with him, and drank a good deal. Several times she had been brought back to Down Street dead drunk. Officers in foreign uniforms would be seen taking her out of a taxi in their arms. She would be put to bed and would immediately fall asleep, to wake up in the morning in bad humor, because she was ashamed of herself. Her name was often seen on the punishment list for having returned to the barracks drunk. Claude pretended to consider this amusing, especially since the noncommissioned officers were rather in awe of her, and rarely carried out the sentences they gave her. Corporal Pruneface didn't dare send her to the kitchen, and Machou wouldn't ask for her. They all knew that Claude was Colonel Max's mistress, and they preferred to be in her good graces. Aside from Max, Claude went to bed occasionally with one woman or another, at Down Street and elsewhere.

The most extraordinary thing in all this was that Claude was essentially a good woman, with an astonishing childlike purity. She could take drugs, get drunk, go to bed with the first man who came along, but she never uttered a cynical word, and she was never blasé. A bouquet of flowers gave her more pleasure than the most luxurious of gifts. One might tell her the most naïve and innocent tales, and her face would immediately light up. If someone were to say, "The Holy Virgin came down onto the altar in the barracks chapel and told Mickey to put on a blue dress," Claude would certainly have been the only woman in Down Street to believe in the miraculous tale.

If any of the girls needed money, she could always ask Claude for it. Claude would give away her last sou, just as readily to a new recruit who had arrived at the barracks only the night before as to her best friend.

And there was another side to Claude. She had gathered among her friends in Down Street an altogether weird collection of women, as different as possible from herself. These friendships were utterly platonic, and these women possessed qualities that Claude alone could see. For instance, there was Paula, the only recruit totally unaffected by the vogue of sex at Down Street. She was the typical old maid of all the ages, the same anywhere in the world. Even in uniform she succeeded in dressing like the "woman in the green hat." Her khaki skirt dragged nearly to her heels. Her cap fell over her nose. A grayish bun bounced against her neck. She was ageless and colorless and even her voice had no recognizable character.

Claude declared that Paula was an exceptional patriot. The Captain was highly embarrassed when she tried to find an occupation for this patriot, for besides all her other shortcomings, she had no training or aptitude for office work, and she was in ill health and couldn't work in the kitchen or in the household. Finally they made a sacristan of Paula. She appeared only at the hours of religious observances, and no one knew what she did in between times. Besides, no one was concerned. Claude was the only person to take the slightest interest in Paula. She even attempted to persuade us that Paula was attractive, and she was continually finding new ways for Paula to arrange her hair, which Paula obstinately rejected.

There was another old maid—an Alsatian, dry, dark, and always in bad humor. Claude pretended that she was good nature itself, and dragged this woman from bar to bar to distract her. The Alsatian opened her soul to no one but Claude. She worshiped her, mending her stockings, making her bed, polishing her buttons. With everyone else she was acid-tempered and always dissatisfied. But with Claude she was completely transformed. The celebrated charm had worked on her too.

There was a little blonde Provençale whom Claude had baptized "Baby" and who was the most stupid, most vain, and most good-natured little thing to be found anywhere. She had rosy cheeks, blue eyes, and a perfect pretty-doll face, and she dyed her long eyelashes pale blue. Baby was interested only in boy friends, whom she recruited with great perseverance from the navy. Claude lent her own civilian clothes to Baby whenever she went on leave, gave her money, and bought her the little cakes of which she was especially fond. And with Baby, as with Paula and the Alsatian, Claude's relationship was never anything but completely normal.

Now Ursula took her place among these neutral and restful friendships. She saw Claude as she was, a disoriented woman filled with rare qualities, and with common faults; a woman who would be old soon enough, but who preserved astonishing areas of youthfulness in her heart. Ursula defended Claude to me. At bottom, Ursula felt, Claude had done her no harm; she had never harmed anyone, for there was nothing destructive in her.

CHAPTER 27

Ann had a date in town with her new love, Lee. She arranged with the hall guard not to mark down the hour when she went out, for Petit watched her ceaselessly. Petit knew that Ann was secretly seeing Lee, and the poor woman's eternally vigilant jealousy had become the newest joke of the barracks. Petit questioned the guard, searched through the register, and was even to be seen lurking in the entry hall, waiting for Ann to come home. And during her lonely hours of vigil she drank at the bar, offering rounds to the girls, and taking one or the other of us into her confidence.

One evening as I was talking to Mickey, Petit got hold of us and proposed that we come have a drink in a military canteen near Down Street. It wouldn't have been healthy for us to antagonize her, and so we accepted, though Petit was generally known as a bore. And when Petit was drinking she became more and more lugubrious, and her air of a little old man became increasingly pathetic.

When Petit opened the door and we entered the canteen, all the soldiers in the place turned their heads to gaze at us, with particular attention to Mickey. They seemed to be sizing us up, wondering if the lively-looking Mickey was in the clutches of the elderly *gousse,* wondering, I suppose, whether I too belonged to that sect.

Mickey tried to give the men the eye, as though to reassure them that she was a real woman; but Petit had installed herself directly in front of us, at a little table, so there could be no side flirtation. Now Petit began recounting her troubles with Ann.

"Yes, it's horrible," Mickey sympathized, with her English

intonation, and opening wide her large blue innocent eyes. Though she was intrigued by someone like Claude, the love affairs of a real Lesbian like Petit were a matter of complete indifference to Mickey.

It seemed to me that our indifference, the indifference of the "normal" world, made the life of such women even more tragic. For they suffered from their loves, like any other woman, but without the balm of sympathy and understanding.

Petit went on with her grief. It seemed that the newcomer, Lee, had acquired a complete dominance over Ann. Lee was very rich, Petit complained, and showered Ann with gifts. When the three of them were together, Ann and Lee behaved as though nothing at all were going on between them. They took pains to turn away Petit's suspicions. Tricky lads, Petit said, but she knew the truth well enough. She knew that Ann was being unfaithful to her. And Lee also, for that matter, for Petit had gone to bed once or twice with the Englishwoman herself. But Petit wasn't going to permit herself to be treated that way. There was going to be an explosion, they'd see! Ann belonged to her! And she went on complaining, and then she began to grieve for her life at home in France, where her two friends were waiting for her, two girls who had always been faithful to her.

Petit knew, of course, that Mickey had made love with Claude, so she addressed herself to Mickey, as to someone who was sure to understand. But Mickey was obviously not listening.

I wondered what Mickey was thinking about. Probably she was letting her mind roam over her years in the barracks, thinking about Claude, about Max, about Robert and the other men, and then coming back to Petit, and drifting from Petit to the Lesbians, and wondering about the soldiers who were eying her, and remembering a theory of love that Claude had once propounded to her.

Love, love, love—even what Petit was talking about was
love, and my mind, too, wandered on this all-absorbing subject. I was still like a bystander at a carnival, watching people
risking themselves on a slippery revolving floor, whirling and
bumping and sliding and falling and half getting up and slipping again, and sprawling on the spinning floor. Why did they
have to do it?

"Come on, come on," the people sprawling on the floor
would cry, laughing hysterically and beckoning to the timorous bystanders like me. Indeed, Mickey had often given me
the most meticulous explanations of her love affairs, and of
Claude's theories on the subject. As Petit's monotonous complaint continued, I recalled one of these explanations for love
between women.

In every woman, Claude had told Mickey, there is a need
rarely satisfied by men, a need for simply caressing, and she
had described how one of her women friends loved to caress
the "neutral parts" of her body for hours at a time. The neutral
parts were the shoulders, the arms, the throat, the back, the
parts that men seemed to forget. The insatiable desire for tenderness was felt most strongly in these neutral parts, which
were so rarely caressed. Men made love each in his fashion,
more or less expertly, according to Claude, and they were
especially fond of those things in women that were different
from their own bodies. When women made love with men, it
was quite often with joy and passion, yet there was almost
always a feeling of deception. It was perhaps the neutral parts
that were disappointed, Claude had instructed Mickey. The
very body of woman seemed to complain, "I want your love
over me, aside from sex, aside from physical desire. I want the
feel of your hand filled with a fraternal affection, forgetting
my sexuality, just resting with pure friendliness on my arm."

When she had made love with Claude, Mickey had said,
there had been long hours when no one was in a hurry, when

it had seemed that the entire night could pass without the necessity of reaching a final point, and she had understood Claude's meaning. This was love between women—to be able to rest their heads together, to hold hands. The stroking of a knee, the kissing of a shoulder-all this was part of love between two women, and this in itself could often suffice.

Inexperienced as I was, I felt that I was becoming something of an expert on love, matching the evidence offered by my friends, and I wondered now whether love had the same meaning for Petit, whether with her also love was a tenderness. And I wondered, almost with dismay, whether all these physical things they talked about could really express love. Sometimes when Mickey rattled on with her technical explanations I felt a disgust growing in me, and had to warn myself that I must not let this grow, or I might become like Paula, colorless, unlovely.

Now I was suddenly interrupted in my reflections; Petit's voice had paused, suspended. I heard Mickey say automatically, "Yes, of course." And Petit resumed.

I knew that Mickey did not believe herself to be a Lesbian, although a sort of understanding had come into being between her and the *gousses*. Mickey was voluble too about her experiences with men, comparing them with her experiences with Claude. She had adopted Claude's technical explanation, that some women could experience only an exterior climax. They were frigid within, and could never be satisfied by men. Claude herself could experience a climax in both ways, and Mickey had immediately declared that she possessed the same gift.

I wondered if it were so simple. Seated facing Petit, I kept thinking how sad her life must be, how sad must be the life of Ann, of Lee, of all these women. Their mournful eyes never laughed, even when their lips laughed. They lived separately from the rest of the world, cloistered among themselves, going out together, living together, going to Lesbian night clubs together, and the only men with whom they had anything to do were pederasts.

Petit was talking about her farm. It was strange how all of them, before the war and in their postwar projects, were centered around this love of the earth. Ann's one dream was to install herself in the country and raise horses. Lee had an estate in Scotland. Most of the others who frequented our bar in Down Street also talked about their farms, or the farms they were going to acquire.

Then I thought that Mickey's explanation was altogether wrong. They were simply more like men, these unfortunate women.

Petit ordered three fresh cups of tea with buns, since no alcohol was served at the canteen. Then suddenly she looked at her wrist watch. She got up precipitately.

"Ann should be getting in now. She hasn't got a late pass. Come on, we'll see what she has to say!"

She rose, paid for all of us, and hurried out, glancing over her shoulder to see if we were following. We arrived at the door of the barracks at the same moment as Ann.

Petit left us to fall upon Ann. The two of them turned from the door and went off down the street, talking. We watched the two women for an instant, disappearing into the fog.

For once, even Mickey's natural exuberance was smothered. We could not help but feel a sort of sadness, growing heavier, a sentiment that there was something rather unjust in Nature itself.

As we went into the dormitory, I realized that among all of the women in our little group there was not one who was involved in what I had always dreamed about, in childhood, as love. There seemed to be only frenzied sexual adventures, promiscuity, or these sad, strange inversions. I wondered unhappily whether such love could exist in our upset wartime world, the plain, faithful love between one woman and one man. I thought of Jacqueline and her passion for her captain, almost as a desperately wanted token that such love was no childhood myth. I needed their love to succeed.

CHAPTER 28

Jacqueline now had moved all her civilian clothes to De Prade's house in Kensington. Every Saturday evening she went to the house, changed into a civilian dress, undid her little bun, brushed her hair; she became once more a civilized young lady, and went to give orders in the kitchen, supervising the menu. She loved this role, and luxuriated in the respectful attention that she received from De Prade's officer friends. Here, at least, she could forget Machou's curses, Ginette's vulgarity, the curt commands of her superiors, and the common atmosphere of the dormitory.

Every Saturday night De Prade came to her room to say good night, and then went off. Every Sunday morning Jacqueline, in her pretty flowered linen nightdress, went to sit on De Prade's bed and to wake him by tickling him. This had become a ritual. Each of them pretended to ignore the obvious; each played the innocent. Jacqueline would say that she was cold, and slip into bed beside him, while discussing literature or the weather. De Prade, feeling her warm body next to him, behaved as though it had no effect on him. There was a tradition of honor in him, a tradition of hardened generations of strong-willed men who did not readily accede to any desire that they could not control with their minds. And in his mind, De Prade had decided that he would not be unfaithful to his wife; because of honor, because of religion, because of a sense of duty—a mixture of reasons whose force arose out of his very blood.

As both of them were from the same sort of world, neither of them spoke of what was going on within them; of desire, of violence contained, of home, or of love. Jacqueline still called De Prade "Uncle," and De Prade treated her like a young niece, a virgin, and the more warmly he felt her body against his the more persistently he set himself to speaking of politics and to pretending that everything was quite natural.

But the intensity of Jacqueline's desire was as great as De Prade's will to resist. Soon their struggle was to reach a decisive point. In a subterranean way, I felt that the climax was precipitated by a great event at the barracks.

Once more Christmas had passed over Down Street, and the New Year's holiday. Once again we were certain that the invasion would take place in the spring. It was 1942.

The news came that General de Gaulle was to inspect Down Street. During the week preceding this event, one would have thought that his inspection of our quarters was a very important part of invasion preparations. We polished the house just as though General de Gaulle were sure to climb up to examine the tops of the wardrobes and to crawl inside the kitchen stove. Under the command of Petit and the officers, we drilled and drilled. The assembly bell never stopped ringing, and punishments for the slightest infraction came down on us like rain. Our dear captain had launched a veritable offensive in the realm of discipline. If one of us had the misfortune to fail to salute a superior officer in the street, if a sentinel forgot to come to attention at the passing of an officer, if a button didn't shine brightly enough, there came an avalanche of punishment details. And the worst crime of all was to voice an objection, for the officers, naturally, were always right.

The most excited of all of us over the coming of the General was Jacqueline. To her, he represented something beyond the savior of France. He was the justification of aristocracy. He was the living proof that France *had* to be saved through someone who had issued from this superior group. Even her passion for De Prade had in it something of this worship of aristocracy, and I suppose the modern psychologists would say that she was in this way expressing her love and her longing for her aristocratic father, who had died when she was a child. But Jacqueline was so nervous over the coming visit of the General that she became almost as irritating as the officers; if someone so much as left an open newspaper lying on a cot, she would exclaim over the disorder in our dormitory.

On the day of the General's inspection, everything shone in Down Street, and we all stood at attention for an hour in advance. The Captain had assumed her most important air, as though the visit were addressed to her personally.

Finally he arrived, and every feminine heart beat more rapidly, and each of us forgot her years of exile and unhappiness. We felt only the pride of being there among the chosen, among the volunteers, before the leader who at that time personified all of Free France.

From our first day of enlistment, except for the months when Jacqueline was in the hospital, Jacqueline, Ursula, and I had kept our places next to each other in ranks. As we saw the General appearing in the doorway, it seemed to me that I could feel the charge of pride that passed through Jacqueline, a possessive pride.

De Gaulle was as tall as we had expected he would be, and he did not know how to smile. Grave and solemn, he had a face impassive in its severity. But one could see that he was a true aristocrat, born in the great tradition of the high French families. He did not try to exert any sort of charm, to make any conquests, to make himself well thought of. On the contrary, he was austere and hard. He said a few words to each of us, asked each woman her name and what she did, and passed on from one to the other, and our responses seemed to leave him totally indifferent.

All at once a Brittany girl broke the monotony by responding that she didn't like her job, that she had too much to do, working as a waitress in a sailor's canteen. Her honest, prepared little speech came out in one timorous breath, like a complaint to a parent. One could see a shiver of horror going through the Captain and communicating itself to all the other officers, and then down to the noncoms. But the General paid no more attention to this reply than to the others, and passed on to the next volunteer.

During the Brittany girl's outburst I felt Jacqueline become rigid. She was staring at the General in a hurt, puzzled way. At first I didn't understand why she should feel upset. Jacqueline was the last person to feel a democratic indignation. But I sensed that in some way he had failed her; he had not perhaps displayed the concern of a true aristocrat, a god, for every least one of his children.

This incident of the complaining girl had a continued effect on Jacqueline. She remarked about it once or twice, until I understood that for her this incident had meant the loss of an idol. The General had not cared, any more than our captain cared. And she needed someone to care, she longed for someone to care as she longed for a father, and as I suppose all of us long for a faith, a feeling that above us there is someone who is good, and pure, and responsible—as she told herself her own father must have been. And now that the General had disillusioned Jacqueline, he was gone for her, and only De Prade was left.

It was shortly after this, at the end of March, that De Prade received orders to leave on a mission to Africa.

Jacqueline talked of no one and nothing else but this man with his deep intelligent black eyes and his square chin and his courteous manners. And now he was going away—the only person in whom she could believe.

Just because he had resisted her so strongly, just because he had behaved so honorably, according to the perfect aristocratic code, just because he had shown himself superior to impulse, she had to seal herself to him, even if in doing so she caused him to break the code for which she loved him.

On his last evening in Kensington there was a little party in his honor. All of De Prade's friends were there. They danced and drank from a bottle of Armagnac that had been brought back from France by one of our secret agents. They talked of the second front and discussed the latest news of Paris.

Jacqueline was seated on a low chair at De Prade's feet; he was stroking her hair. In a way, she knew he felt himself saved. He was going to leave, and this struggle between them would be over. His honor was safe, the honor of a De Prade, who had never deceived anyone, neither his God nor his wife nor himself. He looked down upon the bowed neck of Jacqueline, looked at her hair, following the few bleached locks that she liked to wind through the reddish-brown mass. He put his hand on her shoulder, and she knew that he must have felt her shoulder lift a trifle in response to his hand. But she did not turn her head toward him. For if he saw her face, he would know that it was not yet over with them; even though he was leaving tomorrow, it was not yet over.

When all the guests had departed and the other three men had gone to bed, De Prade came for the last time to say good night to Jacqueline. She was lying on the narrow couch in her room. A strap of her thin nightgown had fallen, baring a rosy shoulder, and it was this shoulder alone that looked up at him, for her eyes were lowered, and a tear had stopped on her cheek. De Prade sat down on the edge of the bed, as on any other night, and began to talk to her softly. He told her that he would write to her, that he would surely be back in a few months, that she should be sensible and watch her health.

Jacqueline did not answer. The tear still stood on her cheek, and De Prade could not take his eyes from her round, rosy shoulder. He was filled with a terrible longing to kiss that shoulder just once before leaving. He leaned over and laid his lips on Jacqueline's shoulder. She flowed toward him, and suddenly he was holding her in his arms. Without knowing how it came about, he was kissing her on the mouth, repeating, "I love you, I love you."

It was very brief. Not a cry came from Jacqueline, for the short pain was too wonderful, too long awaited. She opened her eyes and saw De Prade's face with his eyes closed, his face of a man utterly outside himself, with his mouth slightly open and his eyes suddenly circled with black. She held him pressed in her arms, happy, crushed by his weight, victorious, her world secure. He fell asleep against the shoulder to which he had surrendered.

The following morning De Prade left on his mission to Africa.

Jacqueline came late to the office that morning. As our offices were still next door to each other, I saw her when she came in, and I at first assumed she looked so distraught because De Prade was leaving. But at the earliest opportunity she took me aside and told me she was worried. Nervously, she told me what had happened. And she was afraid that she might be pregnant. Though this fear was only natural, I couldn't help feeling a sickening disappointment; this was the real love, the real passion I had been watching, and it came down to the same sort of agitated apprehensiveness and whispering that went on in the barracks every night, after the girls returned from their casual affairs. I knew I was being unjust to Jacqueline. Her relationship to De Prade had been anything but casual; her deepest emotions had been involved. And yet, for me, this brought only another dismay, another tightening of my defenses against love. I knew that I should not permit disgust to invade me. I had to believe that I would one day love a man. But the same life that was driving some of the girls to sexual liberty came close to driving me to complete inhibition.

As for the practical side, I was scarcely the one to give Jacqueline advice. We decided that Mickey, who worked on the floor below, would be the ideal person to consult, for strangely enough, despite the loud and common talk that went on constantly at the barracks, we had only the vaguest scraps of confusing information about practical sex matters.

We hurried downstairs and encountered Mickey, with a stack of files under her arm, on the way to the elevator. "I have to talk to you," Jacqueline whispered, and Mickey understood.

"I'll meet you in the washroom at ten-thirty," she said. The washroom was the one place where the secretaries could meet and chatter in peace.

At ten-thirty we found Mickey there. Fortunately, no one else was in the room. Jacqueline explained her predicament. Shouldn't she do something about not having a child? It might be dangerous to do nothing. But what should she do?

For all her experience with men, it seemed that Mickey actually knew very little more than we did about such things. Her lovers always took care of everything. Mickey would simply leave all the precautions to them, and nothing had ever happened. But she was quite sure, she said, that it was too late for Jacqueline to take any effective measures now. She could do nothing but wait and see, and hope for the best. If it developed that she *was* pregnant—well, it was too early to think of doing anything about it now. "You'll just have to wait and see," Mickey repeated.

Jacqueline started to laugh. Leaning against the washbowl, she laughed until I was afraid she was becoming hysterical. "How can it be too late and too early at the same time?" she gasped.

CHAPTER 29

It was spring. A wonderful English springtime, with the park covered with crocuses, with blossoms, with sheep, a spring that sent mounted amazons with their cavaliers, onto the bridle paths, and sent couples rowing in the Serpentine.

Once more people were talking of the invasion. It was surely going to take place this year, and at night all of us dreamed that we were back in France.

We girls were being photographed in Down Street. One of the propaganda services was making a short film about the life of the feminine volunteers in the Free French Forces. The dining room and the dormitories were cluttered with spotlights and cables.

Jacqueline was filmed taking a bath, dressing, making up, and getting in the truck to go to work. The sentinels on the roof were filmed, and the little Brittany girls, enveloped in immaculate white aprons that had been borrowed for the occasion, were shown preparing our meals under the smiling supervision of a Machou transformed into a tender, motherly soul. The infirmary was decorated with tricolors for the occasion. The nurse, a dirty girl with greasy hair, who usually left the sick ones to take care of themselves, was photographed in the act of bringing a tray of food to a fake invalid. Vases filled with flowers were all around the room, and the place was hardly recognizable. In order to create an atmosphere of evening diversion, the film-makers perched a couple of girls on the piano and had them put their arms around each other and sing *"Aupres de ma blonde."*

It was during the time when Down Street was revolutionized by these motion-picture activities that a new crisis arose around Jacqueline. Ursula was the first to learn of it. One day after we had all gone off to our duties, she found Jacqueline crying on her bed. Ursula tried to console Jacqueline, without quite knowing what to say.

Jacqueline raised a ravaged face to her. "I'm going to have a baby," she said, and she began to cry again.

Ursula looked at her mutely, not knowing whether she should believe this, whether it was meant as playacting or as truth.

Then, realizing it was serious, she felt filled with respect for Jacqueline, and looked at her as though the child were already in her arms. It seemed to Ursula a thing that was strange and sacred and rather impossible, like a miracle. It was something that could happen to women—to real women, married, older—but here in Down Street, and to one of the "Virgins," it seemed to touch on the world of unreality.

"Are you sure, Jacqueline?" she said in a low voice.

Jacqueline nodded. She had seen a doctor, and he had told her that the baby would be born in December. It was now May.

Ursula remained seated on the bed, completely incapable of offering any advice. Jacqueline repeated, "I don't want a baby. It mustn't be born. It can't. What am I going to do?"

At first only a few of us knew the secret. Mickey was again consulted. After reflection, Mickey said that she believed there was a drug that was remarkably effective in producing abortion, but she had never heard its name. A pharmacist would know.

Presently half the dormitory was aware of the situation, and a great variety of advice was offered to Jacqueline. Ginette made her take a series of baths in practically boiling water. She was induced to jump from her bed fifty times.

After much searching, Jacqueline found a pharmacist who was willing to co-operate, but the stuff he sold her had no effect. Neither did the hot water or bicycle riding or jumping. And time passed.

Jacqueline never wrote to De Prade to tell him what was happening—perhaps because everything then might have been too simple. De Prade would have sent her money, would have helped, perhaps would have been able to return. Perhaps he would have promised her to get a divorce after the war. But Jacqueline would take only the most morbid view of the situation. The conception of the child was entirely her own fault, she insisted, and De Prade would never get a divorce. If she told him what had happened, she would only make him desperate. De Prade had been filled with remorse when he left. But he had probably gone to confession, done penance, and promised to forget her. She was certain that he would never write to her. On returning to France, he would probably confess their night to his wife, begging her forgiveness, and that would be the end of it.

Perhaps, I thought, she was right in her understanding of him. He was from her world. She had selected him because of that. And she insisted that she simply could not inform De Prade of what had happened. Besides that, she had a sort of presentiment that this affair could not end for her otherwise than in still another catastrophe. Catastrophes were the order of her life. Therefore, in the end, she accepted her situation as part of this established order.

After her pregnancy had become officially noted, Jacqueline once again left Down Street. Once more her bed was taken over by a new recruit. A welfare organization of Free France busied itself with finding a room for Jacqueline in the suburbs of London, and providing her with subsistence funds. It was not the first case of this sort at the barracks, and it would certainly not be the last. But officially, no one knew the identity of the father. For once, the few girls in our little circle seemed capable of guarding a secret. It was of course generally known in the barracks that Jacqueline had passed her weekends in Kensington, but three or four officers lived in the house, and besides, they were always changing, and Jacqueline was known to have a great quantity of admirers.

One morning a little notice was pinned up in the hall in Down Street among the announcements, sentences, and regulations. This stated that Jacqueline had been "discharged for reasons of health."

CHAPTER 30

Summer came, a London summer that lasted about a week. There had been no second front in Europe. The Red Cross messages took longer and longer to arrive, and it was said that the people had nothing to eat in France, that women were wearing shoes with wooden soles, and that layettes for babies were being knitted out of black, gray, or brown wool from men's discarded pull-overs.

In London the men kept looking at the photographs of their wives and their children, trying to memorize their faces, which must have changed so much. They spoke less often of France now, because it was painful to remember, and it seemed now that the exile was to endure for centuries. And still people continued to arrive from France in fishing vessels from Brittany or through Spain, and they told the same stories about the resistance, about the occupation, about the lack of food, and they told the same jokes about the Boche.

For quite a while now the bombardment of London had

almost completely ceased. People went to visit the ruins in the City as one went to visit places celebrated in ancient history.

Emerging from GHQ at noon, we girls in uniform walked down St. James Street arm in arm, despite the fact that this was against regulations. We studied the shop windows, but could buy practically nothing, for everything was rationed and we had very few tickets. People counted purchases in tickets now rather than in pounds and shillings, and it seemed that this too would go on forever.

The richer ones among us didn't go to Down Street for lunch, but went instead to treat themselves to a horse-meat steak with fried potatoes at Rose's. Sometimes I permitted myself this treat. After the steak, our supreme luxury consisted in stopping for *croissants*, real French *croissants*, in a Soho pastry stop. Then we would go for a walk in St. James Park before returning to our offices.

Rose's, the park, the movies, the swank clubs and bars, the concerts at the National Gallery—all this was now part of our habitude of exile. Little by little each of us constructed a life for herself in wartime London. For the years passed, and the war endured forever.

All London was pro-Russian. The theatre where Soviet films were regularly shown was always filled. The newspapers were filled with stories of Russian heroism. And the people of London and the Allied soldiers and the exiles from all Europe believed what was written everywhere—that this was a holy war, that hatred between nations was to be destroyed forever, and that a free world was going to be built.

The end of the war appeared to all of us the supreme good. With the end of the war there would be an end, overnight, to all restrictions, to hunger, and to cold. The United Nations would arise, there would be universal brotherhood, there would be a United States of Europe, for all this had to come to pass, since we were fighting on the side of good, and we were going to annihilate evil forever, replacing it with the invaluable qualities of intelligence, love, and order, which we undoubtedly possessed. But all this was still far away, all this was for "after the war."

The individual would take his place in society after the war, his rightful place. The individual would be respected, safeguarded by laws conceived for his well-being, for his liberty, and for his moral and intellectual development. But for three years and more, in the little world of Down Street, as in all other military barracks, the individual didn't exist. And those who rose in authority, those who became the "cabinet ministers" here, were the people who knew how to get along, the people with connections, the flatterers. Well, then, I asked one night when we were debating all this in the assembly room, why were we always talking of tomorrow, and never of today? What would remain tomorrow of bleeding Europe? There would be those who returned broken from war and concentration camps, the sick, and a young generation raised in a world where heroism consisted of committing sabotage, lying, and killing; and there would be the collaborators, the cowards, and the indifferent. This was the world that was to rise from the ruins tomorrow, the world upon which everybody counted so much.

Late in summer, Ann requested permission to spend her leave in Scotland. She gave a false address to Petit; actually she left for Lee's estate.

Petit was not deceived. Seated at the bar in Down Street, she confided her miseries to Claude and to anyone else who cared to listen. "I know where they are," she said. "But what's the use? If I went after her there, it wouldn't change anything."

She resigned herself therefore to wait for Ann's return, consoling herself with a fat blonde who was a waitress in the GHQ canteen.

Meanwhile Petit drank a great deal of beer, and intrigued to get herself promoted. And despite everything, despite her morals, her swearing, and her intrigues, we all really liked her. For Petit was a brave soul, not very intelligent, but fair with the recruits, and she did all that she could to help anyone who came and asked for aid.

Ann passed the weeks with Lee in Scotland. What happened there, the strange event that was to be whispered about with a kind of revolted glee, seemed to me the saddest of all the things I had heard about the unnatural lives of these women. It was something that happened in the intimate lives of three people, and yet it came out, as everything had to come out in that atmosphere of war and of the barracks. Petit pried it from Ann, and then Petit herself spread the story, in a kind of vengefulness.

Lee came from a very rich family; not far from Edinburgh they owned a veritable manor in the style of the Stuarts. Every year Lee passed her vacation there with her brother, a blond young officer who was used to his sister's ways and his sister's friends. He was a type of young man who seemed to have emerged from the novels of the Brontë sisters. He drank a great deal, belonged to an exclusive regiment in wartime, and spent his leaves in boredom at the ancestral manor in the occasional company of his masculine sister, who went off hunting every morning.

An ancient servant couple took care of the dwelling, which was situated in the midst of woods and lakes among the arid Scottish hills. Lee and her brother found the place tiresome, and went there only through a sort of sense of duty, but Ann was enchanted and astonished by the establishment. She had been raised in genteel poverty, and had never known her father. She had always been attracted by riches. It was her dream to be wealthy and powerful someday. By instinct, Ann always sought connections with people above herself. In the barracks she was friendly with the officers, through her inner need to rise in station; and even her women friends, her Lesbian lovers, were always rich or in some way powerful. I don't think she chose them through cold calculation, but it always turned out that way.

Every morning she went hunting with Lee, or riding in the immense park. In the afternoons she visited the countryside, and on returning explored the innumerable chambers of the manor. She loved to walk barefoot on the bearskin rugs in the evening, and to watch the immense logs burning in the fireplaces. The servants had the reserved and dignified bearing of domestics in a household of consequence, and Ann had the impression of sharing in all this opulence. When she embraced Lee in her hungry arms, it was the entire manor that she was hugging to herself.

The brother smoked his pipe, his feet on the table, a glass of whisky at his side, as he yawned through travel magazines.

Lee studied the fire. The fire danced in her eyes. She looked at Ann, and it seemed to her that she had brought her bride home to her house, the ancient house of her ancestors. Every evening, when the three of them were seated like that in front of the rosy fireplace, Lee had the feeling that with the arrival of Ann she had succeeded in making the manor a homestead, and that the only thing now lacking to her was a child, an inheritor. Then she would really have all that a man could have. She crossed her long legs and stroked her short flat hair. If only Ann could have a child! But that was impossible. It was the one thing that she couldn't give her. Every night when she made love with Ann, Lee felt herself thwarted by this sterility, and in her mind, where all values were disoriented, a project was slowly forming.

She reflected on each detail and carefully considered the staging of the scene. After all, it was her child that was in question.

She spoke of the matter first to her brother.

Her brother had consumed no small quantity of whisky since that morning, and the idea rather amused him. It would be a bit of a change, at last.

Then Lee found Ann, who was walking in the grounds dressed in a thick seaman's sweater and brown corduroy trousers, promenading a pair of spaniels. Lee said to her, "Ann, my darling, you and I must have a child."

Ann looked at her uncomprehendingly. Then Lee explained her plan.

That night all three of them would be together, Ann, Lee, and her brother, Richard. Ann and Lee would make love, and at the last moment Richard would possess Ann, while Lee continued to caress her. The child that would be born would be the child of Lee's blood, conceived in Lee's love; Richard would only have lent the one element Lee did not possess, the seed.

They walked together in the Scottish fog that enveloped the manor. Two women without sex, two women outside of human society, profoundly solitary, even in their love, trying somehow to attach themselves to that life which had no way of continuing beyond them through descendants.

In the evening, before the great fireplace with its crackling logs, Richard watched his sister embrace Ann on the bearskin rug, and Richard was the first and only man to possess Ann.

Two days later, Ann returned to Down Street, her leave ended.

CHAPTER 31

Every afternoon we had tea in the canteen at GHQ. The girls would make bets on whether or not Ginette would arrive before the half hour was over. For Ginette had a lover whom she met every day during the afternoon recess. She would rush off in a taxi to her rendezvous, and she was quite proud of being able to make love and get back by the end of tea. She always managed to arrive in time, a little out of breath, and the bets would be paid while the girls demanded news of the "teatime boy." Mickey found the adventure with the teatime boy absolutely riotous, and laughed over it every day.

Ann also usually arrived late for tea, but only because she was highly interested in her work, and her major often took advantage of this to keep her busy well into the recess. Ann had waited in vain for Lee's baby; the child had not been conceived. This had been a bitter disappointment for Lee, and had seemed to affect their relationship.

Moreover, Petit had arranged a surprise for Ann on her return from Scotland. Petit had managed to get her promoted to master sergeant, and even to get her onto a list of candidates for officer training. Once more Ann and Petit were to be seen leaving the barracks together. Overnight Petit had recovered all of her good humor. She bought rounds of drinks, inviting all the girls, calling out in her deep voice, "Another Dubonnet, Renée, and make it snappy!"

To Claude, Ann had confided that after the war she would probably go and live with Petit and help her with her farm. Claude was still seeing Max, and running around with a variety of officers and women, often taking Mickey along.

Sometimes I thought it was her job that made Mickey more avid than the rest of us for distraction. Mickey typed coded telegrams. For three years, from nine o'clock in the morning until six in the evening, and sometimes much later, Mickey typed all the secrets of the war, with prodigious speed, and without having the slightest idea what she was typing. Only someone like Mickey could have accomplished this task without losing her mind. She had arrived at the point where she could type automatically, without error, all the while chattering with people who passed through the office. The typewriter rattled under her long, strong, agile fingers. She had a well-formed hand, a college girl's hand with flat, clear fingernails, masculine in its length. Mickey laughed, gossiped, called her chief "Uncle Henry," and never stopped typing.

What was extraordinary in her was that nothing touched her, neither her love affairs, from which she never asked the absolute, nor her mechanical labors, which would have driven anyone else crazy, nor the barracks with its intrigues, nor even the fact that the reality of the war had never corresponded to the ideal of the early days that she, like all of us, had felt: to volunteer, to save France, to give all, to sacrifice, to find comradeship. This had become tarnished like all one's ideals, but Mickey had not suffered from the change. She was a realist. That was life—one had to be satisfied with a dead ideal as with an easy love or with a meaningless job. She was, in fact, happy so. She had had fun with Claude, and their parties of three had been amusing, and it was amusing to have new experiences. And after all, it was necessary to type the coded telegrams, numbers following numbers in endless succession; it was an important job.

Sometimes she had her regrets. She would attach herself to a handsome man who made love "like a god," who bought her silk stockings and perfume, and then he would leave her for another woman, or he would go off on some mission and never write to her. Mickey would weep over her typewriter, her beautiful blue eyes, too blue, all drowned in tears. Her fingers continued to type the numerals, her tears fell on the keys, and then Uncle Henry had to take her to lunch at Prunier's for consolation, and this indeed consoled her. She would come back laughing, her little snub nose wrinkled, and she would continue to rattle off the mysterious numbers over which the high commanders pondered in their most secret headquarters.

Then she would go out with another young man and go to bed with him because he was handsome and she would discover that he "made love like a god," he too, for life would have been too sad if one couldn't shut one's eyes so as not to see it.

Everybody loved Mickey. Everybody forgave her for being easy and a bit of a liar; everybody forgave her her facile success. Her lovers retained the best memories of Mickey, even though her accessibility in the end proved tiresome. There were so many easy young girls in London during the war. For a while it was relaxing, and then it became monotonous.

Even Mickey finally came obscurely to sense these things. In the bottom of her heart she would have liked to find the strength to become a woman difficult to obtain, one of those women for whom men made an effort. She would have liked to inspire a great love such as one read about, and sometimes for days at a time she tried to stop flirting, to maintain a dignified air, but it never worked. The truth was that what she wanted most of all was to be like Claude. She laughed with gusto, drank a lot, let herself be kissed in taxis, and then it was too late to hold back; the way from taxi to hotel was too short. Once more she would find herself in the arms of a lad who told her that she had a lovely body, and Mickey would think, What good would this lovely body be to me if I didn't use it?

She admired Claude and Claude's success. Claude went to bed with colonels and generals, and with all the women of London. At the barracks there had been Ursula, and Mickey herself, and Renée, and Arlette, and Lucienne, and any number of others. It was amusing to think about. And when Claude went out, when Claude appeared in the clubs and restaurants, everybody looked at her, people whispered when she passed, and men had a special way of looking at her. Mickey wanted men to look at her that way. And so her good resolutions vanished. She said to herself, Later on, after I'm married . . .

Uncle Henry put her on the promotion list for sergeant. After all, she had done quite a job for three years, a job that no one else wanted. But for some obscure reason the Captain refused her promotion. The reasons for approving or disapproving promotions were generally obscure in Down Street. Obscure as the war itself.

Nevertheless, in her own way, Mickey had made progress. She had lost her awkward and disarticulated look, her boyish movements and pimples. She had learned how to make up, how to do her hair, and how to look well dressed even in a uniform. She flirted a good deal less. During her career as a virgin and *demi-vierge,* Mickey had found it impossible to remain more than a moment in the presence of a male without beginning to exert herself, flirting with her eyes, her mouth, her smile. This had seemed to her indispensable to every masculine encounter. Now she was much more sure of herself, and put herself out less for the boys.

One evening she went dancing with a young Norwegian paratrooper, and the same night, coming home with him, she suddenly got engaged. She came into the barracks and announced it as casually as she would have announced that she had gone to bed with another date. And three weeks later she was married. We were all astonished, and Mickey more than any of us. She had got married almost on impulse, to a boy she scarcely knew, the only one of her acquaintances with whom she had neither flirted nor made love. And the amazing thing was that the boy, who resembled her physically like a brother, could not have been better suited to Mickey if they had known each other for years.

They found a little apartment in town, and Mickey would go home from work at GHQ to prepare their dinner, like any young newlywed. Peter was in London between assignments, and spent most of his time in the little apartment; all day long the radio blared. Every evening Peter's friends came to talk about Norway and the war. Mickey had so much fun with her young husband, who shared her love of laughter, that she ended by falling in love with him. It was an odd young household, for they had the air of two young wolves, avid for life, carefree.

Ursula went often to their flat, and Mickey tried to marry her off to one of Peter's friends. But Ursula was too silent, too calm, and she still had too much the air of a little girl, with her straight hair and her short fingernails. Peter's friends scarcely knew what to say to her, and, uncomfortable at their attempts at conversation, Ursula would bury herself in a book or magazine.

I went to Mickey's sometimes with Ursula, and once we talked about her meager experiences with men. Although a long time had passed, it was strange how strongly she recalled the soldier Michel. There had been a strange calm, a kind of serenity coming from him, and yet she had fled at the first physical contact. Philippe had not frightened her in that way. From Philippe she had felt a force of life and a healthy equilibrium that had been necessary for her, but in Michel there was something else, something that Ursula had not known how to accept. It was as though Philippe had given her all that he could, while with Michel there had been an incomplete communication.

Philippe was a man, a man of flesh, normal in the measure of men. Michel was made of another substance, more fragile, more mysterious, and also closer to Ursula. She talked of the black eyes of Michel, and how sad and yet childlike they had looked. If she had been so afraid of him, it was perhaps because she understood Michel too well. With Michel it would have been all or nothing, and "all" with Michel was infinity. Michel's kiss, which she had refused, had contained all that infinity she had wanted to escape. It was the whole of Michel she had fled; the kiss had only been the pretext that she had unconsciously needed. But why? Why? She was still perplexed over this. I couldn't help her; my own experience was even more limited than hers. For though I had known more men than Ursula, I was still nothing but a date girl, a good dance partner, a pleasant companion for an evening, but essentially, I suppose, disappointing to men in wartime London. As for Ursula and Michel, I felt somehow that she would see him again, because something of her contact with him was still growing in her.

CHAPTER 32

Jacqueline's baby was to be born in December. Until the very end, Jacqueline confided to us, she hoped something would happen to prevent the birth. So many women had miscarriages. But she continued in good health and the child stirred within her.

Sometimes she placed her hand on her belly and felt the movement of the infant. Then she would think of De Prade, and it would seem to Jacqueline that each of these movements of the baby should have been for De Prade, that he should have been there to lay his cheek against his true wife's body, and hear the beating of the secret heart of his child. Now all these movements were quite useless and lost. And it would always be so. The first smile of the baby and his first steps and his first words, all would be lost, without De Prade.

As for the material difficulties, Jacqueline was not frightened. She came from the sort of aristocracy that took additional pride in being able to do common tasks better than common people; she was an excellent cook, and she knew how to design and sew her own clothes. She prepared the baby's layette.

For a time Jacqueline continued to go out in town with a number of her men friends, all of whom were in love with her, and some of whom would certainly have been willing to marry her, even knowing that she was pregnant. But when her condition became quite obvious, Jacqueline ceased to see them; she didn't want anyone's pity. Actually, she slipped quite easily into the role of the unmarried mother, taking a certain pleasure in playing the courageous young woman, poor and abandoned. The family in whose house she roomed was proud of her. The husband was a bit in love with this pretty and unlucky little Frenchwoman. The ten-year-old son secretly offered Jacqueline his ration of sweets, without saving a single ticket for himself.

When the final month arrived, Jacqueline realized that she was really going to have this baby, and that she alone would be responsible for it. And then she began to be afraid. She had play-acted all her life. Now suddenly the role she had been acting became terribly real; indeed, she felt that with the child, the role would be beyond her.

The child came into the world in a hospital in London. Jacqueline told us she would have liked to spend all her life in that hospital, for there were nurses to take care of the baby and to bring food to the mother; she had nothing to do, no worries. Everything was sure, simple, and well-regulated. And in a few days, she knew she would have to confront life, fight for the sustenance of her child, suffer for her child, and she felt herself absolutely alone and entirely without force in the face of this task.

All of us were struck with the little girl's resemblance to Jacqueline; she had her fresh complexion, her shining eyes, and her soft hair, already quite long. Jacqueline looked as helpless as the baby. With her finger, she opened the fist of her little girl, undoing it as one might a delicate flower.

After ten days she left the hospital with her baby in her

arms. A French welfare worker accompanied her. The welfare organization had found a job for her, and a family where the baby could be cared for.

But after a month we heard that Jacqueline had changed her job and found another family to take care of the child. Bit by bit, the little girl became the center of her life. Whenever we saw Jacqueline, she complained that the baby wasn't well enough cared for. And she wanted to have her daughter with her all the time, instead of being able to see her only once a week. Finally she placed the little girl in a day nursery, but only to take her out and leave her with another family. Despite all these changes, the child thrived.

Jacqueline was working in an office. Her job was utterly uninteresting, and she earned very little. But there was an astonishing energy in Jacqueline. After work she sewed clothes for herself and knitted for the baby. She fixed her own dinner when she wasn't going out with some of us. She went to bed late and rose early.

A new fixation began to appear in her. She wanted to find a father for her child. This was now her one idea. Jacqueline was determined to return to France at the end of the war with a suitable father for her little girl.

But this was not easy. Young officers took her out and treated her with respect, as always, and talked to her of love, as always, but Jacqueline now felt that not one of them wanted to marry her.

It was at this time that Jacqueline met John. I had been doing a good deal of liaison work with the British, and now the American Information Service people began to appear on the scene too. I was invited to a reception for them, at which the guest of honor was to be the famous English conductor John Wright, who was doing a good deal of cultural propaganda work. I took Jacqueline along. She was excited, for she had often seen his name on posters, and she had watched him conducting the symphony at Albert Hall. He was a man of about fifty, tall, spare, graying, and rather distant with people. His wife was at the reception, but it was whispered that they had not lived together for years.

The guest of honor glanced toward Jacqueline. She gave him one of her ravishing smiles, and they began to talk. His absorption in the beautiful young Frenchwoman did not go unnoticed. A friend of mine told me something I had not known: John Wright had been in love with a young French girl, who had recently died. She had had just such a ravishing smile.

All that evening they remained together. Wright's wife was flirting in another corner of the room.

"What did you talk about?" I asked Jacqueline on the way home. She said, almost reverently, that John Wright had talked to her of the girl he had loved and so tragically lost.

"I *must* see him again," Jacqueline said.

I remembered De Prade. She was deciding again that a man, this man, had to love her.

One day tickets for a concert at Albert Hall were passed out at the barracks, and Ursula and Mickey and I went together. Mickey's husband was away on maneuvers in Scotland, and was to be absent all week.

It was a beautiful warm day. Once more it was summer. We had been permitted to remove our jackets and to roll up the sleeves of our shirts. On the grass in the park, ATS girls were stretched out beside their soldiers. And again there had been no second front in Europe. No one was even disappointed any more, for everyone had got used to disappointments.

Actually, Mickey preferred jazz to any other music, and classical music generally bored her. But she had come along because in Peter's absence she had nothing to do, and this had seemed to her as good a way as any of passing the afternoon.

At the intermission, we suddenly heard ourselves called.

"Tereska! Mickey! Ursula!" We looked toward the boxes and saw the smiling face of Jacqueline. She was signaling to us. We had lost track of her the last few weeks. Now we hurried to her, delighted to see her again. And we found, instead of poor unlucky Jacqueline, an extremely elegant young woman, as fresh and pretty as ever.

She wore high-heeled shoes, which made her seem taller, and her hair was bleached and worn shoulder-length, à la Veronica Lake. Breathlessly Jacqueline demanded, "How did you like John Wright? Isn't he extraordinary?"

Then I remembered the party. So there had been developments.

People came into the box, kissing Jacqueline's hand and congratulating her. "Jacqueline, he was astonishing!"

Ursula stared at this new Jacqueline, who looked so triumphant and happy. Mickey said, "Do you know John Wright?"

"I'm his secretary," answered Jacqueline, with a particularly glowing smile for me.

We asked her about her little girl, and she talked of her daughter as though she were the only beautiful and intelligent baby in the world. The baby lived with her at Wright's house in Surrey. She had a nurse, who was, of course, the best nurse in all London.

After the concert, Wright came to the box. There was something at once brusque and timid in his manner, but when he looked at Jacqueline his expression softened. He scarcely spoke. We all went out through the stage door so as to avoid the crowd, and Jacqueline invited us to come and spend the weekend in Surrey.

"I didn't know she was John Wright's mistress," said Mickey when we had left them.

"But how do you know she's his mistress?" Ursula asked, astonished. She would never be able to divine relationships of this sort. "Jacqueline said she was his secretary."

"His secretary night and day," Mickey said, laughing.

Ursula managed a small smile. "Well, at last she looks happy," she said uncertainly.

In the car that carried them to Surrey, Jacqueline pressed herself against John. She closed her eyes. Yes, she was happy. She was in a beautiful car that was carrying her toward a house in the midst of a lovely garden, and in the house was her well-cared-for child, waiting for her. She was John's mistress, and all the world was attentive to her. John said he was going to introduce her to his friends in the theatrical world, and that she would certainly become a great actress. Everything in life had become so easy, thanks to him. She was proud of him, and proud also of the role that she played at his side.

Jacqueline studied John's face. His hair was almost white. Her father would have been exactly John's age. And John had given her what a father gives to his child: security.

De Prade had given her passion, and this had hurt her; and then he had left her. But to John she owed nothing but joy. He was nevertheless a strange man, rather unsociable. He didn't like people, and he preferred the solitude of his home in Surrey. But Jacqueline told herself that she would succeed little by little in taming him. After all, he was an artist, a genius, and therefore he had a right to his idiosyncrasies.

John spent all his days working. In the evenings, Jacqueline would come and sit on a stool at his feet. She had told him all about the death of her father, her mother's second marriage, the advances of her stepfather, her broken engagement, the war, her attempt at suicide, the hospital, De Prade, the baby, her solitude, her struggle for life. John stroked her face and told her, "It's over now. You shall never suffer again, my dear. You are with me. Don't worry about anything."

Long afterward, she told me that their sexual contacts

were quite rare. John didn't seem to feel frequent sexual needs, and Jacqueline didn't really care for the physical side of love. With De Prade she had experienced the joy of having conquered, nothing more. And physical love-making had always seemed a sort of degradation to her. She felt flattered that John loved her "without that." For "that" was the barracks, the sailors, girls who came home drunk, Ginette and her lovers, everything that was coarse. John gave her music, art, sensitivity, the beauty of this house, and that sufficed.

She knew that there would be no marriage. John had told her that he would never get a divorce. Jacqueline knew this, but she didn't believe it. Nothing had ever withstood her will; whatever she wanted she could obtain, even though she had to pay dearly. And she wanted to marry John, she wanted John to adopt her little girl, she wanted to re-enter France, her head high, with her husband and her child, and with no one knowing anything of what had happened to her.

As she fell asleep that night, Jacqueline thought of us, her friends from the barracks. She was glad to have seen us again. We were her best friends from Down Street, and besides, we were sure to tell everybody at the barracks that she was the mistress of a famous man, and that she was rich and happy. She smiled in the dark. At last she had her revenge on life. She no longer needed anyone, and everybody would know it. She decided to invite us to dinner.

Yes, everything was simple now, and she was happy.

CHAPTER 33

There were many new recruits, and the dormitories were full. In the Virgins' Room, Monique, our chemistry student, finished reading a passionately exciting chapter on enzymes, without hearing what was going on around her. Ursula took a last look, to be sure that her bed was properly made, and went down to her place at the little table in the hallway. She opened the registry to write down our names as we left the barracks.

Claude was not at the switchboard that day, as it was her day of leave, and Ursula was glad of it. Claude had become increasingly irritable of late, seeing nothing but enemies all about her, and it had become quite exhausting to listen to the endless repetitions of her quarrels.

Little by little the house emptied itself. Women came to scrub the hall; they were newcomers, passing their first weeks in taking care of the barracks. A corporal went by, and managed to find an excuse for making them redo the hall, which she considered badly scrubbed. One of the new recruits objected, and the corporal pierced her with a black look and a few well-chosen words.

Ursula recalled her first days in Down Street, three years ago, when she had been so proud of this uniform and had felt that she was surely going to help save France.

Did she still think so? At bottom, yes. She had not yet lost all of her illusions. She realized that most of us no longer believed we were being useful to our country by living in Down Street. And yet we all still believed that after the war everything would change, that the golden age would begin, and that there would be love between nations. The traitors would be punished, the collaborators would receive their due, the United Nations would be created, there would be a world government. New leaders, utterly pure, would emerge from the resistance—that at least was certain. Just as certain as the abundance of oranges and bananas and eggs and milk that one would find again. Ursula closed her eyes and deliciously recalled the distant taste of an orange. A beautiful orange, juicy, perfumed, and sweet.

She was sitting like that with her eyes closed when she heard herself called. "Good morning, Ursula." She opened her eyes.

Just as on that first occasion three years ago, Michel was standing in front of her, with his slightly astonished look, his round face, his full mouth.

"Michel!" cried Ursula joyfully, and she jumped up, reaching her hand to him. An immense happiness flooded her. Michel had returned. Michel was found again.

Michel remembered everyone's name; he asked for news of Mickey, of Claude, of Jacqueline. As for him, he had been in Scotland all this time; now he was stationed in London again, and the Army was giving him free time to attend courses at the university. He was a corporal, he informed her, showing his stripes laughingly.

"Can you come to dinner with me tonight?" Michel asked.

It seemed to Ursula that everything had become the same as before. Once again she would ask for an eleven-thirty pass, she would go to dine in a little restaurant in Soho with Michel, and he would talk very little. She still knew little about him; but there was one difference—Michel had been so often in her thoughts that he now seemed close to her, and it was almost as though she were recovering a part of her childhood.

Evening came. Ursula found herself facing Michel over a little oilcloth-covered table. Michel spoke more freely than he had before. Suddenly Ursula too had a great deal to say. And it seemed to her now that Michel's replies were real replies. She asked him whether he believed in God. Michel hesitated for a second, and then said yes. He didn't make any imposing speeches, he had the same soft voice, and his eyes were as calm and sad as ever under their look of astonishment, but it became clear that he was interested in a great number of matters about which Ursula had never before thought him concerned.

Michel too believed in the reconstruction of the world after the war and in the United Nations, and when it was Michel who spoke of these things all doubt seemed truly impossible.

Ursula asked him where his parents lived now, and Michel said, "In Palestine." After the war, he said, he would join them there.

Ursula listened with passionate interest as Michel spoke of life in Palestine. It was something new and strange, for she had always believed that Jews were all either shopkeepers or intellectuals, and now it seemed that in Palestine most of them were farmers living a communal life. After the war, Michel said, there would be a new Jewish state in Palestine.

When Ursula told me about all this, there was one thing that appeared to have touched her most. Michel spoke to her as an adult, she said, as a person with whom one could discuss anything at all, and Ursula felt proud that so intelligent a young man should consider her worthy of listening to all his ideas and projects. She was happy that Michel didn't resent her because of that other time when she had run away, and she was glad that he didn't speak of it.

He took her home to Down Street and said good night, lifting his black eyes toward her, profound and filled with gentleness.

Suddenly Ursula recalled her early days in Down Street, her disgust at all the vulgarity in the house, and she recalled her life during these last three years, with all its sordid aspects. There was the fireside scene with Claude and Mickey, and her experience with Philippe, and her fear of not being normal, and there were the gray days under the demonic smile of the Ambassador of Peru. She remembered one night when she had come home and plunged her face in the washbasin, trying to wash everything from it as though she could wash away all her shame of being human, while so undeserving of humanity.

This evening, for no reason at all, it seemed to her that all that had been effaced.

CHAPTER 34

Jacqueline came to Down Street to take Ursula and me out to dinner on an evening when John was away giving a concert. She emerged from a taxi, carrying a little white dog in her arms. Jacqueline gazed upon the house where she had scrubbed floors, peeled vegetables, and accepted the scoldings of her superiors. At last she was free of it! If she wished, she could stick out her tongue to the Captain. She was free, she was wealthy, she was almost married to John.

In the cab, she told us that John was being asked by the government to undertake a month's propaganda tour in Canada. He would leave soon to conduct a series of concerts for hospitalized veterans. Jacqueline was proud of his mission, of his talent, of his glory, but at the same time she was afraid for him. Perhaps at bottom her fear was not for him but for herself. Her happiness was so new that she still could not believe in it; it seemed to her that it was too wonderful to last. A month was so long a time, and John would be far away from her, among other women just as beautiful, even more beautiful than she. Jacqueline smiled in joy over John's glory, but also trembled in fear. Since she could not prevent his leaving, she was busy weaving bonds to assure his return, attaching him to her by a thousand threads. Jacqueline showed us a sketch for a tombstone that she was designing to be placed over the grave of the little French girl whom John had loved before he knew her. During his month of absence, she intended to have this monument built and the grave arranged. It would all be finished just in time for John's return; the dead one would help the living one to draw him back to England.

Was this, at last, love? I wondered. Would I ever love anyone the way Jacqueline loved John Wright?

Did love have to contain this exigence, this ferocity? Would I someday be like Jacqueline, in terror of losing a man? Could you have such ruthlessness toward another person, if you really loved him? Could you accept any means at all, so long as they held him bound to you? Perhaps it had to be so. Perhaps that was what one didn't understand above love, until the experience came.

I tried to compare Jacqueline's feeling to other loves I had witnessed. Ursula had loved. What she had felt for Claude was love. But it had not been so possessive. And I wondered whether what was slowly happening between Ursula and Michel was love. I hoped it was; I wished it for my sake as well as theirs, for I would feel so much safer if I knew that love didn't have to be like it was with Jacqueline.

Jacqueline ordered a meal for her dog, and the waiter solemnly served it alongside our table. She talked about her infant daughter, who now called her "Mamma," and called John "Papa," and could stand erect, and was already trying to take her first steps. Jacqueline still talked as though hers were the only beautiful and intelligent child in the world, and this irritated me, though it was touching at the same time.

Ursula said to Jacqueline, "You remember Michel, the young Polish soldier I used to see, about three years ago? He's back in London again. I had dinner with him."

"Oh, yes?" said Jacqueline politely, obviously not remembering him at all.

"He told me the most amazing things about Palestine. He's going there after the war."

"Oh, yes?" said Jacqueline again. "He's a Jew?"

It was obvious to both of us that she had no further interest in Ursula's friend Michel; her thoughts went no further
than John, his fame, his connections. And somehow, when she
said, "He's a Jew?" it had been just like slapping Michel.

I thought, for a moment, of saying something. But Ursula
was sitting quite erect, looking at Jacqueline with a maturity
and self-sufficiency that I had never before seen in her. I
thought of Michel's calm round face, and realized what Ursula
must have been feeling—that Michel didn't need to be
defended before anyone.

After dinner we went to a movie in Leicester Square.
Jacqueline insisted on paying for everything, playing the
bountiful lady. This was her latest role, and there was something truly touching in her need for people's admiring surprise.

As we entered the theatre we heard someone call Ursula's
name. We all turned, and there was Michel. We stood in the
lobby talking a few minutes, and Ursula prodded him with
leading questions, drawing him out, showing him off. Michel
still spoke with diffidence, but nevertheless it could be seen
that Jacqueline was impressed by his intelligence.

Two Polish soldiers entered the lobby and recognized
Michel. Their faces brightened, and they hailed him joyfully.
They seemed delighted at having run into him. It was somehow surprising; one would not have thought that Michel
would be popular among the ranks.

When the two soldiers moved off, Jacqueline leaned
toward Michel and said with her seductive air, "Ursula says
you're planning to go to Palestine?"

There was obviously no subject she could have mentioned
that would have pleased Michel more. His eyes grew animated
as he described the collective villages of Palestine.

Jacqueline said, "But I never heard of anything like that.

It sounds wonderful. And you'll live like that?"

Michel said, "Yes." Then he blushed and added, "If I'm still alive at the end of the war."

We went on into the darkened theatre then, Michel still with us. We were seeing *For Whom the Bell Tolls.*

At one moment I looked at the rows of people with their eyes fixed on the screen, their faces lighted by the projection, and somehow the whole scene seemed unreal, as though all of us sitting there were part of some film. It was an odd sensation, and I mentioned it to Ursula later that night as we were getting ready for bed.

"I know," Ursula said. "I've sometimes felt that way too. Sometimes it seems as if every last one of us were playing a part." She sighed. "I wonder if I'll ever learn how to play mine."

CHAPTER 35

During John's absence, Jacqueline often came to take us out— sometimes Ursula, Mickey, and me together, sometimes one or the other of us alone. Mickey was with us a good deal in those days, as her husband had suddenly been sent off on a secret mission. She had no news of him. She continued to live in their little apartment, coming to the barracks only on payday and when it was absolutely necessary to appear at drill.

She had set her heart on the idea that her husband would be back for Christmas. There was a sort of childish hope in her that just because it was Christmas, Peter had to appear.

But Christmas passed, as did New Year's Day of 1944. Peter didn't come back. But one evening a tall blond young man came knocking on Mickey's door, and told her that her husband was in good health, and sent her a kiss. He said nothing else, and disappeared.

Michel went out often with our little band of women, and sometimes Ann came along, too. It was strange that after our four years of life together, it was Michel who finally became a sort of core around which the little group formed. Before Michel's advent, we had passed entire years together, and yet each of us always felt isolated in loneliness. Now we became a group of close comrades revolving around Michel. Each of us was extremely fond of him, even Ann. None of us—not even Ursula, as yet—was in love with him, and yet each of us loved him. Ann loved him as a wonderfully understanding friend. For Jacqueline he was a revelation—a restful friendship. Mickey loved him as she loved everybody, except that for Michel she had a kind of respect that she rarely had for anyone else, even though she sometimes laughed at what she called his Utopian ideas. I loved him as one of the few truly good people I had ever known in my life—good in the sense that he could do no harm to anyone. As for Ursula, she loved Michel as her salvation. It seemed to her that he had come back into her life to save her, and that without him she was lost.

Michel was good-humored, even gay, and yet he still retained the calmness and timidity that had been his chief characteristic three years before. He went to a great deal of trouble to give us pleasure, hunting out books that I wanted, finding works on music for Jacqueline, taking Ursula to the movies, reassuring Mickey about her husband. He navigated in Ann's Lesbian circles with composure and naturalness, and he had become acquainted with Claude, who adored him, kissing him on the cheeks and calling him her little boy.

He spoke as little as always, but never was mistaken in his judgment of people. He never permitted himself to be overwhelmed by a personality, and never let anyone throw sand in his eyes. If Claude began to tell some extravagant tale that she herself had ended in believing, Michel simply looked at her with his large astonished eyes, without saying a word, and suddenly Claude would stop her recitation.

I sometimes watched him leaving Down Street with Mickey, Jacqueline, and Ursula. He had the air of being equally fond of all three of them. This was probably the secret of his ability to keep us all together, for he never flirted. For some of us this was a surprise; for all of us it was pleasing, since it was a change from the wartime compulsion that seemed to possess every other man around us. I think that Jacqueline felt a little vexed at the beginning, used as she was to the immediate and complete worship of every man she met. But afterward she found that it was, on the contrary, rather restful to go out with Michel. With him, one could be natural; there was no part to play.

On the eve of John Wright's return, Jacqueline took a train to meet him, for the airfield where he was to arrive was some distance from London. She had had a new dress made. It was of black silk, cut in a low circle around her shoulders, and it brought out the fresh tones of her delicate skin and set off her shining hair. She was breath-takingly lovely. A young officer in the train began to talk to her, devouring her with his eyes.

Jacqueline was so happy over John's return that she even told the stranger whom she was going to meet, and that she was his fiancée. She wanted to shout from the rooftops, "John is coming!"

The young officer asked her if she could get him an autographed photo of John Wright, and Jacqueline promised to send him one as soon as they had returned to London.

Each of these details she remembered later, for each detail became invested with a final significance.

She daydreamed of John, of his handsome lined face, of

that savage quality that always seemed to hover about him. Now their life together was really going to begin. It was impossible that John should not marry her. She was certain that he loved her, and now her little girl would have a father in him, a father as fine as De Prade himself.

Before John's departure, he had left a letter for her, "My dearest," he wrote, "if you only knew how much I love you! You have given me back the joy of life. I want you to be happy always. You shall never again want for anything. I shall watch over you, my love, as long as I live. You are my joy." In the train, Jacqueline reread all these wonderful words.

His plane was to arrive the following morning. She spent the night in a hotel, and took a taxi to the airfield in the morning.

Everyone smiled at her. Everyone knew that this beautiful young woman was waiting for the great orchestra conductor John Wright.

Beyond that, Jacqueline remembered nothing.

She saw herself again, waiting in the comfortable little room from which one could see the planes landing.

And then she had found herself in a bed in a hospital. Her head ached, and she could no longer remember anything. But little by little a certainty arose from the depths of her body, a certainty that all was finished, that John was dead.

A doctor came to see her for a hurried moment; he told her that she was young, that she would get over her shock. Jacqueline asked for the newspapers. Perhaps there was still hope. But the debris of the plane had been found at sea, near the shore, and the bodies were scattered and unidentifiable.

Jacqueline returned to London. She didn't go to the house in Surrey, but cut her wrists in the ladies' room of a large department store.

Once more we found her in a hospital. Ursula, Mickey, and I went together to see her. Our presence seemed to help her. We tried to remind her that she still had her little girl, but even as we said it we knew that for Jacqueline it was not enough.

I wondered at the strange fate that seemed to hover over her, bringing repeated disaster, as though some monstrous doom insisted that she pay for her beauty, her charm, her aristocratic background. I felt ashamed that I had sometimes been irritated by her ingrained attitude of superiority. It was only the effect of breeding; she had suffered as much as we had, perhaps more than any of us.

The little house in Surrey was sold by John's wife, and Jacqueline found a job in an office. Once more she placed her little daughter with a family. Jacqueline began to do her own cooking again, and to sew her own clothes, and to get up early in the morning. She went out almost every evening. John was dead, and again she needed a father for her little girl. She would find one, for she was still the ravishing Jacqueline.

CHAPTER 36

Our little group formed more firmly around Michel. To all of us Michel represented the future, in a way. He was the future already present. And in a way he represented God. None of us was particularly religious, nor was Michel religious, but he carried within himself a God whose presence we all felt, and this was precisely the God of whom we had need. It wasn't a particular deity with a form delineated by any religion. It was rather an open way that made hope possible.

Michel never really entered into discussions with us. The girls didn't like intellectual discussions. But in the assembly hall in Down Street he had long talks with the chemistry student, Monique. Monique was just twenty years old, like Michel. She was dark, pretty, and serious. She had passed these years in the refuge of her books, entirely impervious to the atmosphere of Down Street. With her, Michel talked about the world of the future and about religion. But in general it was Michel who asked the questions.

Ursula liked to sit by and listen to them. For the first time in her life she felt the need of knowledge. It seemed to her that she had come into the barracks as an absolute child, and the barracks walls had closed around her. But now the world was opening and she could see the future appearing.

Since her acquaintance with Michel, Ursula had greatly changed. Little by little, she had ceased to be a child. She ripened, and sometimes assumed feminine airs, which suited her very well. She told me she had decided that after the war, even though she was not Jewish, she would go to Palestine with Michel. The moment she was offered an ideal, Ursula seized upon it as though her entire being had awaited nothing else.

She was at last freed from her sentinel's post at the barracks, only to fill a similar post at one of the Free French headquarters. I too had had a change of assignment, and now spent most of my time with the Americans, at a newsroom that their Office of War Information had installed in London. I was meeting many new people, and it was there that I eventually was to meet my future husband.

Each day, when Ursula's duties ended, she met Michel. At the time, Michel was working in an office in the Polish GHQ in London.

By this time Ursula had begun to talk more freely to Michel, and one evening, a little to her horror, she found herself speaking of her experience with Claude. She told him everything then—her passion, her suffering, her fear of not being normal. She told him too about Philippe.

Michel reassured her. The affair with Claude didn't seem to shock him, nor the experience with Philippe. He took Ursula's hand in his, and with an awkward gesture plunged both their hands into the large pocket of his coat.

They went regularly now to dine at Rose's, or in a little Italian restaurant in Soho, and sometimes Michel would take Ursula to the zoo, and they would amuse themselves like children.

About that time a whole group of us got into the habit of going out on bicycle trips in the environs of London on Sundays. We girls had all purchased secondhand bicycles, prehistoric machines upon which we were perched at vertiginous heights. Michel borrowed a bicycle from a friend, and we took along bread, cheese, and apples.

One Sunday most of us had dates in town, and Ursula alone left for a bicycle trip with Michel. It rained all day, a thin, acidulous little rain that drowned the countryside. Ursula laughed, raising her face to the rain. She was happy just to be alone with Michel.

Toward four o'clock they arrived in front of a little inn that seemed, as she described it to me, to have appeared out of a fairy tale.

"It's from the story of the witch who had a gingerbread house," Michel said. The roof was thatched, all shining with rain, and just beneath the roof the little windows seemed to peer at them with secret cunning.

In front of a log fire, the two grown-up children were served an English tea. There was no sugar, but there were hot buns and marmalade.

There was no more war. They were two young children who had taken refuge in the forest, far from the rain, far from the night, encircled in warmth and joy. Michel studied Ursula's pure face. Life had not touched her at all, everything had slipped from her as the rain from the thatched roof. She was still the same little girl who had opened the door on that night of the dance, when she had slipped outside to take refuge from the world. A little girl without a past, and with no knowledge of anything. She was like himself, she knew nothing, and he had no fear of her. One day he could take her in his arms and keep her. He had kissed her once, and she had fled; but that had been some years ago, and then there had been Claude. He had even then suspected something of the sort, but he had not been sure. But now Ursula had told him everything, and Claude was no longer a danger.

He looked at her and was filled with a terrible desire for life. Suddenly Michel wanted to live. Yes, why shouldn't he claim her, and afterward take her to Palestine? Everything was possible! There was a whole world to rebuild! He could not die.

Ursula returned Michel's gaze. She too was happy, and she knew that this happiness and peace were in being with Michel. Then quite simply the words came from her: "How good it is here, Michel! I'm so happy! I believe it's because I love you." Then she halted indecisively, still looking at him.

He arose, and together they went to the window. Outdoors the rain continued to fall. Michel encircled her with his arms and kissed her on the cheek. He held her pressed against him. They were exactly the same height, like two children. He told her, "I have nothing to give you, neither a home nor security nor a future." But Ursula had never had any of these. His words made her laugh. Then she saw that Michel's eyes were filled with tears. She placed her thin arms around his neck and kissed him gently on the lips. Ursula had weekend leave until Monday. It seemed quite simple and normal to them to spend the night at the inn.

The bed was wide and very high, with a thick red eiderdown cover. This was a new experience for Michel as well as for Ursula, and both of them were a little afraid. They pressed close to one another and were somehow reassured in sensing each other's fear. After all, it was neither so terrible nor so difficult. Ursula suddenly thought of Philippe, and an infinite thankfulness rose in her because he had left her for Michel.

They fell asleep and then awoke, and this time their bodies were already acquainted with each other. The discovery had begun. It was still rather awkward and slow because they were deeply moved, frightened, and happy. But everything was so normal, so wonderfully and utterly normal, coming out of these mad years.

Now they were two together and the war was going to end.

They were the future.

CHAPTER 37

These were the days of the V-1, Hitler's "secret weapon." First one heard something like the rattling of a plane, but with a difference. The first time we heard it we leaned out of the windows at Down Street, looking at the sky. In the distance we saw a small black point, coming rapidly forward. It passed overhead, and everyone thought, If the noise stops, it will fall on us. But the noise continued, and the fatal little machine went on its way. Farther on we saw it suddenly halt, and the noise stopped, and the V-1 plunged toward the ground. We heard a distant explosion.

Panic was great in London. After the blitz, after four years of war, people's nerves were not in very good condition. They grew wild with fear. As soon as an alarm sounded, one could see the crowds running in the street, people plunging into the subways, into the shelters, mothers seizing their children in their arms. Even the dogs howled. At the zoo, as soon as the noise of an approaching V-1 was heard, the monkeys screamed in terror and jumped around in their cages.

The universal terror arose first from the propaganda that had preceded the secret weapon, and then from the feeling that nothing could be done against it, that there was no defense.

The V-1's caused a great deal of damage—almost as much as had been caused by the blitz. But this time there was a difference. The seat of destruction was moved, and it was the elegant streets that were affected, particularly in the Kensington district and in the area around Hyde Park. Every day I saw more houses in ruins.

Once more there was an exodus to the country. Many of the children who had come back after the blitz were again evacuated. The railway stations were crowded, and people climbed into the trains by the windows.

There was a high increase of nighttime subway occupants. As during the great blitz of 1940, entire families slept underground and on the stairways of the stations, clutching their most precious possessions, which they carried along with them every night in battered old suitcases.

Michel and Ursula had requested permission to be married. As they were both under twenty-one, they had to secure not only the permission of their superiors but the consent of their parents. Michel wrote to his, in Palestine, and Ursula asked Claude to write a letter that she could enclose with her own to her mother in America. It was a year since she had written to her mother, and she had only an old uncertain address. Her father was in China and she did not know his address at all.

Claude wrote a wonderful letter; she spoke of loving Ursula as her own daughter, and declared that she knew Michel as a serious and intelligent young man. She said that she herself was old enough to be their mother, and believed that neither one of them could have made a better choice.

Michel and Ursula went together to post their letters, and then hand in hand they walked through the foggy London streets. It was the end of February. The weather was cold and damp. Ursula and Michel wore huge khaki coats of the same sort; the garments gave them an awkward air.

After four years of military service, Ursula had finally received her stripes as a first-class private. This had come so late that she could not even take pleasure in it. Michel was a sergeant. In the mornings he worked in a Polish headquarters office, and in the afternoons attended lectures at the university. This was an exceptional privilege, which his colonel had managed to secure by reporting him as an outstanding young man of special intelligence and gifts. But Michel had consented to accept this arrangement only on condition that he would be sent to the front with the others as soon as there was an invasion.

Our little group continued to revolve around Michel. Everyone had faith in him. Claude said, "Michel will certainly become someone very exceptional after the war."

And though no one knew quite why, everyone had this impression. Michel himself was outwardly the same as ever— reticent and utterly unassuming. No one knew him at bottom, not even Ursula.

And yet, since she had come to love Michel, she had been seized with a desire for knowledge. She wanted to read, to study. She asked Michel to tell her about socialism, Marxism, about anti-Semitism and about religion. A world had opened; she was no longer a child. The world was filled with unanswered questions. And her love had given her a kind of optimism. Now, it was worth while to study.

One day when we were out with Michel, Jacqueline said to him, "Since I've known you I've come to like the Jews. I never did before."

Michel, smiling his sad serious smile, replied, "That won't solve the Jewish question."

Then Ursula asked, "What will, Michel?"

He replied, "Perhaps a Jewish government in Palestine. In any case, first a normal country, a normal government in Palestine."

"And afterward?" Ursula insisted.

Michel laughed. "Afterward a world government of all people. Otherwise there will always be wars."

Jacqueline had become acquainted with a very rich and rather stupid young Englishman whom she dragged with her wherever she went. He seemed to be very much in love with her. Jacqueline, would watch him with her sparkling eyes, always smiling as she looked at him, but behind her smile one felt her powerful will, as tenacious as ever, and stronger than anything else between them. What did this young man matter to her, so long as he might one day accept her child as his own? She never spoke of De Prade or of John. But something indefinable, a sort of hard shadow, often passed over her pretty face.

CHAPTER 38

At the beginning of April Michel received a long letter from his parents, saying that they were happy that he had chosen a bride, and blessing the young people. They said that in Palestine everything was in flower, that the orange season was drawing to a close, that the heat would soon begin, and that several new communes had been established.

Everything was calm in Tel Aviv, they said, and they were going to enlarge the house for the reception of Michel and his bride. Just outside their windows, the young couple would have a large veranda, so that they could sleep outdoors in the summer.

His parents had enclosed an official letter in English authorizing their son, Michel Levy, to marry Mlle Ursula Martin.

The letter to Ursula's mother came back marked "Unknown at this address," and Ursula sent a second letter to another address in California that she had found among her papers. They were waiting only for this response before beginning their formalities at the consulates, their respective armies, and the registration office.

Michel had a tiny room in the city, a cubbyhole filled with books. Ursula often went to meet him there. But sometimes, while he was waiting for her, he would fall prey to his pessimistic moods. Once all three of us had a rendezvous there, and I arrived a little before Ursula to find him looking strangely depressed. That time he overcame his reticence, and talked to me. Sometimes, he said, when he was waiting for Ursula, he couldn't help asking himself, What's the good of all this? What use is it to study and to get a degree, what use to dream of marriage, when after all nothing in the world has changed? Have I found any answer—the answer that I sought in Switzerland? Men are still fighting like idiots, and there is no end to the war. And after the war, what will be the answer? What's the use of going around in circles, and even of trying to construct something? What's the use of all that, if it's only in a world of hatred and destructive-ness? One might as well die and be done with it.

It seemed to me that the God in whom he trusted so obscurely, and whose face he had never seen, was perhaps rather a yearning in his spirit than a belief

He thought of Ursula and wanted to weep over her, for she

was so young, and so hungry for love, and for knowledge, and for happiness. What did he have to give her? He thought of Ursula's friends. He thought of all of us—young women in search of love and of happiness, and in the end, what could we have? What hope was there for us in a world bent on self-destruction?

And yet, he said, none of us made great demands. What strange confidence we had in this life that ceaselessly deceived us! For we wanted to live, and we were satisfied with our little ersatz loves and with our few years of difficult life, which would in the end lead only to death. And then our children would begin the whole thing all over again.

Yes, Michel was very young, and pessimistic sometimes to the point of melancholy. I thought at the time that, like all of us, he would grow less heavyhearted with age. But his pessimism was more profound than the general unhappiness of the young in the face of mankind's inhumanity. "I am a hypocrite," Michel declared. "I ought to cry out the truth, tell all of you what I really think, tell everyone of my inner despair. Of what use is it that I, too, should lie to you, and Ursula, and Mickey, and Jacqueline? Instead of saying what is true, I talk to you about the future, about love, about reconstruction and peace, when I don't really believe in that at all. And you have faith in me. It's shameful.

"If there were only a man, a man like Christ," he cried out. "If only once more there would be such a miracle, that a man would rise up and speak to the multitude as Christ had spoken! But even that—what use would it be?"

Christ had spoken and his disciples had betrayed him and his church had been betraying him for centuries, and his brethren the Jews would not even recognize him as one of their own, as their greatest teacher. And all this too was part of the immense comedy that had been playing in the world since time immemorial.

Michel felt that he had no right to deceive Ursula about his inner beliefs, and yet he loved her, he wanted her to be happy. At least he could give her a short while of happiness.

The evening arrived gently, stealing in through the window and covering Michel's books. There was a knock at the door, and Ursula entered, looking at him with her limpid eyes. Michel took her in his arms, pressing her against him.

I knew that this was somehow to protect himself as well as her, somehow to keep himself from showing her his deepest bitterness. I knew too that he drew force from her, against his wish for death. She said, "Michel, Michel, I'm happy!"

He smiled gently, kissing her girlish round cheeks, caressing her long glossy hair. In Ursula's eyes I could read an elation that said, He can do anything! He will do great things! And in Michel's eyes there was the effort of all humanity, it seemed to me, to try to live.

As I saw them together, something unknotted in me. I wanted to cry, and at the same time I knew that I was healed of all the doubt and fear that had come into me through these years of living in the barracks. Mickey's marriage had seemed to me to contain mostly the excitement of war. But these were the pure in heart. I would no longer be ashamed of seeking what was pure. I knew that someday I might hope to feel love like theirs, and I could wait.

CHAPTER 39

The first of June brought a response from Ursula's mother. It was a strange, disconnected letter written in a disorderly handwriting, nervous and irregular. She wished her daughter great happiness, and at the same time warned her against marriage.

Men were all egotists, she said; they were all cruel and untrustworthy. As for herself, she was quite ill, but she was feeling better since she had been seeing a noted psychoanalyst. She described her luxurious life in California without ever asking whether her daughter was in need of anything. In closing, she said that she adored Ursula and was sure that she would be happy. "But do be sensible, dear, and don't have any children," she added.

The next day, Michel submitted his marriage request to the Army.

On the morning of June third, he telephoned Ursula at the barracks. He was at a railway station. He had just received his orders, and had to leave within half an hour. He thought it was for maneuvers and that he would be back in a week. He loved her and would write to her as soon as he could.

Ursula was not particularly disconcerted by this sudden departure. She was used to the ways of the Army, and counted on seeing Michel the following week.

The weather was magnificent. At lunch hour our little group went to take sun baths in Hyde Park. We rolled down our stockings, removed our ties, and rolled up our shirt sleeves. Sheep moved among the trees, cropping the grass. Ursula read to us from a book of poetry.

I had a very early errand in Mickey's office. Uncle Henry was already there, perspiring in huge drops before a pile of letters that he was answering. As I waited for some documents, he received a steady procession of visitors at an accelerating tempo, under the indifferent eye of the sentry. From time to time an explosion was heard, but no one paid any attention. It was only another V-2 (for now there were also V-2's). Everyone was buried in the daily routine and life was relatively calm.

Suddenly there was a strange siren—one we had never

heard before. A red-faced lieutenant burst into the room. At the same moment we all knew. We all cried out together, "They've landed!"

"In Normandy! At home!"

"The invasion!"

"They've landed!"

We had known in the last days that it was coming, and yet we had not known, for we had known it for so many years. Uncle Henry's face broke out into a great grin of relief, and he sweated more profusely than ever, for now at last he could confess that he had been in on the secret—a few in our services had been briefed. The lieutenant pounded him on the back. Mickey came in just then, late, with a dazed, uncomprehending expression, and we all fell on her, hugging her. "They've landed!"

It was an unforgettable day. When I went out, the English stopped me in the street, shaking my hand and crying, "*Vive la France!*" People walked with their faces radiant. French sailors crossed Piccadilly singing. American soldiers bought rounds of drinks for the English, and there was joy everywhere. The second front! The second front in which no one had believed any more, so long awaited on both sides of the Channel. Finally it was true! People were happy, as though the war were already over.

In the street, people tore the newspapers out of each other's hands. When I got back to our newsroom I found everyone clustered around the radio. The British and Americans were already advancing on the roads of Brittany and Normandy. The Germans were in retreat. The Maquis was fighting in the interior of France. The FFI had occupied German barracks, and the population everywhere was in revolt.

I didn't see Ursula until that evening. So this was why Michel had left so quickly. Now we understood. Ursula was pale and nervous, but during dinner in Down Street she, like everyone else, talked of nothing but the invasion.

We realized that we would all soon be leaving to work with the Army, driving trucks and helping in all sorts of tasks in makeshift headquarters under the hazards of war. There was a general fever. Who would be the lucky ones to be the first to leave? What would be their jobs? Certain of the girls assumed airs of importance and whispered that in their offices they had been promised immediate embarkation.

That night there was dancing in the barracks, and the noise became intolerable. Finally some of us went up to the dormitories. Monique was meticulously packing her suitcase so as to be ready to leave at an instant's notice. Ursula sat down on her bed and began to take off her stockings. Suddenly she jumped up and went running out of the room.

Worried, I followed her to the bathroom, and found her throwing up her entire dinner. I told her not to be worried, that it was the emotion of the day. But Ursula looked at me with her large eyes and said quite simply that she was going to have a baby. It was just the sort of news to learn on this day!

Ursula had already suspected it for a week. That afternoon she had been to see a doctor. He had told her that he could not yet be certain, but that it was more than likely that she was pregnant.

I said all that I could find to say. That it was wonderful, and that she should let Michel know right away, and perhaps he would be able to come back on compassionate leave, and they could be married.

CHAPTER 40

Ursula received a postcard from Michel, sent from an English port before his departure. It contained his new military address, to which Ursula wrote every day.

In Down Street, packing cases were being hammered closed. Everyone was preparing to leave, and some of the privileged had already left. Petit was among the first to go, to serve as a liaison officer right at the front. We now spent all our lives glued to the radio or scrutinizing the newspapers.

We passed an agitated week. All of us were so unnerved that we quarreled for no reason whatever. One felt that the Down Street period was coming to an end.

At the Carleton Gardens headquarters, bags were being packed, files were being burned, cases of documents were carried off. And every day officers left to join the active forces, while the entire GHQ was getting ready to move.

During the noon hour we all went to the newsreel theatre to see the American tanks advancing on the roads of France. We watched our own people, the people of France, throwing flowers to the Americans, and we saw our villages in ruins.

About two weeks after the opening of the second front I happened to be on Buckingham Road, passing the Polish headquarters, when I saw one of Michel's friends from the office to which he had been attached. The young man said to me, "You know the news?"

I felt a sort of contraction in my heart, for the Polish soldier's face was grave.

"Michel was killed on the first day, during the landing. He got sixteen bullets in him while he was running to help another fellow who was wounded. His body was recovered. He's buried there, at Falaise, in Normandy."

I could scarcely keep from bursting into tears right there in the middle of the street. Ursula, poor Ursula! Poor Michel!

Once more I saw the round face, the great black eyes, the raised questioning brows, and the small plump form of Michel in his heavy khaki uniform. And I thought of all the things he had said to Ursula and Mickey and Jacqueline and me, about the future, and reconstruction, and the United Nations, the things he had not really believed in his heart. So he had been right. There was really only death, all death.

Suddenly I thought again of Ursula and the baby. It was frightening. What should be done? The Polish sergeant told me that a letter addressed to Ursula had been found in Michel's pocket, and that his chief had received the letter and had just informed Down Street that morning.

I had an important errand and couldn't get to the barracks. I had not been there for lunch, and I was afraid that Ursula might have been there and received the news. I hurried to Mickey's office. When I told her what had happened, she started to cry, soundlessly, weeping as we telephoned Down Street to find out if Ursula had come in for lunch. The sentry said no, and we concluded that Ursula could not yet have learned about Michel. We had the rest of the day to think of some way to protect her. We tried and tried to find a solution. It seemed to us that the child would be the only safeguard. She would have Michel's child to raise. Yes, there would be the child, and that would be a help for Ursula. It was life, it had to be accepted.

At the same time, we simply could not bring ourselves to believe that the gentle Michel, the foe of all that was hateful, could have been killed—not that particular boy, immediately, in the forefront of the liberating army. Mickey said frantically that perhaps it was a mistake, that he was a prisoner, that the news was false. I could see that she had to doubt, she had to deceive herself, for if Michel were only the beginning of the list, if Peter too . . .

CHAPTER 41

Ursula had come to lunch at the barracks, after all. The sentry had not noticed her as she slipped in. Afterward, she, along with the rest of us, had to piece together what had happened.

Immediately after lunch, our captain had called Ursula to her office.

The Captain spoke very considerately, and Ursula said nothing. She did not cry. The Captain knew that she was to have married Michel, for the marriage request had passed through her office. But like nearly everyone else, she was ignorant of Ursula's pregnancy.

Ursula was seated, her head lowered; her hair covered her face almost entirely. Her hands tightly grasped her knees. The Captain told her to cry, that it would do her good to let herself go, but Ursula didn't answer and she didn't cry.

There was a long silence, and the Captain could think of nothing else to do with this child whom she scarcely knew and with whom she had almost no contact. She told Ursula that she could have a week's leave, that she didn't have to report to her office, and that she could do whatever she liked. The Captain spoke also of the war, of the hundreds of young men sacrificing life and happiness that the world might be free of oppression, that there might be no more concentration camps, no more refugees on the roads, no more homeless, and no more blood spilled, so that peace and friendship should reign between nations. She no doubt said what everyone else would have said in her place.

When Ursula sensed that the Captain had finished, she rose and went out. She seemed calm. The Captain reflected that the girl was quite young, and that the sorrows of love are transitory.

Ursula went directly to the infirmary. No one was sick just then, and the infirmary beds were vacant. Ursula quietly asked the nurse for some aspirin.

While the nurse went to get the aspirin, Ursula reached out her hand and took two vials of sleeping pills.

Then she went down to the kitchen in the basement. It was about three o'clock, and no one was there. The kitchen was clean, with everything in order. Machou was in town, as were her assistants, for they were always at liberty between two and five o'clock.

Ursula went to the cupboard, took a mug, went to the sink, poured water into it, and then emptied the contents of the two vials into the water. She took a spoon from a drawer and crushed the pills until they formed a white powder that floated in the water like a cloud in the sky.

Ursula must have gone about her task methodically, as if it were only one more of her duties, one more thing that she had to do; for she left no disorder behind her when she finished her bitter drink. There was only the mug on the table, with the spoon beside it, and a little of the white powder at the bottom of the mug.

She went upstairs to the Virgins' Room. How long she remained alone there no one knows. We know she was there, and that she must have been very calm, for afterward we found all her things neatly arranged together on her bed, as though she wanted to make everything as easy as she could for those of us she was leaving. Everything must have seemed quite natural and normal to her. Her life had begun with Michel, and now she was ending it with him. The future was already dead.

When she left the barracks, she slipped out by the kitchen

door, so as not to have to pass before the table at the entrance, where she herself had so often sat guard.

After having telephoned the barracks, Mickey and I felt a momentary reprieve. We decided to get in touch with Ann, to help us break the news to Ursula. Ann was one of the most capable girls in the barracks, and we believed that her presence would have a steadying effect.

I had to hurry to my office. I was able to telephone Ann during the afternoon. She took the news in her quiet, strong way, and saw at once that we would have to help Ursula support the shock. As I sometimes had to remain late at my office, Ann promised to be at the barracks before Ursula might receive the news from the Captain.

All afternoon Mickey was worried and heartsick. It was almost as though the tragedy were her own, as though it were Peter who had been cut down. She had intended to meet Ann at the barracks after work, to be with Ursula, but instead she hurried to her little flat, with the panicky feeling that she would find some message there, some news of Peter. As Mickey hurried along, a young English aviator fell in beside her. *"Bon jour, mademoiselle."*

Mickey gave him an automatic smile, and then walked on faster. She had no heart at all for flirtation; indeed, since her marriage she had been surprised at the change in herself, at the sense of respectability that had come over her. A married woman never responded to strangers on the street. She had flirted like that as a girl, but now the world was suddenly serious; she was married, her best friend's lover was dead, and there was no response in her to flirtation.

There was no mail. Mickey went slowly upstairs. She dreaded the moment of solitude, of opening the door. She would fix herself a bit to eat, and then go to the barracks to find Ursula.

As she climbed, she heard a record playing. It was Charles Trenet singing:

> *"Je chante*
> *Soir et matin,*
> *Je chante*
> *Sur mon chemin . . ."*

Her heart began to beat wildly. She opened the door and rushed into the room. "Peter!"

It was he. He had grown a beard, and looked somehow different, but it was really her Peter, big, handsome, smiling. His expression was grave and matured, as though years had passed, as though he were older. This was no longer the young lad whom Mickey had married, but a man.

Mickey pressed herself to him while he kissed her arched lips. She studied his face, and a kind of pride spread through her. Yes, he was a man now.

"Peter! How did you get here? How could you come back so soon? Oh, darling, I'm so happy!" she burbled half in English, half in French, covering him with kisses.

Peter held her off a bit, the better to look at her. It was still difficult for him to believe that he had a wife, and such a beautiful wife. What times we'll have, skiing together in Norway! he thought. But in the same instant he felt the force of all he had just lived through. He saw himself clambering over a wall in the night, with his grenades belted around him; he saw himself in an icy river; he saw himself bending over a man's body. Peter closed his eyes. A great disgust welled in his throat. He saw the dead, all the dead bodies, the burned villages, the monstrous tanks pushing along the roads; he heard the shells exploding; and there was Eric, whom he loved as a brother, his childhood friend Eric, howling in pain, with his guts crowding out of his belly.

Peter sighed and pressed Mickey close. She looked into his face, feeling him suddenly removed from her, seeking to understand him, wondering at the tightness that had come over his face, and noticing the new creases at the corners of his mouth.

"You'll stay here now, Peter?" she said. "It's finished?"

He shook his head. "No, dear. Only one night. I've been sent back to make a report on a German installation we blew up- -a big one. Tomorrow I've got to go back again."

The phonograph record kept going around, the needle caught in the last groove, repeating over and over, *"Chante, chante, chante."* Peter went to shut it off. Mickey started to prepare dinner. She felt like crying.

Only one night.

She thought of the tragedy at Down Street. She could not smother this one night with Peter under that tragedy. She tried to push away from her the trembling thought that next time Peter might not come back. She would keep this one night for him.

After their meal, Peter made a fire on the hearth. He lighted his pipe, and Mickey sat on the rug, leaning against his legs. In the past, they would have gone out dancing or to a movie. But Mickey felt that all that was over, that she and Peter would never again be the same.

As though he had followed her thoughts, he said gently, almost as though he were speaking to himself, "After the war I'd like to live in the country. Do you think it would be too boring for you, Mickey? I want to have a house. I'll build it myself, in the mountains, at home in Norway. We'll have a whole lot of children. In winter I'll take them to school on a sledge, and in summer—oh, Mickey, it's so beautiful in the mountains in the summer. You'll see. They're covered with flowers, and you can hear the torrents rushing down. I'll raise a lot of things, and we'll ski and hike in the mountains. You're as strong as a man, you're made for that life. Do you want it like that, Mickey? I've had enough of cities, I've had enough—" he hesitated for an instant—"enough of men. I want to forget the war, my darling. I want to live, really to live. The war—it's the worst, the most horrible punishment that man puts on himself. I don't want my children to have to go to war. And there in the mountains we can teach them to love, not to hate, not to kill."

"Yes," Mickey breathed. Then she looked up with an effort and said, "Peter, I have the most frightful thing to tell you. Michel—Michel has been killed."

"He, too," Peter said. Suddenly he cried out, "It's more frightful than that, Mickey, because it doesn't do anything to me any more! I've seen too many dead, too many of my friends. We've all got used to it. Every day you hear that someone else is dead—fellows like myself, young men, who wanted to live, to have wives and children. They believed in the future, like Michel. . . . Oh, Mickey, I want to begin all over again, all new after the war. I've come to understand so many things. I know what happiness is, and that every man can build it for himself. It depends only on us. We can refuse to kill, refuse to die—that has to come from us, and from the life we choose to live. I know now, I've chosen what I want for myself. You understand, Mickey? Say that you understand."

Mickey was weeping. Tears shone in her large blue eyes. "You're talking just like Michel," she said, and she tried to smile. "Yes, dear, of course I understand. And I'd love to live in the country in Norway, and we'll go skiing, and I'd love to have a whole lot of children. . . ." Already she felt lighter, seeing herself surrounded by her sons, a whole flock of them, climbing the rocks.

Peter took her in his arms. His eyes too had recovered their old gaiety. "Get me a piece of paper, Mickey," he said. "Let's draw the plans for our house."

Ann was the first of us to return to the barracks. She looked for Ursula's name in the register. Ursula had been marked out after breakfast, and had not been marked in again. Ann therefore concluded that Ursula was still in town, and knew nothing.

I got home soon afterward. Ann and I decided that Ursula had probably remained in town for dinner. It didn't occur to us to speak to the Captain.

Ursula must have wandered along the streets until her sleepiness became so powerful that she turned into Hyde Park, and found a quiet corner, between two trees. Although it was still early evening, she was unable to see anything; her eyes could no longer focus. She saw everything double, and the images trembled and danced and multiplied and retreated before her eyes. Her head ached, ached terribly; she had a pain in her stomach, and her heart pounded. Then she slipped to the ground, and curled up as wounded animals do, and she resisted no more.

When Ursula had not yet returned at eight o'clock, Ann reported the matter to the sergeant of the guard, who hurried to the Captain. We learned then that Ursula had been there at noon. She knew. Now the police were telephoned, and a description of Ursula was given out to all the stations in London and its environs and along the Thames.

Someone had telephoned Jacqueline, and she rushed over to Down Street to wait with us for the news that we knew must come. None of us in the Virgins' Room went to bed. We all waited in silence. The hours passed.

At midnight, although I knew I wouldn't sleep, I undressed and put on my pajamas. As I shifted my pillow I heard a soft rustling sound, as though the pillow had rubbed against paper. But I had left no paper there. Who, then? Could Ursula have left a note? My heart thudding, I lifted the pillow.

There was no note, but something more eloquent than

anything Ursula could have written. It was a small snapshot that I had never seen before, a picture of Ursula and Michel, standing close together, smiling. It was her only legacy.

Wordlessly I handed the picture to Jacqueline, who had come to stand at my elbow. She stared at it uncomprehendingly a moment. Then her eyes widened. She understood. She gave a wordless cry, dropped the picture on my bed, and ran from the room.

As I gazed after her, I realized that of all of us keeping this hopeless vigil, Jacqueline alone had really expected to see Ursula again. Only Jacqueline had ever made a gesture toward death, and she had failed. There was the night she had lain huddled on the ground beneath the window from which she had jumped, and the day she has slashed her wrists in the department-store washroom.

Jacqueline had tried, and failed, and tried again. For Jacqueline there would always be a new beginning. When she saw the little picture that Ursula had slipped beneath my pillow, I think she realized for the first time that for some, there is only one beginning and one end.

CHAPTER 42

The next morning the door to the barracks was opened by two policemen, who carried in the body of Ursula.

She did not remain long in Down Street. For an instant we looked at her white face, her closed eyes, her blue lips; we saw the head fallen on the shoulder, and the dead hands.

The Captain's door was closed to us all. Only a few officers entered for secret conferences.

The body was taken away at once, no one knew exactly

where, and the next day a lieutenant announced that Ursula Martin had been buried in the French military cemetery outside London. It was all done quickly, without fuss. The incident was quite annoying, very disagreeable. The sooner it was over with, the better.

One of the corporals remarked that Ursula had always been a high-strung child, and that was her entire obituary.

But Claude wept. She wept sincerely with all her heart, and she came to me, to Ursula's best friend, to accuse herself for the wrong she thought she had done to Ursula long ago.

After a few days no one spoke any more about her, for their minds were full with preparations for departure. We scarcely went to our offices any more. We knew now that we were at last going to have active work to do—with the wounded, driving trucks and jeeps on the bombed-out roads, working in the newly liberated towns as telephone girls, as interpreters, in liaison, and as guards. We wanted only to leave as soon as possible.

Some days later, I learned that before his departure Michel had left a thick portfolio with his Polish friends. The portfolio contained poems he had written, as well as his diary. From what we knew of Michel, of his sense of beauty, of his sensitivity, and from what Ursula had said of his poems, portions of which Michel had read to her, it seemed certain that this unique work of Michel's was truly precious. But there was a formal direction left with the portfolio: "In case of the death of Michel Levy, please burn these papers at once, without reading."

The young Polish sergeant spoke about the matter to Mickey and Jacqueline and me. We were all absolutely of the opinion that Michel's instructions should be disregarded, that the poems had to be preserved. We felt that their value—of which we were certain—was more important than compliance with his last instruction.

But the Polish sergeant, a simple, direct lad, knew only one thing. He had promised to obey the instruction, it was the wish of the dead, and therefore he had to burn the papers. We attempted to explain our point of view to him, to plead the cause of beauty and of poetry. It was the only thing that remained of Michel, we said. Ursula and his child no longer existed; at least his thoughts should remain.

But the sergeant burned the papers.

That night I wept for a long time. I promised myself that at least if I ever had a son, I would name him Michel. With all my strength, I wanted in some way to fill the emptiness that had come into the world where there had been a voice that had something real to say, and that had been destroyed.

I thought of all of my friends from this little room, and what had happened to them. First Jacqueline had lost John, and now Ursula and Michel were gone. And it had only begun. I felt them coming as though within myself, all the young, the girls and the men who approached in an endless line, the dead, all the dead who were being sacrificed without anyone knowing why.

EPILOGUE

It was eleven o'clock in the evening. We were tired, and nearly all of us were already in bed. Ginette was brushing her hair, and Ann was still in the bathroom.

The guards were on the roof, watching for bombs. They telephoned to Claude to ask for hot coffee, and Monique, who happened to be in the hall, said she would go down to the basement to prepare it. Monique had just gone down to the kitchen when a terrific explosion resounded all around us. In the same second the lights went out, and stones and planks and chunks of plaster and pieces of window rained down upon us. I heard Ginette scream, and cries went up from all over the house.

After a time that seemed endless to us, we came to realize that a V-2 had fallen on Down Street. I remember that I was first of all stricken with astonishment. For four years we had seen buildings crumble all around us, but it seemed impossible that such a thing could happen now to us.

I moved carefully and stood up. I was unhurt. Ginette was bleeding, but she could walk. We felt our way forward in the darkness, climbing over piles of rubble until we found the door of the room. When I opened it, I saw that the hall was filled with women in pajamas. Someone had found a candle, and its flame cast a flickering light over the scene. The entrance to the building had been torn out, and with it the entire front of the house.

Already groups were climbing over the debris to reach the street. Presently we were all outdoors, and people came running toward us with flashlights. We were cold, and Ginette was wiping her bleeding forehead with a piece of cloth torn from her nightgown.

Opposite us was the big hotel, where a dance was going on. It was there that the ARP took us, and we made a sensational entrance in our torn nightclothes, with our faces covered with dust and blood, with our scratched bare feet and our still half-awakened air.

We were put to bed in the Turkish bath.

The next morning, in the graying dawn, I looked again on Down Street. The house was a ruin of blackened bricks, disemboweled, open to the sky, with its rafters torn from their moorings, its stones crushed, its windows smashed, its doors hurled from their frames. In a cluttered hole there was a barrel from which a red stream dribbled, forming a puddle, and under this mass of wreckage, of planks and iron and glass and shrapnel, the ARP searched with their shovels for the body of Monique, entombed in the ruins of the kitchen.

This was my last memory of Down Street. I gazed for a long while at the annihilated switchboard room, at the great assembly hall open to all the winds, at the bleeding, crushed house.

Standing beside me, I saw the Ambassador of Peru. And he too was gazing, with a very thin smile, scarcely perceptible, on his overred lips.

Three days later we landed in France.

INTERVIEW WITH TERESKA TORRES
by Joan Schenkar

The following text has been compiled from two interviews conducted on September 26 and October 2, 2004, in Paris, France.

JOAN: *Women's Barracks* has a history as long, as complicated and almost as interesting as your own. More than most novels, it seems to be inseparable from the life of its author. Can you explain why and how you started working on it?

TERESKA: I will tell you from the beginning, the very beginning. I have always kept a personal diary since I was nine years old. I started the diary the day of my ninth birthday and I continued it when I was in the army. I didn't write it every day, but every few days. Whenever I had a moment I would sit and write down the stories of the girls—we really were girls, I was eighteen and a half when I volunteered for the Free French Forces in London—who lived with me in the women's barracks on Downing Street.

My husband, who was not yet my husband at that time, the writer Meyer Levin [Chicago-born novelist, journalist, and filmmaker (1905–1981)], was a war correspondent. He arrived in London in 1943, I think, with the American Army, and as he knew my parents very well, and as I knew him since I was four years old, I went out to dinner with him. And I remember that even at our first dinner I started telling him stories that came from the women's barracks. And he was fascinated. Almost every time we saw each other he was asking, "And what happened to that girl? And to that girl?" And I went on telling him.

After the war—my young husband, Georges Torres [stepson of Léon Blum, France's first Jewish Prime Minister], who was also in the Free French Forces, was killed in the fighting four months after I married him and I had our daughter five months after that—Meyer Levin and I married in 1948. And I was still telling him stories about the army. And Meyer started saying to me, "But write it down! Write it down!" And I said, "But I am writing it, I keep a diary and it's in my diary." And he said, "No no no. Write it as a book. Make a novel out of it." And he continued to insist that I write a novel, which was very amusing to me. Because just at that period I was reading a life of Colette, who had married a much older man, Willy [Willy Gauthiers-Villars, fourteen years Colette's elder], and Meyer was a much older man—he was sixteen years older than I was. And Willy locked Colette up because he wanted her to write down the stories she was always telling about her school friends. So in a way—well, Meyer didn't lock me up—but he kept insisting strongly that I write the novel.

JOAN: Yes, the first words of your foreword to *Women's Barracks* are "My husband tells me I ought to write my memoirs . . ." To my generation of women writers, that phrase is like a red flag waved before a bull . . .

TERESKA: [*laughter*] That's very funny, that's really very funny! But, you know, Colette would have said the same thing. "My husband Willy tells me to write Claudine."

As a matter of fact, I met Colette's last husband, Maurice Goudeket, because I wrote a novel based on Colette's life up to the time she signed her books "Colette" instead of "Willy."

I went to Biarritz where Goudeket lived after Colette's death so that he could read the manuscript. He was very nice, very elegant, and he said he would not allow me to publish the novel because, strangely enough, I portrayed Colette as a lesbian. He wouldn't allow it. Everybody in Paris knew she was a lesbian! She never hid it! So instead of calling my novel *By Colette*, I called it *By Cécile*—and it was published.

Anyway, Meyer and I were in Brittany in the summer of 1948. Some days when it was raining, Meyer would say, "Why don't you go in a room and write your book. Write your book. Write your book." And so I began to write. I have the feeling I wrote *Women's Barracks* just during that summer, maybe it took me two or three months.

JOAN: And did you consult your diaries while you were writing?

TERESKA: No. Not in the sense that I went directly to the diary to see what I wrote here. Not at all. But the diary, those girls were very close to my mind. It was 1948, the war ended in 1945, so all the stories were still there with me.

Anyway, I kept on writing and Meyer didn't see anything until it was finished. And when he read it, he liked it very much and said he would translate it and try to sell it in America.

JOAN: Your description of the origins of *Women's Barracks*— a little bit of Scheherezade, a little bit of Colette—makes me wonder if you weren't writing the book for your husband. And it also makes me wonder just how much the American translation might have been "voiced" by him.

TERESKA: Well, you see, *Women's Barracks* was not my first book. When I was seventeen years old, before the war, I had started a novel and during the whole five years of the war,

besides the diaries, I was writing this novel. And immediately
after the war, Gallimard published the book. So I had behind
me an experience of writing a novel. I don't think I was writing *Women's Barracks* for Meyer, although I was writing it
under his pressure. It was for me. The same way I wrote the
first one. For me.

As for the translation, I didn't see Meyer's translation
before the book was accepted. Because he went to America,
translated it in America, and sold it in America while I was in
Paris. When I came to America, the translation was already
accepted by Mr. Carroll at Fawcett [Dick Carroll, editor of
Fawcett's Gold Medal imprint]. Although my English was not
so good at the time, I read the translation and it seemed fine to
me. Now, when I re-read it today, there are some changes
I might make. But it's the translation that sold 4 million
copies—so what can I say?

But the translation was true to the text. It was absolutely
literal and faithful.

JOAN: So those highly sexualized scenes—which I was
naively thinking might perhaps have been enhanced by your
male translator or requested by your male editor—were
entirely created by you. And, in fact—as I think you're going
to explain—it was the men who tried to tone the book down.

TERESKA: [*laughter*] You know, I must tell you a funny story
about that. After the agreement with Fawcett had been made,
I needed someone to type the book up. (The manuscript was
handwritten.) And I met an American girl in Paris and proposed to her that she type it. My first child with Meyer had just
been born and while Meyer was dictating the translation to
this American girl, I was sitting there with my little infant in
my arms listening. And every so often the poor girl would
raise her head from her typing, look at me, and say, "I can't

believe it. She looks just like the Virgin Mary. I can't believe she wrote what I'm typing!"

JOAN: [*laughter*] Where did you imagine *Women's Barracks* would be published?

TERESKA: I didn't imagine anything at that point. I knew that Meyer wanted to show it to a publisher in America and I didn't think it was at all a book for Gallimard, my first publisher. Many publishers in America were tried and no publisher wanted to touch it because they felt it was so shocking. I thought it was a very innocent book; I didn't see anything shocking about it. Finally it seemed that Fawcett would publish it. And when the first edition came out, they printed 200,000 copies. And I thought I would collapse! My first book at Gallimard, I think they printed 2,000 or 3,000 copies. 200,000 copies!

I went to see the editor at Fawcett in New York, Mr. Carroll, and I said to Mr. Carroll, "You've published 200,000 copies already. How long will you continue to publish *Women's Barracks*?" And Mr. Carroll answered me, "We are going to publish it forever, just like the Bible."

This I remember absolutely clearly.

JOAN: And did Fawcett ask you to make changes in the manuscript?

TERESKA: Fawcett accepted *Women's Barracks* with one condition. They were extremely worried about lawsuits over immorality and they felt it would make the book more "serious" if a girl soldier would have a sort of look at what goes on in a more moral vein. She would say, "Oh, I'm sorry. This is so bad. And this is so sad." And, of course, I didn't approve of this but Meyer wrote to me from New York to ask if I would mind if he added some narrative lines here and there to satisfy the publisher. And since he told me exactly how he would do it and since it really did not change the story, I said he could go ahead with it.

JOAN: So the judgmental narrator—I've always been uncomfortable with this character—wasn't in your original manuscript?

TERESKA: Not at all. Not at all. I didn't moralize at all. Today, I think the narrator is so untrue. She is supposed to be me and even her biography is not mine. She says she comes from a very bourgeois background; my family was a family of Polish Jewish artists who converted to Catholicism before I was born. And I was not allowed to tell my Jewish grandparents in Poland that I was a Catholic . . .

JOAN: So you were not a hidden Jew? You were a hidden Catholic? [*laughter*]

TERESKA: That's right . . . And of course the moral judgments of this narrator are false. And it is this that got the book published in America.

JOAN: Then I'm going to think of her as "the American character." It's interesting that the only "false" character in Women's Barracks is the one who is supposed to be you. In a way, she represents . . .

TERESKA: . . . the kinds of judgements that an American of that time would have wanted in the book. But in the original manuscript I told without judgments and as only I could the stories that had happened to the five girls I knew best: Jacqueline, Micky, Bela . . .

JOAN: Bela is the name of the character in your published war diary. In *Women's Barracks* the character is called Claude.

TERESKA: That's because I changed the names of the girls three times. In the unpublished diaries, all the girls have their real names. In *Women's Barracks* I gave them other names. When I published the war diaries under the title *Une francaise libre,* I changed the girls' names again. Still, two or three of the girls recognized themselves and one of them was furious: "You wrote that I had white hair! Couldn't you have removed my white hair?!!" Well, I wrote much more objectionable things about her than that. I wrote she was a drug addict. But not a word from her about that, just the hair. And I published another book recently, *Le Choix,* where I again speak of the war, so once again, I changed, not all, but some of the names.

JOAN: Now this business of the transformation of the names interests me because the book has already undergone some considerable transformations. It gets transformed from a diary into a novel. A character is interpolated. It gets translated from your pure French to your husband's . . .

TERESKA: Literal English . . . [*laughter*]

JOAN: And in *Une francaise libre,* your published war diaries, you, yourself, have a "real" relationship with Bela—who becomes the fascinating Claude of *Women's Barracks*—which then becomes very much the "fictionalized" relationship that Ursula has with Claude in *Women's Barracks.*

TERESKA: Right. Well, if I have put myself somehow into any character, I could say I put much of my real emotion at the time into Ursula.

JOAN: She was so pure . . .

TERESKA: Well, I was very pure. Although I was not helpless in the way that Ursula in *Women's Barracks* was. I had just come out of convent school where I was so used to answering the nuns by "Oui, ma Mère"—"Yes, Mother"—that I responded to my captain with the same phrase: "Oui, ma Mère." So I took the real Ursula's physical characteristics and her experiences and I mixed them with something of myself. But the real Ursula was also very interesting in another way: she was the great granddaughter of the Russian revolutionary theorist Kropotkin. And years and years later, a man who had been in love with Ursula wrote to me that the Ursula in *Women's Barracks* reminded him very much of his real Ursula.

This kind of thing happened quite frequently with *Women's Barracks*. The character of Michel, who in real life was a friend of my father [Marek Szwarc, Polish French painter and sculptor] and in love with me (although I didn't know it at the time), died heroically in the war. Ten years after *Women's Barracks* was published, I met, entirely by accident and for the first time, Michel's mother at a small party in New York. And she turned to me absolutely as though I had been her son's lover.

JOAN: What intrigues me is how *Women's Barracks* flirts with what is "true" and what is "real"; with what is invented, and with what actually happened. I'm thinking now not only of Ursula, but of the character of Jaqueline—the Colette of your diary who was actually living with the English film star Leslie Howard. She has a parallel—but fictionalized—life in *Women's Barracks*. And you do this with all the women: you translate them into characters while keeping the "truth" of their lives intact. And then they become "real" again in the reactions of the people who knew them in life and find them once again in your novel. It's a novel that comes from life.

TERESKA: Yes, yes. And it returns to life.

JOAN: And then there's that detail of the "false name" Meyer Levin uses in his "Translator's Preface" to introduce the work as a "true" account of, as he puts it, "women who have to live together without normal emotional outlets." I feel a bit as though I'm at a masquerade ball here.

TERESKA: Well, he used the name George Cummings as a kind of joke. Fawcett didn't want him to sign Meyer Levin; they didn't think *Women's Barracks* was the kind of book that should have a Jewish name attached to it . . . [*laughter*]

JOAN: I can't think of another woman writer who has made a novel out of her war diaries; it's really unique. But it's odd that it wasn't published in your native language.

TERESKA: You know, *Women's Barracks* was published in fourteen or fifteen languages and never published in France. Because I felt that if anything should be published in France, it should be the "real" experience, the war diary. And the great question that I ask myself all the time is: How did I manage in the war to write a novel and keep a diary? I don't know. But I did.

JOAN: And you were a teenager.

TERESKA: A teenager writing a diary and a novel and working as a secretary—a great many of us were secretaries—in the Free French Forces. Later on, I became a liaison officer with the American Army and my group was going to disembark on D-Day, but by that time I was pregnant, and I didn't want to lose that baby. So I didn't go. At that point, four people in my family were in the army: my father, who was in the Polish Army; my husband, Georges, who entered Paris with General Leclerc's Armored Aivision on Liberation Day; my step-mother, Suzanne Torres, who was head of Leclerc's Ambulance Division; and me.

JOAN: Now, let's talk about the scandal. I believe *Women's Barracks* is the only novel published in the second half of the twentieth century that required the ministrations of a Catholic priest?

TERESKA: [*laughter*] Yes, but only in a personal way. And only after the trials started. The first trial was in 1953 in St Paul, Minnesota when a salesman was charged with selling "indecent and lewd literature"—*Women's Barracks.* The case was decided in favor of *Women's Barracks* with the testimony of many literary critics, but it was only one of several trials— including one in Germany. And at that point, my parents—I think Meyer and the publishers must have said that it would be a good idea to ask for a monk's opinion and my parents perhaps needed a little reassurance themselves—turned to Père Avril, an admirer of my father's sculptures and a very well known Dominican priest in France, and asked him to read the book and to give a decision as a monk as to whether the book was pornographic or not. And, as I remember, Père Avril's letter was in Italian—I have no idea why—but it was a very good opinion. He said the book was absolutely not pornographic; on the contrary.

But now I want to tell you about another trial. A man appeared, not exactly out of the blue, but almost. And he had produced films for Errol Flynn. And he took an option on *Women's Barracks* to make a film. About a year passed, and during that year I found out he was really not at all the kind of person I wanted to make a film of *Women's Barracks*. He asked Harold Robbins to write the screenplay—and then sent me the synopsis Robbins had written. It was a horror! The vulgarity was just unbelievable! And the option date arrived, and no money with it. So I was delighted to notify him that his option had expired. And you know what he did? He took me to court. And I lost the case because my contract was missing five words: "Time is of the essence."

So, even though the film was never made, this producer continued to send me letters with encouraging information like, "I have Marlene Dietrich to play Claude!" [*laughs*]

JOAN: Marlene Dietrich as Claude? What a film that would have made!

You know, I can't help thinking that the history of this book—which, by the way, I first encountered at the age of ten in a sneak attack on my father's "forbidden" library—more or less mirrors the instabilities of women's history since the War. It crosses genre, linguistic, and continental lines, it is filled with impersonations of all kinds, it has had both a moral character and moral judgments imposed on it. It seems—like yourself—to have survived so much by being a little bit of everything.

TERESKA: Well, you can be a little bit of everything up to a point. It's a great richness. But I think I would rather say that I am not a little bit of everything—I am quite a lot of many things.

AFTERWORD

Alison Hennegan has described how, as a British teenager in the 1960s, she learned how to spot books of potential lesbian interest. "I became aware of and learned to rely on a phenomenon which I can only call a pricking of my thumbs," she writes, "a capacity which led me, unfailingly and time and time again, to the 'right' book for me, however unlikely its disguise" (166). Hennegan evokes the memory of buying a French novel—perhaps Daudet's *Sapho* or Zola's *Nana*—that might have been perfectly respectable were it not for the cover, depicting "two women sprawled across a table and each other, hair, eyes and teeth all straight off a 1950s pin-up calendar" (165). Hennegan was instinctually drawn to pulp novels (often re-editions of French novels with themes that lent themselves well to the pulp cover treatment), and for many years it was assumed that such books appealed exclusively to a male, sometimes sleazy, audience. Reprints of French novels constituted one chapter in the history of paperback publishing in both England and the United States, and subsequent developments offered generations of lesbian readers many opportunities to feel their thumbs pricking.

Tereska Torres's novel *Women's Barracks* was an important part of the history that made lesbian lives and lesbian desire a central part of paperback publishing in the United States. The title alone might well have inspired some thumb-pricking, suggesting as it does a community of women left to their own devices. The subtitle, "A Frank Autobiography of a

French Girl Soldier," was even more promising, since the French have served as convenient shorthand in the American cultural imagination for all things sexual and risqué (just as Hennegan's examples of Daudet and Zola attest), and a "frank" autobiography suggested that no details of life in the barracks would be glossed over. The clincher was the cover: Several women are posed in various states of undress in a locker room, while a fully clothed woman soldier sits in the foreground, smoking, and exchanging a knowing glance with one of the women. The book first appeared on American newsstands and drugstore shelves in December 1950. It was the first lesbian-themed pulp in the United States, and its enormous success—over two million copies sold by 1955 (Tuttle: 349)—launched a veritable boom in lesbian pulp publishing.

Women's Barracks was published by Fawcett's Gold Medal division (established in 1949), the first imprint of paperback originals in the United States. Armed Services editions of classical and popular novels (small, digest-sized paperbacks available free to members of the military) had been popular during World War II, and suggested that there could well be a wider audience for cheap, paperback editions (see Bonn: 47; Lupoff: 165–66). Reprints of best sellers, like Pearl Buck's *The Good Earth*, and of works of classic literature (especially by those racy French writers), were popular, but paperback originals offered a wider range of topics. The publication of paperback originals was a plus for writers, especially first-time novelists, who reached many more readers (and made more money) than they would have otherwise, as well as readers, who were able to buy books cheaply. *Women's Barracks* was a huge success for Gold Medal, the imprint's first bestseller (Bonn: 70).

An advertisement for Gold Medal books appeared in the *New York Times* on December 10, 1950, with bold letters announcing "9 Million Copies in Six Months," with the explanation: "That's the amazing record of the Gold Medal Books program of bringing NEW, ORIGINAL books to the public for 25¢." *Women's Barracks* was one of five novels announced in the advertisement, and together these books suggest the eclectic range of paperback originals: a suspense novel, a western, a detective novel, and a "humorous but authentic guide for mixing drinks." Among these recognizable genres is *Women's Barracks*, which has the tag line "A woman in the Free French army."

Women's Barracks merits our attention as a first—the first lesbian-themed pulp, the first best seller among paperback originals. But the novel is also noteworthy in its own terms, and not just for what it made possible. Its exploration of a community of women against the backdrop of war is daring, original, and provocative. Yet while most observers of the development of lesbian pulp fiction in the United States acknowledge the importance of *Women's Barracks*, the novel is rarely discussed in any detail. A common assumption is that, as Jaye Zimet puts it, "*Women's Barracks* made an impact, but *Spring Fire* started the trend" (20). Author Vin Packer (the pseudonym under which Marijane Meaker, also known as Ann Aldrich, published *Spring Fire*) has become well-known as a lesbian writer, while Tereska Torres does not have a corresponding "name recognition factor" in the history of lesbian letters, and the fact that her husband, Meyer Levin (using the name George Cummings) translated the book, may well make some readers a bit suspicious of its provenance, suggesting as it might that *Women's Barracks* is a heterosexual fantasy (see Adams).

Even though the author's real name is indeed Tereska Torres, the name sounds like it could be a pseudonym, with its alliterative *T*s and its repeated *res* syllables. Little was known about Torres at the time of the book's publication, and misconceptions about her have persisted through the decades. Jeannette Foster's meticulously researched *Sex Variant Women* *in Literature*, for instance, notes that "Toreska" Torres was the pseudonym of an established author (332), and a current web site describes Tereska Torres as a name used by a lesbian novelist (Bianco).

Tereska Torres is indeed the real name of the author of *Women's Barracks*. She has had a distinguished literary career, and she is alive and well and living in Paris. *Women's Barracks* was her second published novel. (Her first novel, *Le Sable et l'écume*, was published in 1946, under the pseudonym of Georges Achard.) After *Women's Barracks*, she published two more lesbian-themed novels, *Dangerous Games* (which carries an endorsement from Vin Packer) and *By Cécile* (a fictionalized account of the life of Colette). Oddly, although Torres writes in French, only one of these three novels was ever published in France. (*Dangerous Games* was published as *Le Labyrinthe* in 1959, two years after its American debut.) In addition, Torres is the author of five other novels, and she has written autobiographical works as well.

Torres was the daughter of Guina (a writer) and Marek (a celebrated artist) Szwarc. Torres's parents were Polish Jews who converted to Christianity. Her father had studied in Paris, and the couple moved from Poland to Paris, where Tereska was born in 1920. The conversion to Catholicism was kept a secret from family members in Poland for as long as possible. As Torres writes in *The Converts*, her parents always considered themselves "Jews of the Catholic Faith," and throughout her life Torres defined herself as both Jewish and Catholic. At the outbreak of World War II, while her father served in the Polish army, Tereska and her mother moved from one place to another. (In her autobiography of those years, young Tereska keeps a running count of how many different beds she slept in during a short amount of time.) They landed temporarily in Portugal, and they were able to move to England, where Tereska promptly joined the women's unit of the Forces

Françaises Libres, the Free French Army.

While in London, Tereska met and fell in love with Georges Torres. The two married just before he was sent to France, where he was killed. Thus at a young age, Tereska Torres found herself not only a widow, but also pregnant with her first child, Dominique. During the war years, Tereska had some contact with Meyer Levin, a family friend whom Torres had known as a child, and after the war they married and had two more children. Levin was an established journalist and novelist, and he served as Torres's translator. While Levin too was a prolific author, he is best remembered today for his obsession with Anne Frank and his lawsuit against Frank's father. (Levin wrote a play based on the diary of Anne Frank, which was rejected in favor of the version written by Frances Goodrich and Albert Hackett.) Much of Levin's life was consumed by what he saw as the injustice accorded him, and the distortion of Anne Frank's work. Torres herself has written an account of Levin's obsession, the title of which—*Les Maisons hantées de Meyer Levin* (The Haunted Houses of Meyer Levin)—indicates how much Levin's, and Torres's, lives were affected by the affair.

At the age of eighteen, Torres became a soldier, and her experiences in the women's barracks in London became the basis of *Women's Barracks*. While the novel might have been advertised as an "autobiography" so as to give the stamp of truth to the adventures of the French women, we do a disservice to Torres and to the novel by reading the text as nothing but the transcription of a diary. Of course, in Torres's own foreword she claims herself to be a somewhat reluctant memoirist, and only claims the title of "novelist" in order to efface her own presence: "I shall from time to time pretend, like a novelist, that I was an invisible witness to the private moments of my comrades" (5). Ironically enough, as we learn from Joan Schenkar's interview with Torres in this volume, the first person "I" that narrates the novel was the one addition made by Meyer Levin at the behest of Fawcett Publications—in other words, the most obvious mark of autobiography was a fabrication by the translator. Schenkar's interview also seems to confirm what some readers may already have suspected: that Torres shared many feelings and experiences with her most finely drawn character, Ursula.

Torres began keeping a diary at the age of nine, and her journals of her experiences during World War II, and particularly in the Free French Army, have been published in France (*Une Française libre* [A Free Frenchwoman]). Readers of *Une Française libre* will recognize numerous events and individuals in *Women's Barracks*: De Gaulle did indeed come to visit the women at the barracks and a young woman made a complaint to him, much to the embarrassment of the others. The women did attempt to make fashionable garments out of their military-issue underpants. Most of the characters in the novel have counterparts in the memoir. But the experience of reading these two texts is very different. Torres's memoir reads as an incredibly rich document of how a young woman experiences not only war, but also autonomy, separation from her family and her homeland, and developing sexual identity. The novel, however much it reflects Torres's own experiences, is shaped by the relationships between the women in the barracks, in particular by the ways in which this motley group of women relate to each other emotionally, sexually, and culturally. From the truth of Torres's experiences, the author has created a narrative that deserves our attention not just—or even primarily—as a version of her own life, but as a work of art that puts women and their desires center-stage.

The women's barracks provide a stage that represents a new environment for the exploration of communities of women, and in that sense the post-World War II publication of *Women's Barracks* is significant. The setting offers readers the opportunity to reflect upon historical change insofar as women in war and women's autonomy are concerned. *Women's Barracks* evokes two different narrative traditions of women left to their own devices: boarding school fiction (Leontine Sagan's film *Maedchen in Uniform* [1931] and Colette's *Claudine at School* [1904] are particularly well-known examples, and Vin Packer's *Spring Fire*, which takes place in a college setting, adapts the pattern), and the women-in-prison film (*Caged*, a popular U.S. film about what happens to women in a prison setting, came out the same year as Torres's novel, and the genre had some popularity in France, as well, in film like *Prison sans barreaux* [1938] and *Prisons de femmes* [1938]).

The boarding school and the women's prison offer obvious opportunities for the exploration of same-sex desire. Girls in boarding school fictions often develop crushes on their teachers and on each other, and sometimes the teachers are themselves lesbians (as in *Claudine at School*). The all-female setting encourages experimentation among the girls and a way of life among the adults, and often the "passing phase" motif is central to the genre. While the women-in-prison story contrasts in obvious ways with the setting of the girls' school, it too has a "passing through" quality, since the story of the woman who is heterosexual on the outside but who becomes lesbian on the inside (whether through choice or coercion) is also a staple of the genre. Generally the women in the women-in-prison stories are adults, and of course their confinement lends itself easily to stories of brutality and domination. A common element of women-in-prison narratives is the mixing together of women from radically different class and racial backgrounds, who committed very different kinds of crimes.

The women of *Women's Barracks* are neither schoolgirls nor prisoners, but traces of these genres persist in the portrayal of young innocents, as well as sophisticated adults, subjected to the authority of the military officers in the barracks on Down Street. Part of the originality of the novel is the depiction of a space where women are confined, willingly, and where they act, both as young women on the verge of adulthood and as adults who bring with them complicated histories of love and loss. Borrowing from the genres of the girls' school and the women's prison, *Women's Barracks* creates a very different kind of space for women's dreams and desires. It is different because it portrays women's agency as more than youthful experimentation or the result of forced confinement. Historically, the novel appeared at a transitional period, after World War II, when American women had experienced more autonomy than ever before, and when the military provided not only a safe haven but a discovery zone for lesbians. But it also appeared at the beginning of the 1950s, when fears of female autonomy (not to mention lesbianism) proliferated (Faderman chs. 5 & 6). As a novel about women's experiences in wartime, *Women's Barracks* seems to allow readers to have it both ways--to see the experiences of American women reflected in the lives of the women in the barracks, but to also be reminded that these are *French* women, doing the kinds of things that the French are so often assumed to be doing.

If the women in the novel seem to be much more preoccupied with their love affairs than with the affairs of war, it is not just a function of what was more likely to sell in the American paperback original market. Women's participation in the fight to free France from Nazi occupation was not necessarily welcomed. The women's division of De Gaulle's Free French Army was founded in December 1940. For the most part, women were assigned to nursing or secretarial duties, and it was explicitly understood that women participated in the military so as to make more men available for combat (Weitz 147). The women in *Women' Barracks* are united in their feeling that "their military life had brought nothing but a series of disillusions" (120). Alluding to De Gaulle's reputed disapproval of a women's army, as well as the argument that the real reason for its creation was to free male recruits for "more useful activities" (121), the first person narrator of the novel observes: "We had imagined that the uniform would somehow put us right into the middle of the war, but it was not at all like that. The war was taking place far from us; we were not participating in it" (121). The women are caught, then, in a peculiar limbo, in that most of them have volunteered as French patriots, and yet they are not permitted to take on the active roles that they imagined.

The focus on the romantic, sexual, and emotional intrigues in *Women's Barracks* could, then, be seen as a literal transposition of the women's frustration: unable to soldier, they do what women are presumed to do best, and that is obsess about romance. While it is undoubtedly true that the appeal of the novel was based on this stereotyped notion of women as more interested in love than war, such a view does an enormous injustice to the novel. For the group of women whose lives intersect in the barracks on Down Street have not chosen to ignore the war; rather, the war has marginalized them. In the meantime, the community of women in the barracks forge modern identities as women on their own, who are still caught up in the expectations of a pre-war culture.

Women's Barracks begins with a brief exposition of the journey of the narrator, "I," from Paris to Portugal to London, and her assignment to the women's barracks once she joins De Gaulle's women's army. We are quickly introduced to the individual women who become the major characters of the novel, and they are introduced initially as physical and behavioral types. Mickey, a "tall girl, with the gawkiness of a figure just out of adolescence" (12), is slim, boyish, and loud. Ursula is just sixteen, with a "frail and childlike air," whose shyness initially masks the independence that has characterized her life (14). Jacqueline is a beautiful aristocrat with "delicately rounded hips and exquisite round breasts" (15), who possesses an "impersonal beauty in which every other woman feels she is somehow represented" (16). Ann is a "strapping large girl with a boyish haircut" (15) who is confident and sad at the same time. Soon Claude arrives, and our first perception of her is through the eyes, not of "I," as is the case with the other women, but of Ursula: "Ursula stood stock-still, a wisp of a girl wrapped in her long beige smock, watching the passage of this beautiful creature. The woman had such a marvelous scent!" (28). Beneath Claude's beauty and apparent sophistication lies a sometimes crude and cruel disposition. While Claude is the most extreme example of the gap between the women's appearances and their inner beings, all of them possess characteristics that belie their looks. For all of her innocence and timidity, Ursula has succeeded on her own for some time; Jacqueline is the picture of class privilege and bearing, but she is a deeply troubled woman desperate for attention.

These six women (including "I") form the core of the novel. Each corresponds to a specific type, the most obvious of which is Ann, whose butch appearance is very quickly revealed to be the badge of her sexual identity. The narrator observes the interaction between Ann and the warrant officer, Petit, early on in the novel: "I thought, They've never met before, but they recognize each other; they know they're the same kind" (20). Leaving aside for the moment the narrator's own knowledge, it's clear that Ann and Petit are easily identifiable as what would then have been called "inverts"—women's bodies possessed by men's desires, women whose sexual desire for other women is a biological and genetic condition. They are members of the "third sex," the most obvious literary precedent of which is, of course, Stephen Gordon in Radclyffe Hall's *Well of Loneliness* (which found its own way into the lesbian pulp scene when it was reissued in 1951 by Permabooks). Ann is the unloved, illegitimate child of a poor woman, and she understood very early on in her life that she was unlike other girls. She didn't play with dolls, she wasn't interested in boys, and she had crushes on women, either teachers or friends of her mother (88). As Ann gradually discovered her own identity, she understood that lesbian love "circled on itself, like a cat chasing its own tail. But that was how she was made. And Petit also. And the childhood of Petit had been the same. And the youth of all these women had all been the same, and no one could ever change things for them" (88).

Ann and Petit do indeed become lovers. While they are drawn to each other, they are also drawn to the army as a place where lesbians can feel at home. Indeed, Ann's decision to join the military seems to result from an uncanny sense—a pricking of her thumbs, perhaps?—that it was the right direction for her to take, after she ends up penniless and alone in London. "As soon as she had seen Petit, she had felt herself to be at home" (86). This is precisely the kind of tantalizing information that raised fears about what the military could do to women, but in Torres's handling of the story, the military provides a temporary safe haven for lesbians. Torres departs from conventional wisdom about inverts insofar as they were generally seen as attracted to more "feminine" women. True, Ann and Petit separate, but Ann once again ends up with an invert, Lee, who seems lifted directly from a country estate inhabited by the likes of Stephen Gordon.

Despite the fact that Ann and Petit are presented as stereotypically butch, I have to say that when I first read *Women's Barracks*, I thought that Mickey, with her slim boyish figure and her ease in a room full of naked women, would turn out to be "the lesbian." (Mickey is introduced before Ann is.) In other words, the novel appears to reflect the reliability of visible types, yet the relationship between the types and the identities and desires beneath what is visible is not always stable.

Now if Ann and Petit were the only lesbians—and therefore
lesbians identified only as "inverts"—in the novel, typology
might be seen to be only momentarily disrupted (i.e., Mickey
as a potential lesbian) in order to be verified with a vengeance.
But in the large scheme of the novel, Ann and Petit's relationship does not occupy center stage, but rather Ursula's relationships do—first with Claude, the beautiful but relentless
bisexual with whom Ursula falls in love, and then with
Michel, the man she eventually decides to marry.

Claude's identity as a femme may have more resonance in
a French context than an American one (and may explain
some of the peculiarly "French" appeal of the novel in the
United States), since she corresponds to the feminine woman
attracted to all things feminine, as embodied by Colette, in
particular, but also by a French narrative and iconic tradition
in literature (Balzac's *Girl with the Golden Eyes*; Zola's *Nana*
in the nineteenth century; Renée Vivien and Natalie Barney in
the early twentieth century). Claude, at forty, is older than the
other women, and she has an air of sophistication that makes
virtually every woman in the barracks respond to her in some
way. She is blonde and beautiful, and she is a sincere pursuer
of pleasure in any form. Although Claude is classified as
bisexual, her relationships with men occupy very little space
in the novel, with only occasional mention of her adored gay
husband. Claude is regularly described in words suggestive of
both the range and the intensity of her desires; she possesses a
"devouring avidity" (38), she embraces her role as a "dangerous woman" (90) and regards lesbianism, group sex, and
opium-smoking as integral parts of her identity (91). Yet
Claude, despite her association with Parisian debauchery and
loose morality, has another side, like virtually every inhabitant
of the barracks: "Claude was essentially a good woman, with
an astonishing childlike purity" (127).

As the initial description of Claude through Ursula's eyes

suggests, Ursula falls in love with the sophisticated older woman. Claude is Ursula's first lover, and through her, Ursula discovers the "independent life" of her body, longing for "the warmth of Claude and for Claude's hands" (60). Their first scene of love-making is lyrically described and relatively understated: "her hand began to caress all of Ursula's body, her throat, her shoulders, and her belly" (49). At the same time, of course, Ursula learns that homosexual women exist (she had only been aware of the existence of homosexual men), yet she is perplexed by the fact that Claude has slept with men as well. If Ann and Petit are classical inverts, born that way and as drawn to each other as twins, Claude herself offers an explanation for the kind of lesbian love she embodies. According to Claude, women have sensuous needs that are rarely if ever satisfied by men, needs to be caressed, to have the "neutral parts" of their bodies touched—their shoulders, their arms, their backs. The suggestion is also a familiarly stereotypical view of lesbianism, that women unready or unprepared for "adult" (i.e., heterosexual) experience seek out the comfort of affection and warmth with other women, unprepared as they are to confront and accept the difficulty of (male) difference. Eventually a particular psychological portrait of Claude emerges. When she was two months pregnant and unsure of whether or not to have the child, she had an abortion, and only when it was too late did she want to change her mind. Hence, our narrator concludes, Claude sought out with younger women the maternal connection that she had never been able to enjoy, and for which she held herself guiltily responsible (125).

What, then, of Ursula in all of this? Ursula adores Claude, but Claude is a fickle lover, and Ursula herself feels enormous confusion in her discovery of lesbian love. At the same time that Ursula and Claude are involved romantically, Ursula meets Michel, a Polish soldier who takes an interest in her. But

Ursula finds herself disgusted when Michel kisses her, which only adds to her confusion about her own sexuality. She eventually sees Claude as a negative presence in her life, and when Ursula goes on leave, she meets Philippe, a French sailor who functions as a transition between Ursula's experiences with Claude and her reconnection with Michel. Ursula is tempted to have sex with Philippe, but she doesn't, yet she recognizes that she does indeed desire heterosexual sex. Once she returns to the barracks, Ursula is ready for a relationship with Michel. Where he once seemed ugly and unattractive, he now seems just the opposite. Michel, it turns out, suffers from many demons and has had a difficult life, and he and Ursula are drawn to each other from a common shared past of pain and depression. Michel and Ursula fall in love and plan to marry.

Ursula's connection with Claude sounds an awful lot like the boarding school romance—lesbianism as a stage on the way towards better, more mature things. But I'm more tempted to read Ursula's discovery of heterosexual love as some feminist psychoanalytic critics have read Freud's descriptions of a girl's acquisition of heterosexual identity: if it's all so "normal," it certainly requires a lot of twists and turns to get there. And in any case, Ursula's romance with Michel is far from idyllic. They are unable to marry before Michel is sent away to participate in the Normandy invasion, and he is killed. Ursula discovers that she is pregnant, and once she knows of Michel's death, she kills herself. The women in the barracks had regarded Ursula and Michel as the future, as the promise of regeneration and rebirth. But their child will not be born, and even Michel's papers, including his poems and his writings, are destroyed at his request. Put another way, in Ursula's passage from lesbian to heterosexual love, heterosexuality is not a magical cure, but a state fraught with perils of its own.

Yet despite the tragic end to their romance, Ursula and

Michel are presented as truly in love and committed to each other. The other heterosexual relationships in the novel do not fare so well. Jacqueline, the aristocratic beauty with the "perverse need to impress everybody" (40), either fails in romance or loses her partner (she, not Ursula, has a child). Additionally, the distinction between lesbian and heterosexual women is belied by the characteristics shared by women on opposite sides of the fence. Of the core cast of characters, for instance, Jacqueline most resembles Claude. Both of them are from a social background that separates them from the other women (Jacqueline's is aristocratic gentility, Claude's Parisian privilege), and both share a sense of sexuality as power. Early in the novel, Jacqueline is described as having been born not only into the world of aristocracy, but into the world of "aristocratic sex": "it was the woman who could always decide, always command, in relationships with men" (43). Indeed, one senses that with Claude and Jacqueline both, it is the sense of power that is most important in matters of sex, rather than the sexual partner. In other words, the two women mirror each other across the divide of sexual identity.

Women's Barracks has lesbianism, and it has stereotyped views of lesbianism, but it doesn't stick to a single, pathological view of what lesbian identity entails. And perhaps most strikingly, the lines between heterosexual and lesbian desire are not neatly drawn. Mickey becomes involved with Claude, as do other new recruits at Down Street. There is a community of lesbians in the barracks, and even though, in her war memoirs, Torres describes the barracks as evenly divided between the "women's women" and the "men's women," the fictional barracks, simply by virtue of the interconnections between the women's stories, present a far more heterogeneous space. As I've noted, the major lesbian figures in the novel—Ann and Petit, the inverts; Claude, the narcissist with unfulfilled maternal urges; and Ursula, the young innocent—correspond to stereotypical notions of what lesbians both "looked" like and "were" like. Yet there is no single coherent view on lesbianism in the novel. Rather, lesbianism and heterosexuality exist on a continuum, and there are consistent parallels between them. Ursula's and Michel's child does not survive; Ann, who is convinced by her lover Lee to have sexual intercourse with Lee's brother so that they can have a child, never gets pregnant. Ann may be the most recognizable "invert" among the new recruits, but Ursula turns out to have the most significant lesbian relationship in the novel. *Women's Barracks* may well reflect certain stereotypes about lesbianism, but it's the way these stereotypes are pushed, prodded, and complicated that makes the novel such an important contribution to our understandings of lesbianism and cultural representation.

For if *Women's Barracks* borrows from twentieth-century definitions of the invert and the femme, its rendering of them, in this diverse community of women, suggests new understandings of desire between women. The invert is no longer the eccentric man/woman on a country estate sitting with her dogs in front of the fire; she is part of a community of lesbians. The narcissistic femme goes about her business, but the women she seduces do not die or go crazy because of their involvement with her. (Ursula was always a troubled young woman, and the novel does not in any was suggest that her suicide was "caused" by Claude; it was caused by the war.) And perhaps most important of all, despite the occasional moral lectures delivered by "I," who often seems torn between empathy and judgment, lesbians and heterosexuals and everything in between reflect each other, and reflect upon each other.

Of the central cast of characters, Mickey is perhaps the most interesting suggestion of the connection between heterosexual and homosexual love. She is determined to have sex with a man, which she does, and is somewhat disappointed by the act. She eventually connects with Claude (thus following a different trajectory than Ursula, who moves on to men after her relationship with Claude), even though she didn't consider herself to be a lesbian (133). Yet she is as fixated on Claude as the other women in the barracks, and "the truth was that what she wanted most of all was to be like Claude" (153). My point is not that Mickey's desire to *be like* Claude is the same as desire *for* Claude, but rather that in the world of the barracks, the women's sexual identities are shaped by a wide range of influences, and while there may be exclusive lesbians and heterosexuals, there is plenty of mobility and flexibility along the way. And despite the moralistic tone that the narrator (awkwardly) acquires, no one is really punished for discovering, and being, who she is.

Recent attention to lesbian pulps of the 1950s and 1960s—and in particular to the juicy covers that contemporary lesbian audiences seem to find modern in their appeal to lesbian sex and enjoyably retro at the same time—tends to view *Women's Barracks* as a first stepping stone to the real beginnings of lesbian pulps, Vin Packer's *Spring Fire*. Published in 1952, Packer's novel explores love among women in a college sorority. Author Marijane Meaker has told the tale of how Fawcett director Dick Carroll asked her, after she published a short story in *Ladies' Home Journal* about girls in a boarding school, if there was much lesbianism in boarding schools. When she replied in the affirmative, he asked her to write a lesbian novel with a boarding school setting. She said she was more familiar with college sororities, and thus Spring Fire was born (Packer; Server: 51–55). The success of *Women's Barracks* made Gold Medal eager to publish more lesbian-themed works. It may surprise contemporary readers to learn that despite the fact that Packer's novel is now designated as the "real" beginning of the lesbian pulp, Barbara Grier and Lee Stuart's *The Lesbian in Literature*, in its first (1967) and subsequent editions, give *Women's Barracks* an "A***" rating (the highest rating available, indicating not only substantial lesbian content but a must-have for any serious lesbian reader), and *Spring Fire* an "A**." Perhaps the tragic ending of Packer's novel is what makes the novel somewhat less important in Grier and Stuart's account. For by the time Packer's novel was published, it was considered imperative that lesbian novels have bad, unhappy endings for their lesbian characters.

Such an imperative was the direct result of the increasing concern in American society that "pornography" was running amuck. In 1952, a congressional committee on "current pornographic materials" published its findings, and *Women's Barracks* was one of the committee's key exhibits. The report consists of testimony and commentary from a wide variety of sources on the ill effects of novels, magazines, and comic books. Paperback books were subjected to particular scorn: "The so-called pocket-size books, which originally started out as cheap reprints of standard works, have largely degenerated into media for the dissemination of artful appeals to sensuality, immorality, filth, perversion, and degeneracy" (3). Homosexuality may well be just one of the vices that comes under scrutiny in the report, but its very proximity to polygamy and drug addiction suggests that the report is as much about classifying homosexuality (as an "uncivilized" custom such as polygamy, or as a pathology like drug addiction) as it is about banning pornographic materials. (In case, the report had little effect on the actual sales of books; insofar as homosexuality is concerned, publishers kept on selling the titles but insisted upon including "moral lessons" in the form of tragic endings, thus skirting obscenity prosecutions.)

Ralph Daigh, the vice president of Fawcett Publications, was called before the committee, and the questioning of him focused on the treatment in *Women's Barracks* "in large measure, and rather frankly, of homosexual relations between women" (37). The novel had already been declared obscene by one judge in Canada (40). Curiously, Daigh's defense of the novel rests largely on the question of authorship (he attributes the novel to its translator, Meyer Levin) and describes the novel as a "diary biography…not, as you might think, a fiction story" (37). Levin, according to Daigh, "rewrote" the original diary. Tereska Torres is mentioned by name, but only to be described as "not a professional author" (37), but rather a young woman who kept a diary never intended for publication. Daigh's argument seems to want to have it both ways, to declare the novel a "fact story" by a young French girl, and as a work of fiction by an accomplished and established author. (Interestingly, Meyer Levin's name is used, not the pseudonym of George Cummings.)

The original tantalizing cover of *Women's Barracks* (by illustrator Baryé Phillips) has already found its place in the visual history of lesbian pulps (Zimet, Stryker). The re-issue of the novel gives contemporary readers the opportunity to discover the novel itself, and to explore a time in American culture when stereotypes about lesbianism might have been visible, but were at the same questioned and rendered unstable through the observations of a writer like Torres. When asked about writers who influenced her own writing of lesbian pulps in the 1950s and 1960s, Ann Bannon replied: "Tereska Torres' *Women's Barracks* showed me a writer who didn't just write about women in uniform. She made me realize what they might have been doing with each other in their off hours, and took my breath away" (Forrest). It's common to warn contemporary readers that what appeared "scandalous" in the 1950s seems tame today. But my guess is that at the very least, some of those readers will feel a strange sensation in reading *Women's Barracks*, perhaps a pricking of the thumbs.

Judith Mayne
The Ohio State University
December 2004

Works Cited

Adams, Kate. "Making the World Safe for the Missionary Position: Images of the Lesbian in Post-World War II America." *Lesbian Texts and Contexts: Radical Revisions*. Ed. Karla Jay and Joanne Glasgow. New York: New York University Press, 1990. 255–74.

Bianco, David. *Planet Out History*. 2004. Planet Out. 15/09/04 <http://www.planetout.com/news/history/archive/07191999.html>.

Bonn, Thomas L. *Under Cover: An Illustrated History of American Mass Market Paperbacks*. New York: Penguin, 1982.

Davis, Kenneth C. *Two-Bit Culture: The Paperbacking of America*. Boston: Houghton Mifflin, 1984.

Faderman, Lillian. *Odd Girls and Twilight Lovers: A History of Lesbian Life in Twentieth-Century America*. New York: Penguin, 1992.

Forrest, Katherine V. "Acts of Individual Valor: Katherine V. Forrest Talks to Fifties Pulp Fiction Queen Ann Bannon." *Lamdba Book Report* 10.7 (February 2002): 6.

Grier, Barbara, and Lee Stuart. *The Lesbian in Literature*. San Francisco: Daughters of Bilitis, Inc., 1967.

Hennegan, Alison. "On Becoming a Lesbian Reader." *Sweet Dreams: Sexuality, Gender, and Popular Fiction*. Ed. Susanna Radstone. London: Lawrence & Wishart, 1988. 165–90.

Keller, Yvonne. "Pulp Politics: Strategies of Vision in Pro-Lesbian Pulp Novels, 1955–1965." *The Queer Sixties*. Ed. Patricia Juliana Smith. New York and London: Routledge, 1999. 1–25.

Lupoff, Richard A. *The Great American Paperback*. Portland, Oregon: Collectors' Press, 2001.

Packer, Vin. "Gold Medal Days." *The Fine Art of Murder: The Mystery Reader's Indispensable Companion*. Ed. Martin H. Greenberg Gorman, Larry Segriff. New York: Carroll & Graf, 1993. 340–42.

Server, Lee. *Over My Dead Body: The Sensational Age of the American Paperback: 1945–1955*. San Francisco: Chronicle Books, 1994.

Stryker, Susan. *Queer Pulp: Perverted Passions from the Golden Age of the Paperback*. San Francisco: Chronicle Books, 2001.

Torres, Tereska. *Le Sable et l'Écume*. Paris: Gallimard, 1946.

——. *By Cécile*. New York: Simon & Schuster, 1963.

——. *Le Choix: Mémoires À Trois Voix*. Paris: Desclée de Brouwer, 2002.

——. *The Converts*. New York: Alfred A. Knopf, 1970.

——. *The Dangerous Games*. New York: Dial Press, 1957.

——. *Une Française Libre*. Paris: Phébus, 2000; rpt. of *Les Années Anglaises*, 1981.

——. *The Golden Cage*. New York: Dial Press, 1959.

——. *Les Maisons Hantées de Meyer Levin*. Paris: Denoël, 1991.

——. *Not Yet*. New York: Crown, 1953.

——. *The Only Reason*. New York: Simon & Schuster, 1961.

——. *The Open Doors*. New York: Simon & Schuster, 1968.

——. *Le Pays Des Chuchotements*. Paris: Séguier, 1987.

——. *Les Poupées de Cendre*. Paris: Le Seuil, 1979.

——. *Le Sable et l'Écume*. Paris: Gallimard, 1946.

Tuttle, George. "The Golden Era of Gold Medal Books." *The Fine Art of Murder: The Mystery Reader's Indispensable Companion*. Ed. Martin H. Greenberg Gorman, Larry Segriff. New York: Carroll & Graf, 1993. 343–51.

United States Congressional House. *Report of the Select Committee on Current Pornographic Materials*. 82 Congress, 2nd session. House Report 2510. Washington, D.C.: Government Printing Office, 1952.

Weitz, Margaret Collins. *Sisters in the Resistance: How Women Fought to Free France, 1940–1945*. New York: John Wiley & Sons, 1995.

Zimet, Jaye. *Strange Sisters: The Art of Lesbian Pulp Fiction, 1949–1969*. New York: Viking Penguin, 1999.

A daring new series uncovers the forgotten queens of pulp—and subversive new viewpoints on American culture

Femmes Fatales: Women Write Pulp celebrates women's writing in all the classic pulp fiction genres—from hard-boiled noirs and fiery romances to edgy science fiction and taboo lesbian pulps.

Beneath the surface of pulp's juicy plots were many subversive elements that helped to provide American popular culture with a whole new set of markers. Much more than bad girls or hacks, women authors of pulp fiction were bold, talented writers, charting the cultural netherworlds of America in the 1930s, 1940s, 1950s, and 1960s, where the dominant idiom was still largely male, white, and heterosexual.

The pulp fiction revival of the last decade has almost entirely ignored women writers. Yet these women were sometimes far ahead of their male counterparts in pushing the boundaries of acceptability, confronting conventional ideas about gender, race, and class—exploring forbidden territories that were hidden from view off the typed page. The novels in the Femmes Fatales series offer the page-turning plots and sensational story lines typical of pulp fiction. But embedded in these stories are explorations of such vital themes as urbanization and class mobility, women in the workplace, misogyny and the crisis of postwar masculinity, racial tensions and civil rights, drug use and Beat culture, and shakeups in the strict codes of sexual conduct.

The Feminist Press at the City University of New York is proud to restore to print these forgotten queens of pulp, whose books offer subversive new perspectives on the heart of the American century.

For more information or to order books, call 212-817-7925.

Small-town girls and big-city passions collide on the brink of the 1960s
THE GIRLS IN 3-B
Valerie Taylor
232 pp., $13.95 paperback, ISBN 1-55861-462-1

◆ ◆ ◆

A double romance—
with the boy next door and the career in the gleaming tower
SKYSCRAPER
Faith Baldwin
288 pp., $14.95 paperback, ISBN 1-55861-457-5

◆ ◆ ◆

Classic noir—the basis for the 1950 film with Humphrey Bogart
IN A LONELY PLACE
Dorothy B. Hughes
272 pp., $14.95 paperback, ISBN 1-55861-455-9

◆ ◆ ◆

Thrilling WWII espionage with a hard-boiled heroine
THE BLACKBIRDER
Dorothy B. Hughes
288 pp., $12.95, paperback, ISBN 1-55861-568-0

◆ ◆ ◆

A tale of terror and treachery as a mother searches for her daughter
BUNNY LAKE IS MISSING
Evelyn Piper
240 pp., $12.95 paperback, ISBN 1-55861-474-5

◆ ◆ ◆

The all-time classic drama of a woman reborn
NOW, VOYAGER
Olive Higgins Prouty
288 pp., $13.95 paperback, ISBN 1-55861-476-1